the
DEVIL'S WIND

ALSO BY STEVE GOBLE

The Bloody Black Flag

the
DEVIL'S
WIND

A Spider John Mystery

STEVE GOBLE

SEVENTH STREET BOOKS®
AN IMPRINT OF PROMETHEUS BOOKS
59 JOHN GLENN DRIVE • AMHERST, NY 14228
www.seventhstreetbooks.com

Published 2018 by Seventh Street Books®, an imprint of Prometheus Books

The Devil's Wind. Copyright © 2018 by Steve Goble. All rights reserved. No part of this publication may be reproduced, stored in a retrieval system, or transmitted in any form or by any means, digital, electronic, mechanical, photocopying, recording, or otherwise, or conveyed via the internet or a website without prior written permission of the publisher, except in the case of brief quotations embodied in critical articles and reviews.

Cover design by Nicole Sommer-Lecht
Cover illustrations © Shutterstock
Cover design © Prometheus Books

Inquiries should be addressed to
Seventh Street Books
59 John Glenn Drive
Amherst, New York 14228
VOICE: 716–691–0133 • FAX: 716–691–0137
WWW.SEVENTHSTREETBOOKS.COM

22 21 20 19 18 • 5 4 3 2 1

Library of Congress Cataloging-in-Publication Data

Names: Goble, Steve, 1961- author.
Title: The devil's wind : a Spider John mystery / by Steve Goble.
Description: Amherst, NY : Seventh Street Books, an imprint of Prometheus Books,
    2018. | Series: A Spider John Mystery ; book 2
Identifiers: LCCN 2018016708 (print) | LCCN 2018019981 (ebook) | ISBN
    9781633884854 (ebook) | ISBN 9781633884847 (paperback)
Subjects: LCSH: Pirates—Fiction. | Murder—Investigation—Fiction. | BISAC:
    FICTION / Mystery & Detective / Historical. | FICTION / Historical. |
    GSAFD: Historical fiction. | Mystery fiction.
Classification: LCC PS3607.O27 (ebook) | LCC PS3607.O27 D48 2018 (print) |
    DDC 813/.6—dc23
LC record available at https://lccn.loc.gov/2018016708

Printed in the United States of America

For Rowan, my lighthouse.

JANUARY 1723

"**D**o not take the cutlass, Odin. It makes you look like a bloody pirate."

Odin stopped before the Phoenix Tavern's swinging doors and glared back at Spider John Rush. Caribbean sunlight streamed in around him, and he stood in silhouette, with the wide-brimmed hat on his head and the cutlass dangling from his belt making him look every inch the sea thief. "And what should I look like, Spider John?"

Spider swallowed his tot of rum—his third of the young morning—then swiveled on his barstool to stare into the one-eyed bastard's face. The hideous scars where half of Odin's face had been ripped off long ago were hidden in shadow, for which Spider was thankful. He had come to regard Odin, crazy though he may be, as a friend after all their shared adventures, but still had difficulty looking at the man.

"I am serious, Odin. There are navy fellows out there looking for us. You think them dull, but they may be sharp enough to reckon we would show when Dobbin swings. They will be watching for us."

Odin drew the cutlass from its scabbard, stirring the sun-drenched dust motes. "Then I reckon I just might need this bloody goddamned thing. Aye? Ha!" Odin rushed out of the tavern.

Spider winced. "Bloody stubborn Scot." There was no talking sense into a man who had survived piracy as long as Odin had. The man was at least sixty, judging by his appearance and stories.

"Is that fellow always so reckless?" Duncan, the barkeeper, deftly mopped up a spill on the scarred oak.

"Aye," Spider answered quietly. "He owns an unlikely lifespan, for a man who was—was, I say—a pirate for most of his life. Dangerous profession, to be sure, yet Odin still lives and breathes. It has made him rather fearless, and he won't heed reality."

"Reality?"

"Odin and I are wanted men, Duncan."

The barkeeper nodded.

Spider peered out a window and watched Odin shamble down a dirty road. The old man often bragged of sailing with Blackbeard and wrestling giant squid and screwing mermaids. If Odin wanted to wave a blade in front of King George's valiant fellows, there probably was no stopping him.

Most days, Spider found Odin's unrepentant attitude amusing. Today was not one of those days.

"You stay the hell away from me and the boy, then, Odin," Spider muttered. "Me and Hob, we ain't bloody pirates no more, even if you want to be one."

"More rum, John?" Duncan held up a bottle. The man leaned across the bar and whispered. "And, for God's sake, quit talking out loud about pirates. I can vouch for most of these folk, but not all."

Spider took a quick glance around the taproom and nodded.

"Maybe you have had enough rum," Duncan said, scratching his neatly trimmed beard.

"Jesus, no," Spider replied. "I'm going to watch a friend die. And I may bloody well be next. There is no goddamned such thing as too much rum."

Duncan, an old sailing mate from long ago, sighed heavily and poured Spider another. It was gone within three heartbeats.

An hour or so later, after slipping through the puddle-riddled streets and alleys of Port Royal and hopping aboard a wagon full of people eager to see pirates swing, Spider felt utterly alone in the crowd that gathered before the gallows.

That could be my noose, he thought.

The gallows, still dark and dripping from the morning's brief rain, stood strong and sturdy in the brisk Jamaican wind, a counterpoint to the swaying palms nearby. Spider looked at the solid timbers and the dangling nooses and imagined himself up there, shaking, silently asking God's forgiveness while awaiting the sudden final drop.

That image had haunted him a long, long time. It haunted most pirates.

Spider tried to convince himself that most of the danger to him and his friends had passed. His Majesty's Ship *Austen Castle*, the frigate that was supposed to have carried them to England as prisoners on charges of piracy and espionage, had sailed from Port Royal a week ago. On that score, at least, his escape was complete. But years on the piratical account had taught him to be ever wary, and there was another navy frigate anchored in the harbor. So long as the king's men were here, and so long as criers spoke of bounties, no pirate was safe. Not even one whose most fervent wish was to leave piracy behind and return to his wife and son. He touched the carved pendant dangling from his neck, and, for a moment, pictured himself handing it to her.

Since the escape, Spider had assumed a false name, that of a good friend who had passed beyond this life and no longer had need of it. John Coombs, he was called now. Not John Rush.

Spider also had been careful to alter his appearance; his long brown hair was now cropped short, and he had allowed his beard to grow shaggy to hide the vicious sword cut across his chin, earned in winning his unlikely freedom. That beard got in the way when he sawed wood, hammered nails, or did other tasks common to ship's carpenters, and he vowed to cut it the first chance he got, but it was worthwhile as long as he was trapped here on land.

Spider kept his hands tucked into his pockets as much as possible these days, to hide the stub where the small finger of his left hand used to be. That was the kind of telltale detail eyewitnesses might remember.

Despite all those precautions, and even though he and his shipmates had managed to hide out at his old shipmate's tavern, Spider was nervous. The unsettling nature of being ashore, where danger might step out of the crowd or any looming door or alleyway at any moment, always rattled him. But it was worse than usual now. The dangling nooses seemed to beckon him. He deserved to swing on the gallows as much as any of the poor souls who would be hung today.

He'd never wanted to be a pirate, of course, and he prayed to God he would never have to be one again, but he'd been caught up in that world and he'd done the bloody work necessary to survive in it.

A ship's carpenter by training, he'd been forced to join a pirate band at a young age. The choice then—as it remained throughout the years of his pirate career—was to rob, fight, and kill, or be tossed overboard.

Only good fortune had placed him here among the watchers instead of on the gallows.

I will not squander this chance, he thought. *I will work my way home, to Em and little Johnny. I will live a better life, by God.*

Spider scanned the throng gathered for the hanging, seeking soldiers or sailors or witnesses who might recognize him, but his eyes were constantly drawn back to the skeletal timber frame and to the long, ugly, choking ropes. One of those ropes soon would break the neck of a former shipmate.

Spider inhaled deeply, hoping the familiar scents of fish and sun-heated tar riding the sea breeze would calm him. He wished he'd drunk a good deal more rum this morning, too. Instinct told him to flee this crowd that had hiked or ridden from Port Royal and Kingston to see the dreadful spectacle, but he needed to be here. Dobbin deserved at least that much.

Several men accused of piracy were to swing this day. Such hangings were common now in Jamaica, though the island once had been safe refuge for those who made their own law and lived by their own wits on the high seas. Even notorious pirates such as dapper Calico Jack Rackham and his famed pirate woman, Anne Bonny, had not eluded the law. Rackham had ended his piratical reign on the gallows. Bonny had been jailed and, if rumor was true, had escaped hanging only by pleading her belly. Not even the bloody English government would hang a pregnant woman.

"Watch when they drop," said a fellow nearby, talking to a girl of about eight. "The eyes bulge, pop out sometimes. You'll see. One lad's eye plopped into my aunt's lap, it did! Couple years ago. Damned truth, that is."

Spider figured a knife in the slobbering boor's neck might make some eyes pop, too, but that would draw attention he could ill afford.

"Is that true, about eyes poppin' out?" Spider turned to see young Hob, munching on a sugar apple. He had not seen the boy approach but was glad to have him here now. "No. Eyes do not pop out of their heads. Not that I have ever seen. Now hush."

Spider peered at faces and listened to whispers. He saw one fellow, not far off, who had a sailor's tan and a familiar look. Had he been one of the salts aboard HMS *Austen Castle* when Spider and his friends had escaped? Spider could not be sure, so he tugged at Hob's sleeve and edged farther away, then tilted his hat to hide his face from the man.

Some folks in the throng seemed eager to see justice done, while others bemoaned the end of the days when pirates gave Jamaica's economy a bigger boost; there were many ashore who benefited from the illegal business conducted on the outlaw sea, and some here who even loved the men about to die. Spider noted a tear on one deeply tanned woman's face, then wiped away one of his own.

"The noose, Hob, is the inevitable destination for a man who sails the devil's wind," Spider whispered to the young man next to him. "You remember that."

"Are you unwell, Spider John?" Hob tilted his head, scrunching his boyish face against the sunlight.

Spider gulped. "Be still, I am fine. I am glad you are here. You need to see this. Learn from this." At fifteen years of age, Hob still had a great deal to learn.

"I liked Dobbin. He doesn't deserve this."

We all deserve this, Spider thought. *We just got lucky, and Dobbin did not.*

Spider knew the sweat that dripped from him was not caused by the hot Caribbean sun. He was accustomed to hot weather, and the strong breeze would have been enough to cool him under normal circumstances. This sweat was the result of nerves and tension. The urge to simply turn and go raged in his mind, but he willed himself to remain. Dobbin would pass through the gates of hell today, once the sun reached its zenith. Spider would see him off.

A quick glance at the sun over the waving palms behind him told Spider it would not be long now. A drumroll confirmed it, and the crowd hushed. A dozen English soldiers, armed and stoic and dapper in uniform, led four men to the gallows. Bayonets flashed in the sun. The gathered laborers, smiths, fishermen, bakers, whores, and sailors opened the way for the troops with practiced ease. This was not their first hanging.

Beyond the gallows, ships anchored in the harbor began firing guns to mark the occasion. Those from the frigate HMS *Southampton* seemed to Spider to be the loudest, and rang out with a sense of omen. That was a navy ship, here to escort a merchant convoy to Boston. Spider, Odin, and Hob would be sailing with that convoy, and Spider hoped *Southampton* would keep her distance.

Black smoke drifted swiftly across the waters, accompanied by thunderous echoes, and in moments Spider could smell it. The familiar odor prompted memories of combat, and he inhaled deeply. For one ridiculous moment, he envisioned himself stealing a sword from a soldier and hacking his way to the gallows to cut Dobbin free.

Fairy tale thoughts, he told himself. *This is reality. This is what happens to pirates.*

He caught sight of Odin nudging his way closer to the gallows. The horrid old bastard was easy to pick out of the crowd, being taller than six feet and wearing a ridiculously broad-brimmed hat he hoped would hide the ghastly scars where his right eye used to be. And, of course, he still had the goddamned sword. Spider wondered where the man had stolen the rusty thing.

Odin wiped at his brow constantly with a white cloth, not to mop up sweat but as a further measure to hide his wretched face. No one who had seen that face was likely to ever forget it, and recognition could mean hanging. Spider noted that Odin's other hand never strayed far from the hilt of his blade.

Odin had heeded Spider's request to keep himself apart, and moved farther away still after noting Spider's gaze. Now the old man peered up at the gallows, which threw a shadow across his face. "Cover that damned gash," Spider growled under his breath—though he was too far away from the old salt to be heard. Even so, Odin raised the cloth again to his face as though he'd actually heard his shipmate's curse.

On the wooden platform, holding an open Bible but reciting its words from memory, a dour minister quietly intoned a message of divine justice. "It is joy to the just to do judgment, but destruction shall be to the workers of iniquity," he said, eyes gazing toward heaven. To Spider, the bastard looked as though he'd never known a happy day.

After that opening, the dark-haired minister made no effort to be heard above the murmurs of the crowd, and few people paid him attention. The preacher gabbled on, softly, but most gazes were fixed upon the condemned men.

Spider did not know three of the men being led to the nooses, but the third in line was Dobbin, the unlucky soul who had been captured while Spider and a few other prisoners escaped. Spider wondered how Dobbin had ended up in captivity. The last time he'd seen the man, Dobbin was being pulled into a rowboat by another fleeing shipmate while musket balls whizzed past them.

Spider scarcely recognized Dobbin. The man's face was all wrinkles, sweat, and ash, his hair matted like a gray tangle of dead seaweed. His eyes were closed, and he merely walked forward, stooping, and let the soldiers guide him. Dobbin mumbled softly, and Spider recalled how difficult it could be to discern the toothless sailor's words. Spider was certain Dobbin's words now were addressed to the one who would not have that difficulty, and he added his own small prayer as well. *Be merciful, Lord. Lend Dobbin courage and strength.*

Poor Dobbin. Why had luck abandoned him, yet smiled upon others? Until a couple of days ago, when the impending hangings were announced and the names of the condemned were bandied about in taverns and on wharves throughout Port Royal, Spider had not known what had become of Dobbin. Spider had started drinking harder upon hearing the man was waiting for execution on the gallows. He scratched at his own neck, where he could feel the imagined rope's bite.

"Dobbin looks bad," Hob whispered. "No life left in him."

Spider turned to the boy, who had become something of a surrogate son to him during their deadly adventures.

"Aye. He is resigned," Spider said. "Maybe that's for the best. No use fighting now."

Hob whisked his wind-whipped blond hair from his wide blue eyes and took in the scene, his gaze following the condemned men up the steps and beneath the waiting nooses. Hob's vision of piracy was fueled by too much imagination and romance and not enough hard reality. Not even the bloody capture of their ship and the ensuing arrest had wholly changed the boy's mind. Spider hoped that seeing Dobbin die on a noose might shake those damned dreams of pirate glory.

They had a chance now, legitimate jobs lined up on a merchant vessel shipping molasses and rum to Boston, thanks to a good word from Duncan. Spider would be a carpenter and Hob a carpenter's mate—although the lad couldn't saw a straight line if Jesus himself assisted. They would be able to start new lives.

The idea bored Hob, of course, who preferred pirate gold and living beyond the reach of kings to learning how to join two pieces of wood. Hob thought he would live forever and win every cast of the dice.

These condemned men had thought themselves beyond the law's reach, too, but events had proven otherwise. Spider hoped Hob realized that now. *Sometimes you learned the most by staring reality in the goddamned face.*

The minister closed his Bible with a stern "amen." Spider, lost in his own thoughts and silent prayers, had not heard a word the man had said. Less than average in height, Spider tiptoed forward to get a better look. Wind-borne sand lashed at his face and neck, and he snatched with long, thin fingers at his broad-brimmed hat before the wind could carry it away. He congratulated himself on remembering to keep his maimed left hand in his pocket.

Spider tried to catch Dobbin's eyes. He wanted him to know that he was there. Dobbin, however, kept his eyelids clamped shut and continued mouthing his invocation. One of the other doomed men sobbed uncontrollably. Another spat and then stared into the sky with eyes that seemed already dead. The fourth, unable to pace under the clutch of his guards, let his eyes do it for him. He scanned the throng as though trying to decide whom to kill first.

The lieutenant in command was reading the charges, and Spider started paying more attention.

"On this day, Tuesday, January 12, in the year of our Lord 1723 . . ." Spider missed a few words as he tried to peer between taller men. "First, that these men piratically, feloniously, and in hostile manner did attack, engage, and take seven certain fishing boats and merchant vessels belonging to the kingdoms of England, France, and Spain . . ."

Movement in the crowd nearby caught Spider's attention. He looked and cursed. That familiar face he'd spotted earlier was peering straight back at him—and then the goddamned son of a bitch pointed at Spider and Hob.

"Hey!" The man shoved his way through the crowd, straight toward Spider. "Pirate!"

"Damn it!" Spider grabbed Hob's arm. "Run, boy!"

Quick as Spider was, Hob passed him, and the boy shouldered aside a fellow who was pulling a gun from his belt. Behind them, gasps and alarms rose.

Several horses were tied just beyond the crowd. Spider freed one. "Hop up with me, Hob!"

"No, Spider John! I will ride on my own!" The boy was clambering atop a roan mare and wielding a pistol he must have stolen from the fellow he'd bowled over.

"Goddamn, Hob, we'll be split up!" There was no time for further argument, though, because Hob's horse was spinning like a dervish and the lad fired a shot that Spider prayed had not killed anyone. Then Hob's horse dashed down the road toward the city, and Spider somehow managed to make the beast he rode follow suit. Mounting a horse was easy enough. He'd done that before. Riding at full gallop, however, was a new and frightening experience.

"Full onward! Ho!" Hob whipped the pistol back and forth above his head. Spider, meanwhile, crouched low on his horse as the sound of muskets erupted behind them.

Spider caught up to Hob, who grinned like a fool. "They cannot catch us now!"

"Lead balls might catch us!" Spider slapped his mare's flank. The horse raced ahead, and Spider hoped it would just follow the damned road, for he had no idea how to control such a beast. After a few seconds at a gallop, he wondered if his ass would survive the pounding. But the horse, at least, seemed to know its way.

The thundering hooves could not quite hide the sound of drum-rolls and cheers from the gallows. Spider listened for the creaking hinges, thrumming ropes, and snapping necks that would tell him his friend was dead. He heard none of those, but he did hear the crowd's collective gasp, followed by a loud cheer.

I am sorry, Dobbin. I wanted to see you off. God damn this pirate life.

Spider, a veteran of many scrapes, shoved the guilt pangs aside and concentrated on staying alive. He could hear the pounding of hooves behind him and was willing to bet his pursuers were better riders. The road bent, trees lined both sides, and Spider decided to seize an opportunity, desperate though it was.

"You know how to stop a horse, Hob?"

"No!"

"Well, then, jump!"

It would likely mean injury, but that was better than hanging. Spider leapt from the saddle, and Hob did likewise, both of them tumbling into underbrush. Branches and thorns scraped at Spider's face and arms. The excited horses galloped onward.

"Are you hurt, Hob?"

"Just bruises and scrapes, Spider."

"Then follow me!" Spider grabbed his hat from the ground and plunged deeper into the underbrush, shoving aside branches. Hob followed.

Once they were well away from the road, Spider grabbed Hob's sleeve and they stopped. Crouching together, they heard the pursuit thunder past and continue down the road, hooves pounding like drums. Spider exhaled the breath he'd been holding.

"May God damn a world that won't let a couple of gentlemen see their old friend off to hell, Hob. It ain't just."

"Aye." The boy wiped at a scrape on his cheek. "It ain't just."

"Come, Hobgoblin, let us sneak our way back to the Phoenix. We've got other business ahead of us."

"Aye."

"Legitimate business," Spider added, and he was damned proud to say it. "Not more of this pirate business. We are done with that. Honest men, by thunder! But rum first. God, yes, rum first. A toast to old Dobbin."

2

"**S**pider, Odin seems worried about something. Truly worried."

Hob, breathing hard and wiping disheveled blond locks from his face, stood in the doorway of the cramped room they shared above the Phoenix Tavern. They would leave this safe harbor for good today. Tonight, they were to sleep aboard *Redemption*. In the morning, they would sail with the tide as part of a convoy bound for Boston. Spider, finally, would sail away from a life of piracy and toward Emma and his son. And he prayed he would never see Port Royal again.

Spider closed his eyes, and he could see her—the long hair, brown or blond depending on the light and the season, the broad smile that brightened his heart every time he saw it, the nose that crinkled when she flashed that smile. He could not envision the boy; little Johnny had been bald and wrinkled and pink in Em's arms the last time Spider had seen him, before walking away to board a whaler. He was supposed to have been gone only a couple of years. Pirates had intervened, and two years became something more like eight, although he had lost track. By now, little Johnny was dreaming of the sea, most likely.

Spider opened his eyes, and Em was gone. He gulped. *Dear Lord, whatever it is that troubles Odin, don't let it keep me from home.*

If Odin was worried about something, that was a bad omen. Odin had shown no concern when *Red Viper* headed into battle with another pirate vessel, and none when the king's frigate *Austen Castle* had come swooping down on them, and none even when he was in chains aboard that very same naval ship. Odin, who had sailed with the notorious Blackbeard and made sure everyone he met knew it, worried?

That worried Spider John.

Spider, sitting on one of two cots set up in the upstairs room and leaning against the wall, sucked on his pipe and let the fumes fill his head. In his right hand, he held a French throwing knife, a gift from Odin. The old man had stolen it and presented it to Spider with a wink. Spider had always been good at throwing knives, and this balanced beauty was the best he had ever owned. He'd been practicing with it this morning to help him stop thinking about Dobbin, two days dead. He shifted his gaze to the water spot on the wall ahead of him, then casually flipped the knife right into the very heart of that stain. The tip sank into the wood with a satisfying thunk.

"Damn," Hob said.

"Ten in a row," Spider replied. "Fetch the blade for me. Now what is it that concerns Odin?"

"I do not know," Hob answered, scurrying over to the wall and pulling Spider's knife free. The boy ran a finger across the tight grouping of slots left by the blade. "Jesus, Spider, you could cover all these with a shilling." The boy examined the weapon for a few seconds, eyebrows arched in admiration, then handed it to its owner. "Wish I could throw like that."

"I shall teach you. It'll be easier than teaching you to saw a plank, because you'll actually pay attention. Which reminds me . . ."

Spider reached into the sack by his cot and fished out a walnut-handled knife. "This is for you." He handed it over to Hob.

"This is very nice," the lad said. "It has my name on it!"

"Aye," Spider acknowledged. He'd carved the letters into the handle himself, after getting the tavern keeper to write the letters for him to use as a guide. Hob could not read much beyond his own name, but in this case, it was enough.

Hob tucked the knife into his belt. "Thank you, Spider John."

"Now, tell me of Odin, lad."

"We were up on the mizzenmast, making sure all was snug, and Odin was showing me some knots, and some new fellows came aboard. Odin went white as a ghost, I swear, and he turned away so the new men could not see his face."

"Nobody wants to see Odin's face," Spider said.

Hob scowled. As someone who had sailed with the notorious Blackbeard and lived on the Spanish Main longer than Hob had been alive, Odin was a bright star in Hob's universe. "Odin told me the lesson was done, real sudden, though we'd scarcely got started, and he said to go away. He seemed very, very concerned. Scared, I should say. Britches-shitting scared."

Spider took another deep inhalation of tobacco smoke, then let it stream from his nostrils. "I do not like the sound of that," he said, "not at all. Odin would laugh at the devil himself if ever they met. Hell, the devil might run from Odin."

"I know," Hob said. "That's why I am here, instead of waiting for you on board. What the hell shall we do?"

Spider stood and tucked the dagger into his belt. "I suppose we'd best get to *Redemption*, and see what it is that has Odin fretting. Perhaps one of the new fellows knows him of old, and he worries he'll be found out as a pirate."

Hob gulped. "Will we be revealed as well?"

Spider stared into the boy's blue eyes and put a hand on his shoulder. "I do not believe Odin would tattle on his shipmates, if that is what concerns you, not if burning bamboo shoots were thrust under his fingernails, not if a flaming brand was rammed hard against his balls. You may rely on that, Hobgoblin."

The boy smiled. "He is a tough son of a bitch."

"Toughest I ever knew. Sailed with Blackbeard, he did. Ha!" It was a fairly good imitation of Odin's raspy voice, and they both laughed. "Let us go to the ship. We'll see what has Odin fretting, and if we can do anything about it, by thunder, we will."

Spider grabbed his hat, which smelled of sea and salt, and the small leather sack that held his few belongings. He checked to make sure the heart pendant he'd carved for his Em was still hanging from his neck, then headed through the door behind Hob.

Spider's chest felt tight as he descended the stairs. He did not look forward to the walk through Port Royal. In his reckoning, every alley hid a thief, and every pair of eyes belonged to a spy. But he had to traverse those streets one more time to reach the ship, and Em, and so he would.

They stepped into the taproom. Hob headed for the swinging doors that led outside, but Spider stopped as Duncan proffered a bottle of rum. "Fair winds, my friend. It was good seeing you, Spider John." He placed the bottle on the bar and reached for a pair of wooden cups.

"Thanks for the port in a hell of a storm," Spider said as Duncan poured. "And thanks for easing my way with Cap'n Brentwood."

"Just promise you won't squander it," Duncan said. They both drank.

"I will not," Spider whispered. "No more pirate life for me. I go by the name of John Coombs now, honest ship's carpenter."

"So you will be paying for the rum this time?"

"I will, by thunder." Spider poked around in the sack and pulled out some coins. He plunked them down on the bar. "Heh, feels strange to do that."

"Well, now. Never thought I would see this." Duncan scooped up the coins quickly, as though they might vanish if he didn't.

Spider followed Hob out the door and into the overwhelming Jamaican sun. He tilted the hat until its wide brim shielded his eyes. A few steps later he emptied his spent pipe and tucked it into the band of his hat, and together he and Hob strode toward the wharfs. Spider's good mood of a few moments ago was gone now, dashed on the rocks like a ship in a storm. This was a city of spies and thieves, with many people willing to cut a throat or turn a pirate over to the authorities for a few coins or to gain favor, as if the favor of those in power ever really meant a goddamned thing.

The town, once known as a pirate haven and decried as a wicked rebirth of the biblical Sodom, was arranged rather haphazardly, with taverns propped against brothels next to churches in narrow alleys and winding streets. People of every hue between white-burned-to-red and darkest ebony moved quickly between the shady areas. They fanned themselves, or huddled beneath parasols, and drank steadily from flasks and wineskins. Sutlers rolled carts, setting up to sell everything from hats to nuts, fruit to gunpowder, plantains to cockatiels. Spider growled when one of the birds squawked at him.

Hob laughed. "Why do you jump from birds so?"

"They move too goddamned fast, and have too many sharp parts, and I think the devil created them to shred men. And have you looked in their eyes? No more soul than a shark."

Hob just shook his head.

Piles of shingles and busted timbers lined the streets; those and a number of boarded windows and cracked walls testified to what must have been a hell of a recent storm, although the weather had been fair since Spider arrived. Even cobblestones had been ripped up in places.

Mules pulled a creaky wagon laden with crates and barrels toward the harbor. Children threw stones at rats, and women emptied chamber pots from upper windows in brothels while men tried to drag the ladies back to bed. The breeze, although cool on Spider's skin, carried a disturbing mix of scents—urine, fish, sweaty animals, and perfume. His stomach reeled a bit, and he momentarily regretted the rum.

"Once we sort out Odin's concerns, Hob, you can show me if you've learned to fashion a proper dovetail joint."

"Jesus, Spider, do I really have to learn all that?"

Spider stopped dead in his tracks. "Do you know why I am not a dead man right now, Hob?"

"Because you are too stringy for sharks?"

Spider slapped the back of Hob's head, but laughed. "Because I have a skill. When Jed Carter's bloodsucker crew came pouring over *Lily's* rail—I was not much older than you when I was mate to *Lily's* carpenter, you know, and then carpenter myself after Herman got sick and died—Jed didn't take on many of our crew. He already had plenty of men who could fight, plenty of men who could sail. But he needed a carpenter, by thunder. That saved my life. Jed sent most of *Lily's* crew overboard to fight against the sea for their lives, but he kept me aboard. I would be dead and deep, boy, but I knew how to wield a saw and a hammer. That, and that alone, saved my life."

"You know how to wield a gun and sword, too." Hob nodded hard, as though he had scored a point. "That has saved your life more than once, and I was a witness."

"When I met Jed Carter, I didn't know any fighting ways." Spider drew a deep breath. "I learned all that after. Because I had to, not because I wanted to."

They continued walking, but Spider's mind was turned inward now. The dark memories made him wince. Spider had hoped to mind his own business, work hard as a carpenter, and avoid the bloodshed until he could find means to escape. But he had quickly learned that every man aboard a pirate vessel was expected to fight, and he had just as quickly learned that in the thick of things he'd rather fight than die. Spider had gotten blood on his hands right away, and it would never all wash off. Never.

Hob whistled softly. A winking trollop crossing the narrow street in front of them left a sweet scent in her wake, and Spider punched the boy in the arm. "No time for that, and no money."

"I have money. I have been saving," Hob said. "I have enough, anyway. And Cap'n Brentwood gave me liberty, told me to enjoy my last day in Port Royal."

"And what of Odin's worries?"

"Thinking they might be the kind of worries that might get me hung or shot, I would as soon take my leave for a bit and follow her. Might be my last opportunity." The woman, gazing back, turned away with a smile, a flash of green eyes, and a swirl of blond curls that were wilting in the morning heat.

Spider relented. "Very well, then. Go enjoy life. It can be god-damned short enough, I guess. I will try to have all our problems settled by the time she has emptied your purse and your balls."

"Thank you." Hob scurried off, and Spider headed toward the wharf.

Spider turned to watch the boy go. He understood Hob's eagerness. He had been younger than Hob when he had first become enthralled with Em's charms. He had been unable to think of anything besides bedding her. He remembered those times now, the long looks, the sneaking away, the frantic lovemaking. Hob's dalliance was not the same, of course. It would not likely result in a wedding. But Spider certainly understood the lad's urges.

Like an apple at the end of a branch, Port Royal sat on the tip of a long spit called the Palisadoes. The spit divided the harbor from the Caribbean; as Spider proceeded westward, the busy harbor lay to his right beneath a bright, cloudless sky and swirling gulls. Farther above, a majestic black-and-white frigate bird tilted toward the open ocean. Spider's distaste for birds did not apply to this fork-tailed wonder. He assumed it had dagger claws and a sharp beak just like every other bird he'd seen, and perhaps even the same evil eyes, but he'd never seen a frigate bird up close. Indeed, he'd never seen a frigate bird do anything but soar aloft, and he longed to know that kind of freedom. So long as frigate birds kept their distance, Spider could get along with them.

He kept his eyes on the damned gulls, though.

In a short time, which seemed longer because Spider averted his eyes anytime he encountered someone looking in his direction, he came within view of *Redemption*, sitting at anchor in water shining in the bright sun. If Spider was to know freedom, *Redemption* was the key. He hoped Odin's concerns would not be an obstacle. Perhaps someone aboard suspected Odin's pirate past? That could end with Odin, Hob, and Spider in manacles. So he was eager to learn what worried the one-eyed rigger.

But first, he had to cross a harbor of ghosts.

Spider stepped from the wharf and into a tender, flipping a coin from his sack to one of the two oarsmen. "*Redemption*," he said, pointing toward the triple-masted, Dutch-built beauty some two hundred yards away. Pointing probably had been unnecessary, since harbor men always knew every ship by name, perhaps better than they knew their own children, but Spider liked calling attention to the fluyt. She was the finest ship he'd ever served, tall and straight with woodwork that only impressed more the closer one got. She was a floating work of art. As the men slipped the lines and dipped their oars, Spider

tried to concentrate on the ship that was their destination and to keep
his mind off the dead in the waters below.

"You worried about the ghosts, sir?" The bald oarsman nodded
toward the water.

"No."

"You seem worried."

"Just row."

It had been about thirty years since an earthquake and the resulting
tidal wave had laid waste to Port Royal. The quake—hailed by many as
a justly deserved divine retribution for the people's wickedness—had
leveled two-thirds of the town, and the wall of water had reduced the
hard-packed sand beneath Port Royal to sludge. Buildings and people
slid into the harbor, to be buried beneath the stirred mud.

At least three thousand people had died, if the tales were true.
Spider doubted every one of those people deserved God's wrath, but he
was no expert in such things.

The storm had assaulted the dead, too. Hundreds of graves had been
ripped asunder and dashed into Kingston Harbour. Henry Morgan,
famed privateer and once governor of Jamaica, had been among them,
and his spirit was now said to haunt these waters. They'd talked of it
over beer and rum at the Phoenix, Hob wide-eyed, Odin nodding, and
Spider trying to convince himself that ghost talk was just talk. He realized now he had not quite succeeded.

Spider kept his hands away from the gunwale, because he had seen
men lose fingers and hands to sharks in this very harbor. Local harbor
men insisted the ever-present sharks hardly ever bit a man, but Spider
wouldn't trust a fucking shark any more than he trusted a naval purser,
or those hovering gulls.

Spider fixed his gaze on *Redemption*. She towered there, and
because her bow was aimed at them, her shape was evident. Narrow
above and wider below, the Dutch fluyt had been built to haul cargo
efficiently. She would never be swift in any sea, but she was steady and
sturdy and could be handled by as few as eighty men. She had no guns
mounted, but she would be part of a convoy of East Indiamen escorted

by the naval frigate HMS *Southampton*. The frigate would pack guns aplenty, by God, and would be a nimble ship. Spider could see her beyond the harbor, riding the wind smartly under full canvas, brilliantly white, and no doubt her captain was drilling the crew with disciplined efficiency. Spider could envision *Southampton's* men running out guns, firing broadsides, loading and running and firing the guns again and again, until it could be done to the captain's satisfaction. He'd never been in the navy, but he'd been on the opposing side in such battles and had a deep respect for navy skill. He and his pirate mates had escaped capture or death mostly by luck, and by racing their sloops into waters too shallow for the king's ships. But vessels like *Southampton* had rid the seas of most pirates.

Redemption *should be safe enough*, Spider thought, before spitting overboard for luck.

Most of the heavy stores—barrels of water, salt pork and salt fish as provisions, cordage, and the several tons of molasses and rum to be sold in Boston—were stowed in *Redemption's* large holds already, but three boats crowded the ship to starboard to load trunks, cages of squawking chickens, additional canvas that Odin had insisted upon, and more.

Other tenders plied the waters, too, and so the shortest path to the ship was not available. The tender gave *Redemption* plenty of leeway and took Spider around the ship's stern. The captain's cabin doors were open onto the stern gallery, perhaps Spider's favorite feature of the ship. That stern gallery, akin to a back porch on a home, allowed the captain to step directly from the confines of his cabin and into the open air, where he could take his tea, gaze upon *Redemption's* wake, and ponder whatever plans and dreams crossed the minds of captains.

Captain Josiah Brentwood was not out on the gallery now, but Spider could hear the man's gentle voice emanate from the cabin, intoning, ". . . nearly forty yards in length, and ten abeam, and as sturdy a ship as I've ever sailed. Beautiful. You'll find her quite accommodating, and we've worked below to see to every comfort."

The ship would be any captain's pride and joy, Spider thought, and he was glad to realize Captain Brentwood, a recent widower and much distracted by the loss of his wife, had noticed. Spider hoped this journey would give the captain some spark, and this was certainly a ship to inspire a seafaring man.

The fluyt had once been used as a pirate's flagship and had been captured by the Royal Navy and sold off. Brentwood now owned it and had personally overseen the work done to erase what he called the "stamp of thievery and debauchery" left by her previous crew. Spider's key task in recent weeks, aside from all the ordinary carpentry jobs involved with getting a ship ready to sail, had been to make certain the cramped passenger quarters below were as comfortable and attractive as possible, and to sequester one section for the captain's daughter, Abigail. Captain Brentwood had been quite clear that his daughter should be as comfortable as possible, and Spider had gone so far as to build a rolltop desk for her, with copious drawers for papers and such and deep wells for ink jars, where she could write in her journal. Spider also had gutted an adjacent passenger cabin and turned it into a sitting room of sorts. Captain Brentwood had smiled and deemed it all acceptable.

Spider couldn't help but feel proud. *Redemption* wasn't his ship, but he'd earned many blisters and small cuts in making her as beautiful and solid as he could. He'd learned a few things, too. The Dutch built fine ships.

The tender sidled up to the ship, and Spider clambered up the larboard rope ladder, sack over his shoulder.

"Ho, John!" The sailing master, Nicholas Wright, peered down at Spider. "Care to toss a dirk? I would like to win my money back." Even the simple motion of freeing a kerchief from his belt to wipe his brow prompted muscles to ripple in Wright's arms. The man's chest swelled beneath a gray shirt stained with dots of tar. Spider, not a large man, envied Wright's physique.

"Best not to do it today, sir," Spider answered. "I have been practicing, and I swear I can't miss. You might as well just give me your coins now if you insist on more bets."

"Very well," Wright said, beaming a wide, bright smile. "We shall have a go tomorrow, though. I will never believe a man can hit the mark so often as you think you can."

"I would think you've seen me throw enough times by now to keep your money safe," Spider answered. "I mean it, sir. I am very damned good at it."

"Indeed." Wright laughed. He was about Spider's age, somewhere in his twenties, but even though he was second-in-command, he wore authority easily, like a cloak he could doff or don as needed. As sailing master, Nicholas Wright had charge of most day-to-day matters aboard, and he'd commanded other vessels for Captain Brentwood. Others aboard *Redemption* who had sailed with him before spoke well of him. He got on well with the men, because he worked as hard as any of them and treated them as equals, even though they were not.

Wright smiled. "But tomorrow, aye? I feel lucky."

"Aye, sir." Spider hopped nimbly over the rail and headed to the forecastle. Once he'd stowed his belongings in his chest, he looked aloft to find Odin.

The man was perched on the foremast, straddling the topsail yardarm, inspecting lines and blowing great clouds of pipe smoke into the Jamaican breeze. Spider, an able climber, clutched his hat brim in his teeth and ascended the ratlines. Soon, he was perched on the yardarm next to his friend.

"Hob tells me you have misgivings," Spider said, returning the hat to his head as a guard against the bright sun.

"Aye," Odin said quietly while looking around. That alone made Spider nervous, for Odin seldom cared who overheard him. Ordinarily, caution was alien to the old codger, something for lesser mortals to worry about.

"Well," Spider said, smelling Odin's pipe and wishing he'd taken a moment to light his own. "Are you going to tell me your worries, or am I going to have to cut it out of you?"

"Some new folk came aboard," Odin said. "And one of them, a paid passenger, is the very goddamned devil. The very goddamned fucking devil."

The old man brushed his long ash-colored hair away from his face and gazed toward the bowsprit, almost directly below. Then he pointed. "There."

Spider looked and saw four men leaning against the starboard rail. "Which one?"

"Fellow with the pipe and the brimstone vapors swirling about his head."

One of the four, indeed, seemed enveloped in dark clouds emanating from his pipe, nostrils, and mouth. Gray beard and long hair framed a craggy, cruel face.

Spider spat out toward the sea, and watched the spittle fly on the breeze. He snatched the hat from his head, so as not to lose it. "Why does he worry you?"

"I'd rather see headless, dead Blackbeard crawl up from the ocean than to see that son of a whore." Odin sucked on his pipe hard, and the bowl flamed like a volcano.

"Who is he?"

"Passenger. Named Samuel Lawrence," Odin said, "but we called him Sam Smoke."

"You sailed with him?"

"Aye," Odin said softly. "With him, and with Wicked Pete Reese, and with one worse."

"Worse than Blackbeard?" Spider shuddered.

"Ned Low." Odin inhaled deeply and held pipe smoke in his lungs a moment, then blew out a monstrous fog. "We all sailed with Ned Low."

"Jesus," Spider said.

3

Ned Low had been the subject of many a bloody tale by the Phoenix hearth during Spider's weeks in Port Royal. Men spoke of cruel tortures and pointless killings, and surmised that although Blackbeard, Bartholomew Roberts, and Calico Jack might all be gone, Ned Low would prowl and infest the seas forever. No one would ever bring goddamned Ned Low to justice. He was the devil's son.

Spider remembered one such story vividly. "We found a jolly boat, adrift, full of sliced men," one old French gent with haunted eyes had sworn. "Ned Low's flag rolled up, tucked between the thwarts, with heads in it. Heads. Five heads."

Much of the common-room discussion had revolved around the killer's current whereabouts, whether he was on the Spanish Main or had run up toward Charleston, or off to the Azores. No one really knew, of course. But Ned Low had the Admiralty's attention these days, and the pirate had been playing the mouse. The sea was a wide expanse, an endless sheet of water. Ned Low could be anywhere.

Or he could be right out there somewhere. Spider gulped and stared at the harbor mouth. If one of Ned Low's henchmen was on this very ship, then Ned could be very close, indeed.

"Seen any signs of pirate vessels in the harbor here, Odin?" Spider blocked the sun from his eyes and scanned the ships around him. Most were cargo ships; some were clearly cut out for little more than fishing. He did see one sloop, built for the kind of speed and maneuverability that made pirates love them, but this one had no apparent guns and had obviously seen much tender care. It was an unlikely pirate ship.

A crescendo of feminine laughter from below interrupted Spider's thoughts. A small group of people wandered along the starboard rail, and the laughs rose from the lone woman in the group. She had to be Brentwood's daughter, Abigail. She was dressed like a man in britches and a simple shirt, probably a practical decision to make moving easier aboard a crowded ship, but her long blond hair and slender figure deserved a fine skirt and a lacy blouse. She battled the wind for possession of a flowery hat, briefly, before tucking the thing under her arm. Her laughter was music, incongruous with the cursing of sailors and the screeching of gulls. Yet here she was, aboard *Redemption*, with the likes of Sam Smoke, whose mere presence chilled the soul of Odin.

"Pretty, is she not?"

Odin spat. "I guess we're a goddamned hen frigate. I do not see a single goddamned thing good about having a girl aboard."

Spider gave Odin a hard look. As usual, he found it difficult to assess the man. He could not know what Odin was thinking or even guess how old the codger really was. In repose, Odin was a nightmare figure, an ancient warlock with a horribly scarred and sun-leathered face. But his long fingers could handle knife and knot as easily as anyone, and he could scramble up a mast like a monkey. Odin made light of things that made other men shiver deep inside.

But he did not make light of Sam Smoke.

"Jesus," Spider muttered again. "Lend me your pipe, and tell me about this bastard Smoke."

"Christ," Odin growled, handing his pipe over to Spider. "Give me bloody Blackbeard before Ned Low or any of his right-hand men. Blackbeard was a monster, but he killed for reasons. He had reasons, by God! Kill some, viciously, get known for that, and people knew they'd best just kneel and give him what he wanted. A man could maybe deal with Ed Teach, maybe even predict him. He was human enough for that. You didn't have to wonder if he was going to kill a man for no goddamned reason at all. But Ned. That is another thing. Ned is another thing."

Spider passed the pipe back to Odin.

Odin's jaw clenched on it, and he talked through his tombstone teeth.

"Not human, by God! Not Ned, nor his bloody helpers Wicked Pete and Sam Smoke. That's what bonded them, those three. Not being human."

"And you are certain he's one of Ned's men?"

"Aye. You do not forget a bastard like Sam Smoke."

Odin took a deep draw and then handed the pipe to Spider. His gray eye stared out to sea, as if that was where the memories hid. "It was before I signed on with Barlow on *Plymouth Dream*," Odin began.

"Ned, Sam, Wicked Pete, and me, we were all crew under George Lowther, plundering where we could and making our own laws. Bloody pirates, aye? We were well off the colonies, near some damned island, and Lowther sent a sloop to take some men ashore to cut some wood. Ned Low commanded that sloop, and me and Sam and a few other gents went with him."

Spider inhaled deeply from the pipe, then handed it back to Odin.

"We got the wood cut, loaded it on the sloop," Odin continued, "but Ned thought one fellow, named Ed Pigeon, hadn't hauled his fair share of lumber. Probably true. Ed was lazy. But he got going pretty good when Ned smacked him. He barked back, said something about guns or swords on the beach, take your pick. Ned punched Pigeon in the jaw and knocked him on his arse. Should have known it was all fucking going to hell from there."

Spider had questions, but decided to let Odin ramble on.

Odin exhaled a stream of smoke and watched it fly on the breeze. The vessel swayed slightly, and ropes hummed in the wind. "Ned hauled the man up, gave him a look that chased all the fight right out of him, and ordered Pigeon's wrists bound. Pete and Sam, they drew guns and stood guard. Ned, he twisted a slow fuse between Ed Pigeon's fingers, weaving-like. Ned forced the man to his knees, then asked Sam Smoke for his pipe. Always smoking, Sam was. Sam Smoke laughed, because he knew what was coming.

"Ned lit that rope with Sam's pipe and watched it burn between Ed Pigeon's fingers while Pigeon screamed, guns to his head. The poor bastard tried to fall on his hands, smother the fire with his own body, but Ned kicked him in the face. 'No, no, no,' Ned says. Then Ned knelt in front of the poor son of a bitch, so he could smell the man's hands cooking. He fucking smiled, he did. Breathing deep, burning flesh, and he smiled. Any of us that thought we might help, we thought twice, because Sam Smoke and Wicked Pete were standing guard, guns in hand. You could see it in their eyes; they could hardly wait for an excuse to shoot somebody. They fucking hoped we would help Pigeon. It wasn't really a gunshot we feared, of course. It was being the next mouse those cats played with. That was the fright that stayed our hands. Unmanned us."

"Damn," Spider said. He looked below—and saw Sam Smoke staring right back at him.

"Odin . . ." Spider counted silently to five. Smoke's hard gaze remained locked on him the whole time.

"Bugger," Spider exclaimed. "He's spied us! He might have recognized you."

Odin freed his work knife. "Son of a bitch comes up here, I'll gut him."

"Shove him," Spider suggested. "A knife wound would be tough to explain, but a slip . . ."

"Aye."

Spider freed his own knife and looked below. Sam Smoke was gone. "Fuck," he said. "Smoke is not there."

"Is he coming up?" Odin sounded nervous. Spider had never heard Odin sound nervous.

"I do not know." Spider grabbed the mast and leaned forward, straining to look below. "I do not see him climbing up, but . . ."

"He might be aiming a pistol at us," Odin said.

Odin went higher, and Spider remained where he was. With the knife in his hand, poised for a throw, Spider fought to control his breath. He'd fought as a pirate many times, of course, but he'd never found himself wondering how to kill a man without anyone else aboard noticing. A pitched battle was one thing, but this was new.

He watched the mast below, twisted his neck to eye ratlines and peer around spars, looked across empty air to see if Sam Smoke perched on a yardarm, gun in hand.

There was no sign of the bastard.

After a long wait, his heart drumming a fast cadence the entire time, Spider saw Sam Smoke take up his previous spot. Spider sighed and waved to Odin, who clambered down, knife clenched in his teeth. Odin perched again in his previous spot and put his dirk away.

"Maybe he just went to refill his pipe," Spider said, putting away his own weapon. "Tell me the rest of your story."

"They just played with Ed Pigeon, cats with a mouse. And we didn't help." Spider had never heard Odin speak so quietly before. "I ought to have done something, but . . . something about those men." Odin turned his gray eye toward Spider. "There is more, Spider John."

Spider looked below, where Abigail Brentwood gazed over the rail. Wind blew her hair in at least three directions, and sunlight reveled in it. Sam Smoke stood not twenty paces away from her, lighting his pipe and staring at the pretty blonde. He seemed at ease, master of all around him. He did not look up toward Odin and Spider.

"Tell me," Spider said.

"After Pigeon stopped blubbering, Ned cut the bindings. Pigeon looked at his hands, all black and red and bloody, still smoking, still oozing, and the man could hardly breathe. He looked like he was screaming, but there was no sound, hardly any air. Sam and Ned whispered to one another, and laughed a lot. Then Ned ordered Pigeon bound around his waist and had him hauled up to a yard on a pulley. Men did it, too, figuring they'd be shot, or worse. Which is very fucking true.

"The poor soul dangled there above us, swinging in the wind, just like poor Dobbin but wrapped around the belly, not the neck, so still fucking alive, blood and pus dripping from his hands, tears pouring out of his face, pissing himself, and Ned and Sam laughing. Wicked Pete, too. They laughed. Ned stood under the man, catching the falling blood and piss in his hands and on his tongue, lapping it up. Then he stepped aside."

Odin took a deep breath, then looked away again. "'Drop him.' That's what Ned ordered next. 'Drop him.' And they did, else get shot by Pete and Sam. They just fucking dropped him. Pigeon fell from the yard and smacked the deck like a wet sack of wheat. We heard the bones break and the wind gush out of him, and saw blood spray out of him. But it didn't kill him. God! It did not kill him! He kept moving. The idiot. Flopping. Like a fish tossed on the deck. Just flopping. So Ned ordered him hauled up again."

Spider's fingers brushed the hilt of his throwing knife, and he stared intently at Sam Smoke.

"Three times," Odin said. "That is how many times they hauled him up, and dropped him to the deck, before he finally died. Finally, mercifully, died. Ned, Sam, Pete, all of them laughing at every drop, every new splash of blood. All because Ed Pigeon didn't carry wood fast enough to satisfy Ned Low."

Odin turned his gray eye back to Spider. "I ain't proud. I should have helped that man, should have risked getting shot, should have pulled a knife on the whore sons, but I didn't. I didn't. I do it in my fucking daydreams, I do it in my fucking nightmares, but I did not do it then. I've done some crimes, but that is my worst.

"We sailed back to Lowther, and when George divvied up his little fleet again I went off with Barlow and counted myself lucky to be far away from Ned Low and Sam Smoke and Wicked Pete Reese. The fucking inhuman bastards."

"And now Sam Smoke is here," Spider said. "And maybe Ned Low is in these waters." He scanned the harbor again.

Odin nodded. "Maybe."

Spider had dreamed of freedom, but he was still sailing the devil's wind. Maybe the devil's wind was the only wind there was.

"We can't exactly tell Cap'n Brentwood about this bastard, can we?" Spider sighed. "He'll start asking all kinds of embarrassing questions. 'How do you know this man Sam Smoke's a pirate?' he'll want to know. He'd ask Sam a lot of fucking questions, too. And I suppose Sam Smoke would tell a few tales in return."

Odin nodded. Captain Brentwood had accepted the assurances from Spider's tavern master friend and decided not to ask a lot of questions about their past. The captain struck Spider as a decent and trusting soul who would assume the best in a person as long as he could, but he would not ignore accusations made out loud. If Odin talked of Sam Smoke's piracy, Sam surely would do likewise regarding Odin. And that would, soon enough, lead to speculation about Spider and Hob.

They could not afford that risk, not with a naval escort nearby, not with their escape still the talk of Port Royal, not with New England and Em and little Johnny almost within reach.

"Talking would be foolish," Odin said. "I say we kill him."

"A bit rash, aye?" Spider scolded. "Remember, we've become honest."

"I *honestly* think we should kill him," Odin replied. When he saw Spider's jaw gape, the lone eye widened. "Ha!"

Spider was glad to see a small spark of Odin's usual nature return; apparently, telling his story had helped ease his spirits, if only a little. "Has Sam seen you aboard? I mean, up close? I am not sure if he was staring at you or at me just now, to be honest."

"I do not believe so," Odin said. "I have kept my distance. But I can't hide from his sight forever."

"Certainly not." Spider swung onto the ratlines. "Had you lost the eye when you knew him?"

"No," Odin said. "And I went by my own name then, too."

Spider blinked. "What is your own name?"

Odin shook his hideous head slowly. "Ain't telling you that."

Spider nodded. "Fair enough. Do you think Smoke might know you if he saw you now?"

"I do not know," Odin said. "It was a long time ago, and I was prettier then. But I'd rather not chance it."

Spider sighed. "Well then, if he hasn't seen you yet, and might not know you if even he does, that means I have time to come up with a plan that won't get us chucked in the brig or dancing on the gallows."

Spider started to climb down, then stopped to give Odin one last look. "But if I can't devise something smarter, perhaps Sam Smoke vanishes in the night. Men fall off ships all the time. It can be another great mystery of the sea."

4

Spider dropped nimbly the last three feet to the deck, turned, took one step—and fell on his ass to avoid the screeching yellow-and-white blur flying at his face.

"Thomas, damn and blast ye!" Little Bob Higgins hurled a belaying pin at the chubby cat. Thomas, however, had already scrambled neatly out of range, and the pin rebounded from the ratlines and glanced sharply off Spider's shoulder.

"Fat little bugger!" Little Bob, all three feet of him, stepped past Spider as if to chase the ship's cat up the ropes. Spider grabbed Bob's ankle, gave it a sharp twist, and sent the man tumbling hard to the weather deck. Spider did not particularly care about the cat—he distrusted the creatures, placing them almost as low as birds in his esteem, and wondered how in the hell this one had managed to follow him from the sinking *Red Viper* to the frigate *Austen Castle* and now to *Redemption*—but he had even less love for Little Bob Higgins.

"Damn and blast!" Bob rolled onto his back, hands on his bruised, bald scalp, amid an uproar of laughter from the men on deck. Spider rose, dusted off his hands, and said, "Those pins are not for throwing about, Bob. Beware, or I'll stuff you into a keg and set you adrift. I suspect I'd get a dozen volunteers to help me."

That drew a rowdy chorus of assent.

"Damn your arse, John Coombs." Spider almost startled; in the heat of the moment, the assumed name caught him off guard.

"Just be sure you give me leeway," Spider said curtly as Little Bob rose. "I have never liked you, Bob, you fucking fopdoodle."

Spider bent to pick up the belaying pin, but kept an eye on Bob.

The short man had an equally short fuse. But Little Bob kept his distance as Spider handed the pin to a seaman and asked him to put it in its proper place.

"I say damn and blast ye, Coombs."

Spider grinned. "I'll break your neck like kindling, Bob, if you push me." Spider picked up his hat.

Crewmen laughed, with one or two calling curses down upon Little Bob and at least one cursing the cat. "Where's Mister Wright? He may want to lay a bet on this," someone called.

Spider caught sight of Sam Smoke, standing in the back but tall enough that his face could be seen easily, watching with amusement. Up close, the man's hard blue eyes cut through the tobacco haze that swirled beneath the brim of his hat. Spider thought the devil might look very much like that, peering through the brimstone smoke.

A stern, but calm, voice cut through the din and brought Spider's attention back to the row with Little Bob.

"That is quite enough." Captain Josiah Brentwood strode forward, commanding attention with his six feet of height and hard gray eyes. His hair, long and just as gray, waved like a flag in the breeze, and he stood with his hands locked behind his back and his jaw working back and forth as he looked about. After the men quieted, almost instantly, the captain confronted Little Bob. "Have you been after Thomas again?"

Upon hearing his name, the cat appeared from somewhere above, hurtling himself at the captain. Brentwood, clearly expecting the cat's maneuver, unclasped his hands and deftly caught the animal. He stroked Thomas gently and fixed his icy eyes on Little Bob. "Well?"

"He stabbed my nose," Bob said, staring at the deck. He pointed to his nostrils, both of which had been sharply pricked. Bob looked like half a man standing there next to the lanky captain.

"I've told you to keep your nose away from Thomas," Brentwood said quietly. "Thomas is a very good cat. He won't bother you if you don't bother him."

"He hates me! Little bugger!"

"Enough!" It was the first time Spider had heard Brentwood raise his voice, and it was impressive and shocking, like thunder from a clear sky.

No one else spoke, but a new player pushed his way through the crowd. "I am sorry, Captain," said Nicholas Wright. The master sucked air into his broad chest, and his eyes widened with fury. "I will take care of this, sir. Should not have let it happen." His light blue eyes fixed on Little Bob, who ducked his head as though dodging a blow.

"It is all well, Mister Wright," the captain said. "I do not expect you to be in all places at once. Nor do I wish to delegate all the unpleasant duties to you." Spider didn't think the captain's expression quite matched the conciliatory words, but Wright nodded and seemed pleased. Brentwood turned his attention back to Little Bob.

"I gave you a chance, Bob," the captain said. "I doubt any other captain would have done so. You are a lazy hand, and a miserable cad. As unpleasant as a prickly rash. This is a good cat, bad mouser, but a good cat. Minds his own business. You should mind yours. Are you not supposed to be stowing goods for our passengers?"

"I was, Cap'n, honest; then this little bugger . . ."

"Halt!" Brentwood sighed, scratched Thomas behind the ears, then released the cat. Thomas dropped nimbly to the deck and wandered off, seeking shade. "Bob Higgins, I release you from my crew. Mister Wright will pay you what you've earned, if anything. Don't pay him if he hasn't worked, Nicholas."

"Aye, sir."

"Then, Mister Higgins, you will get off my ship."

Little Bob's eyes bulged. "No, Cap'n, no! Over a damned cat?"

"Get off my ship," Brentwood said slowly and quietly.

"I need to get to Boston, sir, please." Bob raised his hands, imploring the captain with broad pleading gestures and a big smile. The effect of the smile was ruined by six or seven missing teeth. Bob turned to Wright when his pleading failed to break the captain's resolve. "You do not know what it means to me, sirs. I will behave, I swear."

"Get off my ship," Brentwood said, "or be thrown off."

"I'll see it done, sir," Wright said. His tone, low but hard as good oak, left no doubt that he would.

Bob's smile vanished, and his blue eyes grew cold. "Damn ye! God damn and blast ye!"

"Be on the next tender that leaves, or you will swim. As for you, John"—the captain turned toward his carpenter—"what is your role in this?"

"None, sir, other than to be pummeled with a belaying pin Bob threw at the cat."

"I heard a mention of breaking a neck."

"Aye, sir," Spider said. "It was a hot moment. Wouldn't have actually hurt him, sir, not unless my life depended on it." Spider tried to sound sincere and wondered if he'd succeeded.

"You bring such concerns to me, John, or to Mister Wright, and break no necks. We shall have no fighting aboard *Redemption*. You work hard, and know your trade, but that gives you no leave for fighting. Do you understand me, John?"

"Aye, sir."

Captain Brentwood's eyes turned toward the mast, and his gaze followed it upward into the rigging. "*Redemption* knew too much fighting in her day. Too much neglect. A carrier of brigands and thieves." He looked at Spider. "Those days are behind her. She is lovely, John, and you deserve as much credit for that as anyone. You focus on your duty, and let Mister Wright and I discipline the hands, if it should become necessary."

"Aye, sir."

Captain Brentwood turned and headed slowly to his cabin aft, his head down and his hands once more clasped behind his back. After three steps, he let out a heavy sigh and quickened his pace. Spider thought he caught snatches of a hymn, hummed in the captain's low voice.

Little Bob walked, grumbling, toward the hatch that led below. Wright dogged him all the way.

The crewmen went back to work, and Spider, relieved to have

escaped the captain's wrath, thought to go find himself a tot of rum, or maybe two. But he caught a glance of Abigail Brentwood, who sat on a barrel by the starboard rail, and he froze. Across her lap was a wooden contraption, long and slender, and she tapped it with her fingers. Her head swayed slowly as she did so, and her eyes were closed. Spider noted her swaying seemed to be in time with the ship's gentle rocking, and her smiles coincided with each roll to port. Her hair was caught up in a ponytail, which tossed about on the breeze.

She is breathtaking, Spider decided, and then he silently asked both Em and the good Lord for forgiveness for noting that. He was about to turn away, but when Abigail Brentwood opened her fine blue eyes, they were aimed directly at him, and she smiled. He gawked foolishly just long enough to realize simply walking away was no longer an option. He suddenly wished he owned all his fingers and all his teeth, and perhaps a razor and some soap. He lamented the fact he had not yet had a moment to cut off most of the wretched beard.

"What," he said, pointing at the device in her lap after a couple of awkward heartbeats, "have you there?" He hoped he did not sound as foolish as he felt.

"This?" She tapped fingers on the device quickly, then lifted her hands and spread them wide. "It mimics a clavichord. Isn't it wonderful? Mr. Fox built it for me." Her accent was refined, and spoke of London, or at least the London of Spider's imagination. He'd never been there.

"The same gent who built your father's case clock?" Spider had admired the tall, slender clock tucked into the captain's cabin ever since it had come aboard. The chains and pendulums and gears that made it work were tucked away in a chest—there simply was no point in trying to operate the clock at sea on a rocking ship, the captain had explained, much to Spider's disappointment. But the case itself was impressive enough, formed of good oak and trimmed with walnut by an artist who had a way with pastoral images. Leaves and flowers, deer and rabbits, hawks and doves, all were captured in loving detail, and varnished with care by an expert hand.

"Indeed," Miss Brentwood said. "Mr. Fox is most handy and clever. This keyboard, he tells me, is full of hinges and clock springs. The keys all rise again after I push them down, just like the real thing. He made it so I could keep up my practice while we travel. Isn't it wondrous?"

"Yes, very clever," Spider said. He slowly walked toward her, and now he could see the keys up close. Her fingers nimbly danced across them, and they popped up afterward.

"I must hear the music in my head, of course," she said, "but I am getting accustomed to that. And I am composing little songs, too, writing the notes and chords in my journal. I shall have an entire song-book by the time we reach Boston. Do you play?"

"Uh, I have scratched at a fiddle once or twice," he said. "I think the fellows listening might have preferred hearing music in their heads."

Abigail laughed. Spider blinked; the sound reminded him of Emma. "It is as fine a thing as that clock."

"Mr. Fox is a dear man," she said. "Since my mother died, Father has been . . . not himself. Mr. Fox made a gift of the clock, knowing Father admired it. I am sure Mr. Fox might have sold it for a handsome price, but he says that is not why he made it."

"Why did he make it, then?"

"To see if I could." Spider turned to see a man wiping his forehead with a dingy kerchief. Once finished, he pulled the cloth away to reveal brown eyes and a friendly smile, arranged around a nose that might have passed as a small potato. Brown hair was neatly combed back and pigtailed, but beaded with sweat. "I am Rufus Fox," he said, extending a hand to Spider after bowing to Miss Brentwood. Spider guessed the man's age at perhaps twice his own, fifty years or so.

"John Coombs, ship's carpenter." Spider took the proffered hand and shook it firmly.

"Carpenter!" Miss Brentwood clapped her hands together. "Why, you built my sitting room, did you not? The window is such a nice thing! Thank you!"

Spider nodded and wondered if he blushed. "Aye. Not a real window, just a frame and a rod, you know, but . . ."

"But I hung curtains on it, and it looks pretty just the same," she said. "Oh, I am happy to have made your acquaintance, Mister Coombs!"

"As am I," Fox said. "Carpenter!" The man's face ignited with interest. "Oh, I am happy, sir, happy indeed. And do I hear a bit of Boston in your accent, sir?"

"Grew up near there," Spider answered.

"I spent many years there when I was younger, lovely town. Mister Carpenter, I would love to know more about this wondrous vessel's construction, and I shall be begging some oil and other items from you, I dare say." The man's voice was soft and fluid, like a viola played quietly. "I am a hobbyist. I must tinker, you know. Always tinkering."

"If you'll show me how your clock works, I'll show you all about the capstan and rudder and pumps and all else you wish to see," Spider said. "When duty allows, mind you."

"Of course, of course. If we see a calm day, we can rig up the clock long enough for a demonstration, I suppose. The captain might appreciate seeing it at work, too. The clock amuses him. Or always has, anyway." His voice trailed off, and Abigail reached out to touch his hand. They both sighed.

Wind bore a cloud of pipe smoke between them, and Mr. Fox coughed. Spider turned toward the source and noted Sam Smoke walking past. The pirate did not notice Spider, though; his leer was anchored on Abigail Brentwood.

At that moment, Little Bob rose from the hatch with a duffle strapped over his shoulder. "Damn and blast! It is unfair, damn it!"

Wright's voice followed him. "Fair is what the captain says is fair." Wright emerged and stood by Bob, pointing toward the rail. "Off you go."

"A million curses, damn and blast," Little Bob grumbled, but he obeyed. Hoots and cheers accompanied the small man as he descended.

"Good to see him go," Spider said. "He's lazy and poor company, a true burden aboard a ship."

"And cruel. I can't abide a man who is mean to animals. My father loves that silly cat," Miss Brentwood said. She lowered her voice to a conspiratorial whisper. "He says he cannot sleep without it in his bunk. I probably should not reveal that to you gentlemen, as a captain is supposed to be like God aboard his own ship, I hear, but it is true, and I am glad to see him take joy in something."

"It has been difficult for him since your mother passed," Fox said, placing a hand on her shoulder. "He is trying, you know."

"Yes," Miss Brentwood said. "This voyage surely will help. He has missed the sea." She glanced over her shoulder and sighed at the sunlight dancing on waves. "I have seen it, of course, a million times. But I have never been upon it, not since I was a little girl, anyway, and I scarce remember that. It rolls and moves, the sea does, like a living thing. Quite beautiful."

"Beautiful, yes," Nicholas Wright said, rushing by on his way toward whatever task he needed to oversee next. "I wish I could show you all of it, Miss Brentwood."

Spider noted a blush from the girl. "Do you, now?"

"Aye," Wright said. "Lovely islands, one of them your father told me of a while back, and I've seen it since. Like Eden. You would love it. But we shall not come close to it on this journey. A pity, really." He smiled, then rushed off.

Spider suddenly felt like an eavesdropper. "If you'll excuse me," he said. "I will get back to my work." He nodded clumsily, then turned to leave. A raised voice behind him, though, stopped him in his tracks.

"You, I hear, are to give the reading on Sunday? Not I, but you?"

"No offense is meant," Fox said. Spider turned to see Mr. Fox staring into the dour face of the same preacher who had presided at the gallows as Dobbin's soul passed into the next world. "The captain asked me to do it, and so I shall. He and I are friends. I am certain the captain did not mean to slight you."

"Are you even ordained?" The minister spat it as much as he spoke it. "Are you qualified?"

"Well," Fox said, smiling, "I have mingled with the Society of Friends, although I remain stubborn and disagree with them on a few points, and I have studied much on my own, but no, I am not ordained.

It is the Lord's book, however, and he is surely qualified. I shall merely be reading from it. I am more than able to do that. But say, I do not think the captain would be averse to a sermon as well. A brief one, as there is much work to do, of course, and we shouldn't keep the men from it longer than necessary."

The dour man stood a bit taller. "The Lord's work is more vital, I think, than anything that needs done aboard ship, especially on the Sabbath. I would happily provide some expert theological guidance to accompany your . . . mere reading." Spider got the sense that the man had to force himself to even look upon Rufus Fox.

If Fox noticed the man's disgust, however, he gave no indication. Fox bowed. "I was counting on God to do most of the real work, but will accept your help as well, Reverend Down, I surely will. I shall broach the subject with the captain at the first opportunity. We shall have it settled by Sunday morning, and no doubt we all can breakfast on righteousness."

The Reverend Down nodded. "Very well. Thank you. I shall want to go over any points with you beforehand, I dare say, to assure that the message is . . ."

"I plan to do no more than read the Good Book, Reverend. Any message the men get will be from that, and thus from the Lord, not from me. *Sola scriptura.* I am just a tinkerer who can read, and not so arrogant as to assume more than that."

The Reverend Down licked his lips and furrowed his brow, as though trying to determine whether he'd been insulted or not. Spider wasn't certain of that point, himself.

"Of course," the minister said finally. "Very well. Mr. Fox. Miss Brentwood."

He nodded and walked away briskly.

"A very short sermon," Spider said. "I like very short sermons."

Fox and Miss Brentwood laughed.

Spider took a quick glance at Port Royal. In the morning, they would sail away from this city, and if there was any luck in the world, he would never set eyes on it again. He would be with Em and his son.

It is best not to depend on luck, though, he decided. *It is best to keep an eye out for trouble and eliminate obstacles.*

He went to spy on the pirate Sam Smoke.

5

"**I** love a man who puts away his tools properly." Rufus Fox shielded his eyes from the lowering Caribbean sun and leaned over Spider's shoulder.

"Hello, sir. Aye," Spider said, tucking a hammer into its slot in the tool chest, glad he no longer had a long beard to dangle in his way. He had cut it quite short. "Treat them well, and they will serve you well in return."

"And what are you working on here, John?"

Spider, kneeling on the weather deck, looked up at Fox and squinted in the sunlight. *Redemption* was heading east, with Port Royal and the Palisadoes far out of sight. The ship was tacking close to the wind and had been all day. The going had been slow, with much gentle rocking and creaking of masts. Fox looked a tad green in the face and wet with sweat, but he smiled nonetheless. He had a gray blanket wrapped around his shoulders, despite the tropical heat.

"Are you unwell, Mister Fox?"

"It would seem I have yet to acquire sea legs, John. But I shall not spend this voyage in a bunk below. There is simply too much to see and learn up here. And the hammock, well, it sways with the ship, too, so no real respite there, in any event."

"You will grow accustomed to a hammock, sir."

"Oh, I do not know if I believe that." His lips tightened at the thought.

"Well, then," Spider said. "Just mark, sir, there is an entire ocean there, should you need to spew."

The cook, Lazare, had treated them all to an excellent plum duff for breakfast and baked flounder for supper, and Spider had noted that

Fox had seemed to enjoy a great deal of both. Spider, kneeling on the deck, was in a dangerous spot should Fox's food come back up, so he muttered a silent prayer.

"I have made use of the sea once already, friend John," Fox whispered, pulling the blanket tighter against him and leaning closer. His breath bore the evidence of his statement, and Spider struggled to prevent a wince. "Do not fret. I shall certainly remain in control long enough to avoid any unseemly breech of courtesy." The man tried to smile, and Spider chuckled.

Fox pointed toward the contraption on the deck. "What is this you are working on?"

"I am making a target, sir," Spider said. He knelt beside a contraption of wood, like a very small boat, with a rectangle, about a yard square, of pine planks mounted on its mast instead of a sail. The planks were shoddy, the worst Spider could find, for he had determined not to waste a scrap of good wood on this foolish project.

He'd painted a red circle in the center of the square, a small one, because he was equally loath to waste paint.

"Well, not making a target. I have made a target, I should say. I am finished. That's the bull's-eye, there. One of our distinguished guests requested it. I finished my essential duties, you see," Spider said, rising and spitting overboard, with a glance aft at the huge lowering sun, "and so now have time for frivolous ones, or so the master tells me."

Spider tried not to sneer as he explained; the guest who had made the request was none other than Sam Smoke. The pirate had disappeared into his quarters the night before, thwarting Spider's plan to spy on him, but Smoke had emerged in the morning saying he wished to relieve his boredom with some gunplay. Spider thought it a silly idea, but Nicholas Wright had pointed out that Sam was a paying guest, and told Spider to indulge him when time allowed. Spider had kept himself busy all day, which was not easy, because he had gone over *Redemption* very thoroughly before she set sail. He had managed to find some busy work, pretending to sharpen tools that already had perfectly good edges, but he could not put off Smoke's request forever.

He pointed at his handiwork. "The idea is to float her behind the ship, I suppose, and waste a good deal of shot and powder, not to mention time and effort, shooting at it."

"I see," Fox said. "Sturdy-looking vessel, though apparently sized appropriately for Thomas the cat."

Spider lifted the target by a large eye hook in the top of the mast, grabbed the hull, and inverted the tiny craft. "Rudder here keeps the target square on to us, you see."

"Indeed, yes. It is to be towed?"

"Aye," Spider said. "We shall attach a line here." He pointed to a hook at the tiny boat's prow. "She'll ride in our wake, smart as paint, and keep her target aimed at us. If you'll do me a favor and grab that coil there"—he nodded toward a rope—"we will lug this aft and let Mister Lawrence start his ruckus."

"Mister Lawrence?" Rufus Fox closed his eyes tightly for a moment, then fixed Spider with a stare. "The unpleasant fellow constantly surrounded by a wreath of smoke of his own making?"

"Aye."

"I did not appreciate the . . . gaze . . . he directed at Miss Brentwood."

"Aye," Spider said. "Not to worry, sir. The lass is well liked by the crew, and the cap'n well respected. I have no doubt lads will stand in line to slice off Mister Lawrence's balls if he misbehaves."

As soon as he said it, Spider's eyes opened wide. Sam Smoke's presence aboard had rattled Odin, and that fact rattled Spider enough to make him speak like a boor to a paying passenger. "Pardon, sir. Crude sailor talk. Please forget . . ."

"Nonsense," Fox said with a wink. "I have several implements quite suited to the emasculating task, if anyone should have need." He hefted the coil of rope and slipped his right arm through it. The coil held down one side of his blanket-cape while the other side whipped about in the breeze. "Shall we go?"

Fox headed aft but stopped short. A tall, slender man stood in his path, arms crossed and eyes staring angrily from a dark face. "That man might hurt Miss Brentwood? The smoke-wreathed man? Is this what I hear you say?"

"We do not think he wants to harm her, Hadley," Spider said. "He may be smart enough to not try anything with her father on board. But feel free to hurt him if he is not smart enough."

The man nodded sharply and dropped a hand to the knife in his belt. "I will watch him. He will not hurt Miss Brentwood."

"Very well, then," Spider said. "We'll all be on the lookout for trouble from that fellow. Shall we head aft, Mister Fox?"

Fox nodded, letting out a deep breath after Hadley moved on.

Spider pointed toward the ladder. "This way, sir."

"That man seemed very protective," Fox said.

"Aye," Spider answered. "If all the wagging tongues aboard *Redemption* speak truth, Hadley was a slave, not the cap'n's slave, though. Cap'n would not own one. Anyway, a while back a wheel broke on the girl's carriage, and Hadley was on some errand or another and noticed. He come over and fixed the thing, they say, and he impressed Miss Brentwood with his work and manners. She told her father that Hadley ought not be a slave, and the cap'n went and bought the man. Set him free, gave him a job here on the ship, learning the ropes."

"Wonderful," Fox said. "I have known the captain a while now, but never heard that story, nor met the young man."

"Hadley lives aboard *Redemption*, has for weeks," Spider said. "I do not think the cap'n wanted Hadley around his home too much."

"Oh?"

"I believe Hadley has an eye on Miss Brentwood, or would if he could."

"Really?" Fox stopped, turned, and watched Hadley haul on a foresail line. "He seems strong enough to give any rivals trouble."

"Rivals, I suppose, but the real problem is the father. Cap'n will hire the man, but that's about it."

Fox turned back toward Spider. "I see. Hadley, being black and poor, that is the objection."

"Aye. Cap'n helped him more for his daughter's sake than for Hadley's, I reckon. He treats him well, but . . ."

"A pity," Fox said, his face brightening as though he'd just had a pleasant thought. "Romeo, thwarted by parental concerns."

"What, sir?"

"A rather famous story, John. Of Romeo and his Juliet, would-be lovers kept apart by feuding families. Surely, you have heard of it."

"Names sound familiar," Spider said.

Fox gawked. "It is Shakespeare!"

"That name sounds familiar, too."

"Well," Fox said after a gulp. "Perhaps we can do a presentation. It's a play, you know, a very famous one. We do not have a script, of course, but I know it well, and I know Miss Brentwood adores the play. I am no match for the Bard, naturally, but she and I might work something, provide a little entertainment! It would make the journey less tedious."

The man halted, suddenly lost in his own mind, staring up the ladder.

Spider grinned, having decided he liked Rufus Fox. The man had hardly balked at the idea of a black sailor aboard. Spider had sailed with black men many times on pirate ships; indeed, a good many fellows who escaped slavery had nowhere else to go, and some relished the thought of preying on merchant captains as an act of revenge. The dangerous work of piracy also meant manpower was always in demand, so a pirate ship often brought together men of many hues and many cultures in order to assure there were enough hands aboard. Spider had learned that men were just men, and they fought to live, or fought and died, much the same way, whatever color their skin might be.

A merchant vessel was another thing entirely, though, and Hadley's presence on *Redemption* had riled more than a few crewmen. The captain had made it clear he would put up with no nonsense, however, and Hadley worked twice as hard as any man aboard. The man was learning the trade of a sailor, but he had helped Spider with some woodwork, too. *Hell*, Spider thought, *he'd make a better carpenter's mate than Hob.*

Anyway, it pleased Spider that Fox did not seem terribly worried about a black crewman. "Have you and the minister settled your differences, if I may ask?"

"Heh," Fox said. "The good Reverend Abraham Down fears, I think, that I shall lead a good many of you poor souls astray with my uninformed and unschooled approach to theology. He professes contradictory things, in my humble opinion. First, he teaches that the Bible itself is sufficient for a man's salvation, with no need of priestly embellishment. Second, that it somehow matters a great deal whether it is he, Abraham Down, a trained theologian, or I, something of a devoted, but enthusiastic, amateur, who reads from the Bible. He seems to believe my mere reading of it will somehow be far inferior to his reading it and explaining to us all in great detail what it means, according to his doctrine." Fox laughed. "I plan only to read it aloud, I swear. I can hardly hope to improve upon the Author's work. A greater author even than Shakespeare!"

"I am no scholar, sir," Spider said. "But they say it's the Lord's own word. I suspect it is worth reading."

"You have not done so?" There was nothing judgmental in Fox's tone.

"Can't," Spider said, suddenly aware that he had been wasting time. "Never learned my letters." He started up the ladder to the quarterdeck, the float target held off to the side.

"You climb ably, sir," Fox said, "and may I say for a small man you have a goodly strength. Oh, and that is the mizzenmast, correct?" He pointed toward the rearmost mast, rising between the two hatches leading into the captain's cabin.

"Aye, Mister Fox." The man had spent considerable time the day before asking *Redemption's* hands about masts and capstans, backstays and topgallants. "Climb a lot as a sailor," Spider said. "And swinging a hammer builds muscle, I suppose." *As does swinging a sword and fighting for your life*, he thought. He'd done a lot of that in his day.

"Indeed," Fox said, following him up. "We all have our gifts."

As they crossed the quarterdeck, Fox stopped at the large hatch and peered down through the grating. "Ahoy, Captain Brentwood!"

Spider winced and shook his head. "No, sir," Spider whispered, taking Fox by the arm. "That's for hoisting stuff in and out, and giving the cap'n some air and light, but we don't bellow at him through it."

"Oh," Fox said, somewhat mortified. "I did not mean to break ship rules." Even as they walked away, the captain's voice rose from below. "Good day, Rufus."

"You are his friend," Spider said. "He is certain to forgive you. But still, he goes in there to work his brain, or to calm it."

They negotiated another ladder to reach the high aft deck. Sam Smoke, fumes oozing from his nose and mouth, stepped forward. The man had a half dozen men with him, passengers and crewmen not currently on watch, and young Hob as well. The boy carried a bucket containing a canvas bag of gunpowder, bits of wadding, and numerous balls. The crewmen carried guns, and some waited to shoot while others finished packing ball, powder, and wadding into their weapons.

"We have only a little daylight remaining," Sam Smoke snarled.

"I have many chores, sir," Spider said. "I am a carpenter. Whole ship is made of wood, you know. Demands much of my attention." It grated to address Smoke as sir, but the man was a paying passenger and Spider was a crewman. Spider also preferred to keep his disdain to himself, lest Smoke realize his pirate past was known, but it was not easy. "I got to your request as soon as I was able."

"That looks as though it should suffice," Smoke growled, pointing at Spider's target.

"Good," Spider said. He set the target down, took the coil of rope from Fox, and fixed one end of the line through the eye hook at the front. It took only a second for Spider to fashion a good knot, although he was no Odin. "Hand me that, please."

A crewman lifted a coil of light rope and handed it to Spider, who fitted that one through the eye hook at the top of the target's mast. "We'll lower this for you, then, and you can begin wasting shot and powder."

Sam Smoke smiled, if you could call it that, and lifted his pipe to his mouth. He clenched it tightly between yellow teeth, and it quivered as he spoke. "Why, mister carpenter, these are dangerous waters, and we'd best all know who can shoot and who cannot, would you disagree? Might even be pirates about." His eyebrows lifted beneath the broad brim of his hat. "Aye? Heard tell of some nasty sorts that escaped from a frigate in Port Royal. One of them killed a navy officer, the story goes. They caught a few, hung a few, but not all of them, I heard. Some escaped the gallows. Might even be on this ship, for all one can tell."

Smoke punctuated his speech with a quiet, death-rattle chuckle.

"I heard the stories," Spider said, lifting the target. Two crewmen took it from him and carried it to port, where they began lowering it to the sea. Spider fixed the tow line to *Redemption*'s taffrail. Once the tiny vessel caught the water, the crewmen brought up the drop line and Spider paid out the tow line. Soon, the target settled into *Redemption*'s wake, where it bobbed like a drunkard.

"Dangerous waters, as I said," Smoke continued, "and us with our captain's pretty girl aboard. It would not do to let a pirate near that precious cargo. It surely would not." He chuckled. "No, no, no. So, if we be destined to run into pirates, should we not be prepared?" Smoke pulled a pistol from his belt. "Should we not sharpen our aim with a little practice? Be sure we can hit what we need to hit? Load a weapon quickly? The pirates will be trained, that's for certain. You can rely upon it."

"I would not know," Spider said.

"Wouldn't you?" Smoke's hard eyes glistened before another puff of smoke wafted from his mouth and hid them.

"I wouldn't," Spider said.

Smoke's eyes narrowed. "Wouldn't you? Well, I should like to be prepared proper, if I should meet any pirates." His head lowered in what seemed to Spider to be a short nod. "I would not mind shooting one of those damned pirates, you may rely on it." He grinned, and fumes curled through the gaps in his teeth.

"Those gents will deal with any pirates," Spider said, pointing off the starboard rail. There, HMS *Southampton* and her guns followed a parallel course but slightly behind. Sunset light filled her sails, painting them reddish-gold. Spider could not recall the last time he'd looked upon one of the king's ships and thought it beautiful. In the past, a naval vessel was something to elude.

Four merchant vessels had left Port Royal under the frigate's escort.

Aside from the fluyt *Redemption*, the other ships were all former East Indiamen owned by a Boston merchant of German descent who had given them names Spider found difficult to pronounce—*Viel Reisenden*, *Dame des Nebels*, and *Altes Huhn*. The latter, according to Odin, meant "old chicken." Spider had wondered aloud why anyone would name a ship that, to which Odin answered, sounding more the Scotsman than usual, "Who knows why a German does goddamned anything?"

Those ships now were in line ahead, out of sight from Spider's vantage as *Redemption* and the frigate brought up the convoy's rear. The frigate, swift and agile, darted ahead at times and fell back at others, watchful for pirates. It still felt odd to Spider to realize he was comforted by the navy's presence, so long as her captain and crew stayed on their own vessel, and he was glad to remind Smoke that the king's men were within hailing distance.

"Yes," Smoke said, laughing softly. "Those navy boys will protect us. Surely, they will." He lowered his head and shook it slowly back and forth. "Such confidence you have."

"I have never fired a weapon," Fox said, his keen eyes fixed on a pistol Hob held, "but I should be glad of the experience. Is there a spare I could fire?"

Sam Smoke turned toward Fox. "We can trade off. We have a half dozen pistols and plenty of shot and powder."

"Excellent," Fox said, handing his blanket to Hob. "Fascinating contraptions, these pistols."

Indeed, Spider thought, the flintlock pistols stored aboard *Redemption* were quite well made, with sixteen-inch barrels mounted on good walnut stocks, not ornate but sanded smooth. They were solid but too heavy for target work, in Spider's opinion. French-made, if he was not mistaken. They were fascinating enough contraptions.

This exercise, though, was futile. Flintlocks were unreliable, misfiring often, and they weren't of much account if your foe was more than a few feet away. Spider had fired one in battle many, many times and almost always stuck the damned thing right in his opponent's belly before pulling the trigger, just to have a chance at felling his target.

The gun made a right bloody mess at such range, of course, but even that was not foolproof, for the damned things sometimes just flipped a useless spark into the air and the powder never lit. It was always best to follow up a gunshot with a sword or knife in case the damned gun failed to fire.

Spider could not think of a single useful thing to be learned by shooting at a target towed some thirty yards behind *Redemption*. And considering how the ship bobbed and swayed, and the target did likewise in her wake, any hits on the target were likely to be mere accidents.

"It is done like this," Smoke said, nodding toward Fox and then turning suddenly toward the target. The mast and plank were silhouetted against the red arc of the sun on the horizon. Smoke watched for several heartbeats, judging the motion of ship, sea, and target. Then he squinted until his eyes were nearly shut, inhaled sharply so that his pipe bowl fired like a small sun, held his breath, raised the pistol quickly, and fired.

The upper left corner of the makeshift plank burst in a shower of splinters.

"Jesus," Hob exclaimed, leaping and spinning. "I would not have bet you could hit it! I think it the finest shot I have ever seen, sir!"

Fox had jumped from the sparks and the sharp thunderclap of exploding powder. Spider waved away the cloud of gun smoke that brushed his face. "Calm down, Hob."

The lad was right, though. It had been an extraordinary shot, or else a merely lucky one. Smoke's wink and yellow grin professed he could do it again anytime he liked, and Hob basked in the man's confidence and swagger.

Spider would have to sit the boy down for a long talk.

"Excellent shot," Fox said. Others nodded approvingly.

"I'll believe so if he can do it again," Spider said quietly, evoking a chortle from Smoke.

"Now you try," Smoke said.

Fox grinned. "I doubt I will . . ."

"Shoot the damned thing."

Fox nodded. "Very well." He took a gun from Hob, who said, "It is a powerful feeling, sir. This is loaded and ready."

Fox nodded. He examined the gun, stood squarely, wiped a bead of sweat from his brow, aimed, and held his breath. The man's head nodded almost imperceptibly in time with the rise and fall of the ship as he tried to carefully time his shot, and to Spider's eye the man looked a tad green.

They all stood in silence, and Smoke's damned pipe glowed brightly three times before Fox's gun cracked.

The floating plank showed no sign of damage, but a gull squawked.

Smoke laughed. "You fired over your man's head, I think, and he cut you twenty times before you shot at him. You will be of no account in a fight, friend Fox."

"It would never be my desire to shoot a person," Fox said, although he seemed disappointed with himself. He handed the gun to Hob and took back his blanket.

"Shooting a person is what this is for," Smoke said, holding his own gun aloft. "I hope you have the steel to do it if you need to. But . . . you won't, will you?"

Fox stared at Smoke for ten seconds. "I will leave you to your prac-tice, sir." He pulled the blanket tightly around his shoulders and headed toward the ladder without looking back. Smoke laughed quietly.

"Let us try a volley," Smoke said while loading powder, shot, and wadding down the barrel of a fresh gun. "Best way to take a man down at a distance is for all of us to fire at him at once. We all aim and fire together, on my command."

"Do not stand too closely together," Spider warned. "These things throw a shower of sparks. Fire a bunch at once and it is like a rain in hell. We don't want to toss a spark into someone else's weapon, or into Hob's damned bucket."

Smoke winked. "So you know a thing or two about guns, then." Around them, men loaded their weapons.

Spider shrugged. "A man learns things at sea."

"Indeed. How did you lose the finger?"

"Accident with an axe."

"Carpenter's peril, I suppose." Smoke looked Spider in the eye. "One of them piratical fellows that escaped the navy, he had a missing finger. On his left hand. Like yours."

This man's leering eyes would look better with a dirk in one of them, Spider thought. He inhaled sharply, to expand his gut a bit so he would feel the hilt of his knife pressing against it and thus know exactly where his weapon was. Spider envisioned the attack and decided a gut strike would be best, his hand whipping the knife free from his belt and arcing the blade across Sam Smoke's belly. Spider knew he could do it without ever freeing his gaze from Smoke's, and he knew the shock of that first slash would give him all the time he needed to finish the job. Smoke would be over the taffrail and sinking before he ever knew he was dead.

But *Redemption* was a legitimate merchant vessel, not some damned pirate ship, and Sam Smoke was a paying voyager. Spider willed himself to calm down.

"At least three other men on this vessel are missing a finger or two," Spider said. "Don't recall which hands. Sea life is hazardous. We all get hurt, eventually."

"Oh, yes," Smoke said. "All seamen get hurt. Sometimes bad. Real bad." He laughed quietly, and the pipe bobbed up and down.

Spider's spine iced, despite the Caribbean heat.

"All ready, sir," Hob said.

"Very good," Smoke said as Hob retreated with the bucket. Smoke yanked the pipe from his mouth and emptied the bowl into the sea, then tucked the thing into his belt. "Let us see if we can tear up the carpenter's hard work."

Spider turned away, glad for the interruption.

"Ready!" Smoke bellowed. A half dozen arms extended over the taffrail, guns in hand.

"Aim!"

Spider braced himself. No matter how many times a man heard a bunch of guns going off at once, the first volley was always a jolt.

"Fire!"

Six hammers snapped, five flash pans erupted in sparks, and five balls flew out to sea. As near as Spider could tell, not a single ball had hit the target.

"Fuck," said an able-bodied seaman named Jones, staring at his weapon. "It did not spark. I might as well have just pointed a stick at it." He started examining the thing, and Spider snatched it away. "You aim it at the enemy's face, not your own."

Smoke grinned. "Let us have another go. Powder and balls, Hob. Hob!"

"Sorry, sir," Hob said, turning sharply and reddening a bit. He glanced behind himself quickly, toward the weather deck below, then faced Smoke and strode forth with his bucket. "Here we are."

Spider peered below to see what had distracted the boy. He expected to see Miss Brentwood, a sight to distract any man. He whistled softly when he saw someone else instead, just as feminine as Miss Brentwood but crowned with long red hair like a shock of flames. "Who the hell is she? And where has she been hiding?"

"I do not know her name, sir," Hob said, peering back over his shoulder as the shooters gathered powder and balls from his bucket. "But I aim to meet her. I saw her when she came aboard, but she stayed below, until now."

The woman wore a simple dress of gray, and once the wind died, her long red tresses spilled down her back. She had a fine figure, and when she turned her head Spider saw enough to deem her handsome. A small hat, adorned with bright scarlet flowers Spider could not name, tugged in the wind against the hairpins that kept it in place.

"Did you happen to see if she has a wedding band, Hob?"

"She does. But unless I see a husband, I am not sure I care," Hob said.

"You had better care," Spider said sharply. "We don't want trouble."

"Perhaps she's a widow."

"Hob."

Smoke bellowed orders. "Ready! Aim! Fire!"

Spider's gaze remained fixed on Hob's, until drifting smoke forced him to blink.

"It gets lonely at sea," Hob said. "She might get lonely, I think."

"It was not so long ago you spent your pay on a whore, boy. I do not believe you will die if you don't empty your sack again before we get to Boston, but if you are that desperate, grab your own pickle and have a tug. A married woman is trouble."

"I am not a child."

"Then be a man and think," Spider growled. "You give her leeway, by God, do you hear me?"

Neither of them had noticed Smoke's approach, at least not until they smelled the ever-present tobacco fumes. "Well, won't we all be damned," he said, his eyes locked on the mystery woman.

"Do you know her?" Hob frowned, and his eyebrows furrowed.

Smoke smiled widely. "Does anyone really know a woman? They are all mysteries, aye?" Then he laughed, clapped Spider on the shoulder, took Hob's bucket, and walked back to the taffrail.

Hob was already headed down the ladder.

"Damn it, Hob." Spider followed and noted the red-headed woman was approaching Nicholas Wright. Spider hoped Hob had sense enough to not interrupt the master's conversation with her. That was a false hope, though, as the boy rushed to the next ladder, slid down it, and headed directly toward them.

"Fool," Spider muttered. He crossed the quarterdeck and descended to the weather deck as quickly as he could, in hopes of heading off trouble.

He was too late. Hob had already joined Wright and the mystery woman. Wright, always a busy man, was clearly being polite to her but glowered at Hob. The man carried a burlap sack, and for a moment Spider thought he might hit Hob with it.

"Fuck and bugger," Spider muttered.

A meow answered him. Thomas curled against the captain's cabin door, staring at Spider. "Leave me alone," Spider said, stepping away from the ladder. He got another meow in return.

"If you've no duties to attend to at the moment, be off," Wright said sharply to Hob, who turned and ran, leaving a "yes, sir" in his wake.

"I will leave you to your duty, as well," the woman said. She bowed slightly, turned, saw Spider, and bowed slightly again, then headed forward along the port rail. Wright also headed forward but chose the starboard path.

Spider could not tell where Hob had gone. "I am going to saw off that boy's whore pipe," he muttered to himself. "But for now, Lord, I need a drink."

Fortunately, he knew where the cook kept his secret rum stash.

6

"*T*he words of the preacher, son of David, king in Jerusalem."

"Oh, for pity, not that book for this ungodly lot."

The first phrase, intoned by Rufus Fox, was scarcely audible above the morning breeze humming in the lines, as he whispered in rehearsal for his upcoming Bible reading. The second, growled somewhat louder and more aggressively by the Reverend Down, came from somewhere behind Spider and was quickly followed by more. "Give them not the subtleties of Ecclesiastes but rather the purifying fire of Revelation. Perhaps they will understand that."

It was too much for Spider, whose head throbbed with a boozy headache, and he snapped. "Some of us ignorant men can build ships and navigate them, Reverend. Can you?"

Spider received several appreciative nods from his fellow crewmen. The Reverend Down muttered toward him. "You speak of ephemeral, worldly things," the clergyman said. "Your ships, and indeed the stars you sail by, will not outlast the eternal perdition that awaits you if you do not learn the path to salvation."

"Amen," said Hadley, head bowed and eyes closed. Thomas, curled up against a bulkhead, meowed as if in agreement.

The preacher nodded in assent at Hadley, then sneered at Spider. "There is a man with his mind in the right place," the Reverend Down said, pointing at the former slave. "You might follow his lead, else eternity might not be pleasant for you."

For one flicker of a moment, Spider imagined himself sending the Reverend Down on his merry way to whatever eternity had in store for him, but Rufus Fox attempted to quiet things down. Fox looked up from the book in his hands and smiled. "Reverend," he said with a nod. "We talked about this, and I thought it was settled. Good morning. And good morning to you all," he told the sailors gathered for the reading.

It was not a good morning, Spider thought. He had found Lazare's rum, by God, and had carried off two bottles of it. He'd intended to stow one away for later, but as Sam Smoke's hard stare arose again and again in his mind, he'd kept drinking. He'd eventually tossed both empties overboard and stumbled back to his hammock. If he'd slept an hour, it was in a stupor. He'd have slept through the Bible reading entirely if Hob had not been sent below to rouse the hands.

Now, with bright Caribbean sun pouring onto the deck, Spider seemed to sway in one direction as *Redemption* swayed in the other, and Odin had propped him aright more than once.

"I shall call roll," Nicholas Wright said, approaching the crowd with Abigail Brentwood and the mysterious flame-haired beauty following him. Both women wore dresses of white, reflecting the morning sun in a way Spider deemed angelic. "We shall begin the reading once the captain is with us," Wright added.

"Might I suggest a reading of Revelation, sir?" The Reverend Down raised his hand. "I believe it would be the proper message."

"Captain Brentwood left such matters to his Quaker friend," Wright said, "and I am hardly the best man to judge."

"I am rather an expert," the reverend said tersely, "and I assure you . . ."

"I assure you," Wright said, "my duty is to see the captain's wishes done." He turned before the preacher could say another word. "Hiram Allsworth," he called.

"Here, sir."

"Thomas Ames."

"Here, sir." That call came from the poop deck, where a helmsman remained at the rudder.

"Edward Chambers," he bellowed, for the man he called was up in the trees as lookout. *Redemption* was still under way with the rest of the convoy, so some men had to remain on task, though it was a gentle sea and a fine, easy wind.

"Aye, here, sir," the reply came down.

"John Coombs."

Odin poked Spider viciously in the ribs, and Spider answered, "Aye, sir." Still feeling the rum, he'd not been prepared to respond to his departed friend's last name.

"Were you waiting for him to call Spider John Rush?" At least Odin had maintained the sense to whisper that name.

The master continued the roll.

"Chace Lazare."

"Aye, sir, and good bread stolen in the night, sir, and a small cheese."

Mister Wright scowled. "Does any man have an accounting of the cook's bread and cheese?"

"Cook didn't mention the rum," Hob whispered, laughing.

"He's not supposed to have it, himself," Spider reminded the boy.

"Aye," Hob said. "Was the bread good?"

"I didn't..."

Spider closed off his reply when the master's voice rose. "The captain will be made aware, and no doubt will be displeased that stores meant to be shared by all are being pilfered instead. We treat you well, men, and deserve your respect and obedience. Punishment upon the guilty party will not be pleasant. Do not let this behavior continue."

Spider noted that Wright's eyes scanned the entire crew, but fell most often upon Hadley.

The mystery woman's wind-swept red hair caught Spider's attention. She was just a few feet away, talking to Miss Brentwood, and the flash of green eyes and the fine face arrested him. She noticed him staring, nodded slightly, then turned quickly and hurried away. Sam Smoke's odious presence stepped into the space she'd just left, and Smoke watched her vanish into the assembling crowd, his gaze traveling up and down her body.

Odin bowed his scarred head as if in prayer to hide his face. Smoke clamped down tightly on his pipe, shook his head slowly, then muttered something only the devil might have heard. Then Smoke wandered off, too. Spider hoped the man had gone to empty his bowels overboard and prayed for a nice ocean swell to tip the son of a bitch into the depths. That would ease Spider's mind greatly, although he wondered if it wasn't a rather blasphemous thought for a Sunday.

Wright continued calling the roll, from memory, his voice rising as he climbed the ladder to the quarterdeck above.

Spider rubbed at his bearded face. When he pulled his hands away, he saw Abigail Brentwood chatting with Rufus Fox, and he regretted his bloodshot eyes and foul breath.

Wright worked his way through the roll all the way to Edward Williams, then declared, "All hands accounted for. Mister Fox, if you will join me here on the quarterdeck, I think you will find it to be an excellent stage for your reading while the men, and ladies, of course, listen below. The captain will join us shortly, I am sure."

"With pleasure, sir." Fox tucked his leather-bound Bible under his arm and ascended the ladder, while Wright climbed higher to the poop. The Reverend Down climbed up after Fox and wielded a Bible of his own. Thomas the cat gave a surly meow as the men passed by.

"Ecclesiastes," the reverend grumbled quietly, "will be lost on this hoard."

"Ecclesiastes is my father's favorite of all the Bible," Abigail Brentwood said, calling aloud to Fox. "I am quite fond of that book as well. It is poetry, to my mind. I think it an excellent choice."

"Thank you, dear," Fox said, bowing slightly. "I know your father will approve."

The Reverend Down cleared his throat.

Wind sang in the cables, and the ship creaked as they waited for the captain. The sun warmed Spider's face, and he shut his eyes against its brightness. He told himself he would open them again once the reading began. If anyone needed to heed the Lord's word, he figured, it was a former pirate.

He never heard that reading, though. Instead, he heard a single gunshot. Spider winced as the thunderous sound ripped through his rum-soaked head, and he wondered for just a moment if he'd been shot.

Thomas the cat leapt with a loud screech and hurled himself into Hob's protective arms. Abigail Brentwood gasped, then let loose a scream more intense than anything Spider had ever heard during bloody combat or the horrible surgeries that followed.

Miss Brentwood crumbled to the deck, and Spider jumped to help her. He expected to see blood on her blouse or skirt, then realized she was staring gape-jawed at her father's cabin.

All other gazes were aimed in the same direction. The shot had come from within Captain Brentwood's cabin.

"No! No! No!" Miss Brentwood growled the word repeatedly in drum-like cadence as Hadley forced Spider aside and put an arm around the girl's shoulder.

Down and Fox looked down from the quarterdeck rail as Wright missed nearly every rung, plummeting from above and landing on the weather deck with a thud. "Make way! Make way, damn ye!" The sailing master shoved through a crowd of hands who had rushed toward the captain's door. "Captain! Captain Brentwood!"

Wright rattled the latch and growled. "Locked, damn it!"

"This one, likewise," said a man shaking the cabin's other door on the opposite side of the mizzenmast that rose between them.

Wright pulled a leather cord from around his neck, and a batch of keys dangled from it. He fiddled with them for a moment. "Where the bloody hell . . . ?"

Wright flung the keys behind him. "Damned thing is gone!"

The master took four steps away from the door. "Stand back!" Wright rushed forward and rammed his shoulder against the heavy oak. He was a powerful man, but the solid door did not budge. Spider ran to a toolbox near the rail and grabbed an axe. Wright rammed his shoulder into the unyielding oak twice more before Spider got the axe to him. "Use this, sir."

Wright grabbed the tool, men got out of his way, and in four great sweeps of the heavy blade, he shattered the wood and the latch. Another shove with his shoulder, and the way was clear.

Wright was the first inside, and Miss Brentwood tore herself from Hadley's grasp and rushed in behind him.

Spider thought the girl's ensuing wail might haunt him the rest of his life.

"Come, Spider," Hob said, his hand on the carpenter's shoulder. "Let us have a look."

Spider clamped a hand over Hob's fingers. "Aye," he said, though the boy's eagerness bothered him. He pushed his way through the crowd around the door, Hob following in his wake.

The captain's quarters were spacious, as far as nautical cabins go, but so many men had spilled into the space that one stood on a sea chest lashed against the bulkhead, and another would have knocked over the towering case clock in the corner had it not been secured with ropes. It took Spider a moment to worm his way through the men and see what had happened.

It was a scene of horror.

Sunlight stabbed through the grating above to show Captain Brentwood, dressed for duty, slumped on the deck near his desk. Blood had spilled across his desk, run down the front of it, and splashed on the wall behind it. The back of the captain's head was simply gone, and hair and bits of bone clung to the bulkhead.

His right hand had a loose grip on a pistol, and blood had eddied around the weapon.

"Dear Lord," muttered the Reverend Down, peering through the grating. He closed his eyes in prayer while Fox rose from his spot. Spider heard Fox's boots drum on the quarterdeck as the man ran to the ladder.

Spider had seen plenty of gun deaths in his day. It appeared the shot had been at close range and that the ball had rammed through the captain's forehead near his right eye. With his eyes, Spider traced the air where the ball must have flown and found the shattered wood just to the left of the door Wright had hacked to pieces.

Everything smelled like copper. The blood scent was so thick that Spider had half a mind to throw open the doors to the stern gallery and rush out of the cabin. He almost thought he might empty his belly into *Redemption*'s wake, so foul was the blood scent, but there was scarcely room to move within the cramped space. He swallowed hard.

Abigail Brentwood knelt, her dress nearly touching the pool of sticky blood on the deck. She shook with heavy sobs, and Wright stooped beside her, whispering softly.

"Do not touch him, Abby," Wright said. "The navy lads will want to look this over, satisfy themselves as to what took place, as we sail under their protection. They will need to make reports to the Admiralty."

Spider had witnessed many a bloody scene in his day, indeed, he had created more than a few, but nonetheless he fought the urge to be sick. Here was a good but sorrowful man, apparently done in by his own hand. And with the doors closed tight, the blood stench was awful.

"Your father was in great distress, Abby," Wright whispered. "He missed your mother so. He is with her now. It is what he longed for."

Spider blinked hard and fought the churning of his stomach and the boozy maelstrom in his head. *Focus*, he told himself. *Find a fixed point. Settle your attention on that. Breathe normally.*

His gaze fixed on an uncorked ink bottle in its slot on the desk, and then on a quill, and then on a scrap of parchment. Words were scrawled across it, but Spider could not read them. He could tell, though, that the hand that had written them had been shaking mightily.

"Mister Wright," he said, pointing at the desk. "I think the cap'n may have . . ."

Wright rose quickly and seized the parchment. He stared at it for several heartbeats, each punctuated by a heavy sob from the man's daughter. "It says only, 'I am sorry.' Oh, God, Abby."

Miss Brentwood lifted her eyes heavenward. A low wail, starting in a deep tone, but rising quickly in pitch and volume, became an incoherent screech before Fox shoved his way through the gathered hands and into the cabin. He pulled the girl out.

"He would not," Abigail sobbed. "He would not."

"Come, miss," Fox said, tugging her by the arm. "Take the air, the fresh, clean air."

Wright followed in their wake. "Abby. Your father is in pain no longer. And I have a thought that might give you some solace. A special place your father loved. A final resting place . . ."

Once that trio had left the cabin, everyone remaining grew silent.

"Damn me," Spider said quietly, suddenly forgetting his churning belly and inhaling deeply through his nose.

Hob stared at him in disgust. "You suck this foul air in like a bellows," the lad said.

"Aye, foul," Spider whispered into Hob's ear as he tugged the boy out of the cabin. "But not foul enough, damn me."

"What?"

"I do not think the cap'n took his own life, Hob. I will explain," Spider said tersely, "once I spy where Sam Smoke went."

7

*A*s things came to pass, Spider had no time to explain himself, nor to explore the vessel in search of the pirate.

"Church must wait," Wright said to the Reverend Down, who stood clutching his Bible to his chest. Wright looked aloft. "Chambers, signal His Majesty's frigate, if you please," he called. "Distress, and permission to come aboard."

"Aye, sir."

Wright plunged down a hatch, toward the passenger berths. "Abby . . ."

Spider glanced off the port bow, where *Southampton* coursed about two hundred yards away, under reduced sail so as to not outpace her slower charges. *Redemption*, her great, wide hull built for cargo rather than speed, was slowest of all the ships in any wind and thus brought up the rear of the convoy. Spider expected the frigate to signal all ships to close ranks while *Redemption*'s new commander rowed across to *Southampton* to report the dreadful news. Instead, he saw the last thing he wanted to see.

Southampton was readying a boat for launch.

"They are coming to us," Spider said, turning so quickly he almost whispered the words into Odin's nose.

"What?" Hob asked.

"I said the fucking pirate-hunting Royal Navy is coming over here."

A call from above confirmed Spider's words. "*Southampton* answers, sir, but you are to remain here; she's sending an officer." The call was passed below to Wright.

"Ha!" Odin said, heading to the mainmast in no apparent hurry.

Nothing, save Sam Smoke, worried Odin, and he seemed somewhat emboldened by the fact Smoke had not apparently recognized him thus far.

Spider, however, was plenty worried. His last close look at the king's fellows had involved bloodshed and shackles and a desperate escape, and he did not want to risk recognition. *Austen Castle* had sailed from Jamaica earlier, but crew and officers might well have changed hands, and there was at least a fair chance someone aboard *Southampton* might have been involved in Spider's arrest. It was not a gamble Spider wished to take.

A call came from above. "*Southampton* orders, sir, all ships to drift."

Hands were scurrying into the rigging as Wright returned to the weather deck and gave orders to furl sails. The other ships in the convoy were already reducing canvas.

Wright's attention was drawn upward, so Spider decided to go low. "Orlop for us, Hob. Come."

The orlop was as low as one could go on the ship, and it meant foul air, bilge water, stifling heat, and rats. But it was as unlikely a place to encounter a visiting navy man as Spider could envision, and so that was where he would hide.

"Coombs!" Wright called.

"Aye, sir." Spider froze in place, well short of the hatch, and waited to hear the man's order.

"Stand guard, will you, at the captain's door. See that no one goes in or out. We shall have nothing disturbed before His Majesty's fellows have had a good look. Hob, you can assist."

"Aye, sir," they said in unison as Spider's heart did a gannet dive. For once, he wished he were a foretop man. He'd feel much safer up there.

"Well, then, this is a very bad spot," Hob said once Wright had gone off. "I am supposed to help you saw wood and hammer things, not guard a dead man while naval officers take a right close look at us."

"Aye, ye lubberwort," Spider said quietly. "This is perilous. Hush, now. I must think."

They took positions to either aside of the busted cabin entrance, kicking aside the shattered remains of the door, and still the smell of blood was thick—and that was amiss, like calm water in a heavy wind. That fact again roused Spider's suspicions, and his thoughts tossed about wildly.

All he could think of for now, though, was the slow approach of the boat from *Southampton* and the odds of any member of the visiting crew having seen him during his captivity and escape. He'd altered his appearance, yes, but was shorter hair really enough of a change? He suddenly regretted his haste in chopping short his beard. And then there was Hob, taller and browner and stronger, but still the same boy who'd not long ago been a naval prisoner. And Odin, for Christ's sake, could anyone who ever saw that mangled face ever forget it?

No, Spider decided. *We are foundered, shipwrecked, lost if we remain standing here.* No doubt the navy men would want a look into Captain Brentwood's cabin to satisfy themselves as to the situation. No doubt the buggers would march straight toward the cabin the moment they stepped onto the bloody deck, would stare Spider in the eyes, would recognize him as a wanted pirate, and string him up within the hour.

He could almost feel the noose.

Spider's throat grew cold, and with his maimed left hand he reached beneath his shirt for the pendant he'd carved for Em, who now seemed farther away than ever. His mind raced as though gale-driven, trying to conjure some vital carpentry work that would get him off the main deck. "Pardon me, sir," he would call, "but the spars need replaced or the boat needs patched or the capstan needs greased or . . ." It had to be urgent work, and believable, for Wright was not foolish. Unfortunately, the fluyt was in outstanding condition; Spider himself had worked damn hard to assure that. And Wright, a famous ninny at dice and cards but a sailor through to his bones, knew the vessel inch by inch. No bit of made-up busy work was going to get Spider out of this hard spot.

After a long, agonizing wait during which Hob whispered, "We are fucked, Spider," at least four times, the navy officer and his party were piped aboard. Spider cringed. They stood amidships, a handsome young lieutenant and two seamen, and the officer looked entirely too familiar. Wright and the officer exchanged words, and while Spider could not hear what was said, the visitor's mannerisms seemed to stir memories. The confident posture, the aristocratic tilt of the head . . .

No, Spider told himself, *you are fooling yourself. All these young navy men have a certain bearing, a particular manner. Full of themselves, they are. Line up any six of them together and a mother would be hard-pressed to recognize her own son in the lot.*

Spider almost believed it, too, until the tall man's long strides toward the captain's quarters brought the green eyes and hawk's beak nose into full view, and the doffed hat freed a shock of curly brown hair. Lieutenant George Price, by God and devil, one of the very men who'd sent *Red Viper* below into the bloody depths after locking up her surviving crew. That bastard had been among the officers who had stood over Spider when the shackles were clamped to his wrists. Spider swallowed hard and kept his eyes dead ahead.

Wright waved toward the cabin. Price nodded solemnly and stepped inside, taking no notice of Spider and Hob. *Maybe we got lucky*, Spider thought. *Maybe navy contempt for merchant sailors will keep us beneath his notice.*

Wright followed the officer into the cabin. Spider worried his own heartbeat could be heard reverberating within the cabin and tried to settle himself with deep, slow breaths. He hoped Hob was doing the same but would not risk a sideward glance for fear that the motion would catch Price's attention.

Spider and Hob stood still, afraid to move, while gulls pivoted above the mainmast and mocked them with shrill laughter. After what seemed an hour, but surely could not have been more than a few minutes, the men within the cabin started talking.

"Ghastly business," Price said quietly.

"We all thought this journey would be good for him," Wright replied. "His wife's passing laid him quite low, lower than we realized, apparently. He left a note, or started one, but never finished."

"Yes," the lieutenant answered in a tone of disgust that said he'd heard enough. He hurried from the cabin.

Wright followed, and the two men stopped not a dozen steps from Spider and Hob. "We've a chaplain aboard *Southampton*," the lieutenant said after some time. "I can have him perform a service. It would give the poor fellow something useful to do. Although, suicide being a mortal sin, not part of God's plan for us, I am not sure . . ."

"The captain's friend, a Mister Rufus Fox, is a passenger, and he has served the captain as a chaplain, of sorts, certainly as a spiritual advisor. I am certain he will do the honors."

"Is he ordained, this Fox?"

"Quaker, I am told," Wright said.

"Quaker?" Price's nose wrinkled as though Wright had waved shit under it. "Well, then. We shall arrange a gathering of ships and commit him to sea at your Quaker's convenience, provided he not wait very long. We should not dally. This evening would be best, but morning will suffice. Must give the men a chance to grieve, I should say, merchant men not so well acquainted with sudden death, you know. Perhaps, morning would be best."

"I agree, sir," Wright answered. "Coolest part of the day, and it will give his daughter a chance to collect herself. She is horribly shaken."

"Horrible business, and her aboard to see it," Price muttered. "And this is she approaching, I take it?"

Abigail Brentwood, looking determined, strode forth after emerging from a hatchway. Her father's blood had stained her sleeve brown, but she did not seem to have noticed. She also failed to notice Hadley, who sat on a chest near the hatch and watched her intently.

Miss Brentwood stopped before the officer. "Pardon, sir, may I have a word?"

The lieutenant bowed. "Miss Brentwood, on behalf of Captain Shepherd and myself, and indeed our entire crew, allow me to say how very sorry we are to hear of this tragedy. I am Lieutenant George Price, miss, and I am entirely at your disposal." His sudden gallantry seemed practiced to Spider, who noted that the more the man talked, the closer Nicholas Wright moved toward Abigail Brentwood.

Spider thought Hadley wanted to move closer, too, but the man stayed in his spot. He stared with the intensity of a Caribbean sun.

"I am pleased to hear that, sir," Miss Brentwood said in a voice that shook. "I want you to know my father did not commit suicide."

Price looked at her sadly. "I understand it is a difficult thing for you to bear, but . . ."

She lifted her chin. "I know his mettle. I know his feelings on the subject. He would not do it. He would bear any sadness, rather than commit such a sin."

Fox cleared his throat. He approached and stood nearby, trying to catch Miss Brentwood's attention. "You know your father longed to see your mother again," he said. "Perhaps, then, God would not judge him so harshly."

"He did not kill himself. I know it."

"The note, Abigail. The gun in his hand," Wright said gently. "He was locked in there, for God's sake."

"Someone killed him," Miss Brentwood said. "I will find out who, if you men will not."

"We have examined the evidence very thoroughly," the lieutenant said softly. "Sad as it may be, miss, I fear your father, indeed, took his own life."

She waved a hand in dismissal. "I will learn the truth of it. For now, I have a particular favor to ask. My father had a particular place, an island. Loveliest place in the world, he thought, and I believe he'd want to be committed to the deep there, within sight of it. Mister Wright can show you on a map, or a chart as you call it, I am sure. He knows where it is."

Wright nodded reluctantly. "Once through the Windward Passage, sir, we can bear westward and find it easily enough. I know the spot well. It would add but a few days to our journey, and we could sail direct north from there."

Price turned his hawkish nose toward Wright, and the maneuver put Spider within the man's range of vision. "Absolutely out of the question, Mister Wright. I know those waters, and I know many of the islands. Pirate rendezvous points, many of them. Hiding grounds. Cover for predators. My duty is to see this convoy safely to Boston, Mister Wright, not to lead it into pirate territory."

"Aye, sir," Wright said, nodding. "I thought that might be your reply, but I promised Abby . . . Miss Brentwood, rather . . . that I would discuss it with you."

Abigail Brentwood tilted her head. "But, sir, you've a powerful frigate, all freighted with heavy guns, those long nines or whatever you call them. Surely, a pirate would run before the wind rather than cope with all that."

"A wise pirate, yes, but wisdom is a rare commodity among the sea robbers, Miss Brentwood. And they are more bold when they can dodge in and out among island waters they call home. Their sloops can enter shallows where we cannot. It is why they choose such places." He smiled and softened his voice. "I admire your devotion and your courage. Indeed, I do, and if it were but you and I to make the trip, I would gladly escort you to your father's beautiful island."

Good Christ, Spider thought, *he sounds as though he means it.* The lieutenant's eyes, though, indicated he had other reasons to muse about sailing off alone with the girl.

Wright crossed his arms, inhaled sharply through his nose, and stared at Miss Brentwood.

"But it is not just you and I," the lieutenant continued. "We've several vessels to fret about. A fool pirate might think he can sweep in and take a ship unawares, or distract us in one direction with one ship whilst another strikes from a different quarter. They often attack in droves, you know, small fleets. They are quite brazen, these fellows, and swift as *Southampton* is, she cannot be in all places at once. The pirates know this, miss, and may well make a run at us if they think they can succeed. I do not mean to frighten you. . . ."

"I do not frighten easily, sir," she said. "And if pirates attack in numbers, then why have we only one frigate for escort?"

Price stiffened. "There are many demands upon His Majesty's ships, Miss Brentwood. I assure you *Southampton* is quite up to the task, on open water. Provided, of course, that we do not rush upon a dangerous course."

Wright put an arm around her shoulder. She cast a glance at him before returning her gaze to the navy man.

"I see that cowering is not in your nature," Price said to her. "But nor do your pirates cower. Greed makes them take foolish chances. But even if they should fail in taking one of our ships, well, they might yet cost us dear in terms of lives lost. No. I shall not even mention the notion of your father's lovely isle to the captain. Forgive me, but I have my duty. And I have my career to think of." He smiled. "Proposing such a risk would no doubt leave me a lieutenant forever, if not cost me my rank altogether."

"I thought you and your cohorts had done your duty so diligently that piracy was all but dead." Miss Brentwood punctuated her statement with a frown. "Calico Jack, Stede Bonnet, Bartholomew Roberts, even Blackbeard, where are they now? Gone, I am told. Hanged, or shot dead, or drowned. Nary a pirate left on the high seas. I have read of many such victories."

"We have had great successes, indeed, miss," the lieutenant said, trying to hide agitation and failing. "But we captured pirates not very long ago, miss, near these very waters, and we hung a few, by God. But some escaped our grasp. Some men never learn, never give up."

And Ned Low is one of those who won't ever give up, Spider thought. He looked to port and starboard. *Was Ned Low out there somewhere?*

"It is simply too dangerous to ask all these captains to sail their ships into such waters," Price said. "And I cannot very well expect them to give up their escort so that I might fulfill your wish. Nor should they."

Miss Brentwood lowered her eyes. "I see."

"It is for the best, Abby," Wright said. He tightened his grasp on her shoulder and brushed hair from her face. She did not seem to notice. Wright leaned his face closer to hers. "Perhaps you should accompany the lieutenant aboard *Southampton*, get away from all this."

She twisted from his embrace. "How could you think I would leave him?"

"Abby, he is . . ."

"He needs me," she said. "He needs to be made presentable, for his . . . for his burial. Wherever that may be."

"*Southampton* has a surgeon," Wright suggested, looking at Price, who nodded. "He can dress your father's wound, clean him up."

"I am his daughter," she answered pointedly. "I will see to him. And he would not want to leave his command."

Wright, defeated, stepped back and nodded.

"I thank you for your time, Lieutenant." Miss Brentwood curtsied, and Price and Wright bowed, seemingly trying to outperform one another in dignity, to Spider's mind. Then she returned below, Price and Wright strode back amidships—Price giving Hadley a very stern look—and Spider exhaled. He longed for a pipe and a moment's peace. And a jug of whiskey.

"I don't know if I have ever been so scared," Hob said, giggling nervously.

"Aye," Spider said.

"What were you going to tell me?"

"Eh?"

"Before we got posted guard here, you were going to tell me something. You said the cap'n's cabin was not as foul as it should have been, or something of that nature."

"Aye," Spider said, nodding. "The cabin air. It smelled foul with blood, aye?"

"Yes, of course," Hob said. "Damned thick with it, like a butcher shop."

"No surprise in cramped quarters, all closed off. But it was not foul with burnt gunpowder, was it?"

Hob's face scrunched up, until he looked a bit like a seal. "Aye! You are right!"

"Quiet," Spider admonished. "Now you tell me how a pistol fired in such cramped quarters, all sealed up, doesn't leave the whole bloody cabin smelling like brimstone. The hatch above was open, aye, but all else was closed up and air wasn't moving much. Why would gun stench clear and blood stench not?"

"Lord, you think he was shot from outside? From the stern gallery? Or from above, through the hatch?"

"I don't know," Spider said. "The gallery was closed off from inside. But maybe there is a way. I don't know. I need a pipe and time to ponder, and perhaps to snoop. But I reckon it may be that the lass has judged right. Our cap'n did not die by his own hand."

"Lord," Hob said.

"I believe it may be murder."

8

Spider could not recall a more somber evening at sea.

Redemption followed the little convoy north by northeast, plying through the Windward Passage, on a steady breeze. Soon, she would leave Caribbean waters behind and plunge northward through the Atlantic, marking one more milestone on Spider's journey to a normal life with wife and child.

But Spider could not help but think the current situation aboard *Redemption* was a barrier. He imagined naval inquiries, possibly even a diversion to England, stemming from Captain Brentwood's death. Lieutenant Price had seemed to accept the explanation of suicide, and appeared to want nothing more than to leave the whole miserable business behind him, but if the man suddenly picked up on some clue, or heard someone aboard *Redemption* mention murder, that could change everything. That could make the goddamned Royal Navy decide its interests outweighed everything else, and to hell with getting any lowly merchant's cargo to Boston or Spider home to Em. If the navy decided all the witnesses had to go to England, by God, all the witnesses would go to England.

The mere thought latched onto Spider's stomach like a kraken.

Redemption leaned a bit to port as Spider, Hob, and Odin sat on hawser coils and ate ackee and salt cod from wooden bowls. Lazare had made dumplings to go with the fruit and fish, though the Frenchman had skimped on the peppers, in Spider's estimation. Still, it was a fine dish and had been intended as a Sunday treat. It was the kind of small pleasure that meant so much to men at sea.

This day, the splendid food went almost unnoticed.

Rufus Fox sat across the deck, holding his Bible close to his eyes in the dimming light and muttering to himself, his bowl untouched beside him. No doubt he was preparing his words for the morning when Captain Brentwood, now lying wrapped in clean sailcloth within his freshly scrubbed cabin that still smelled of blood, would be committed to the deep. The Reverend Down, scowling at Fox from time to time, paced the main deck and waved his hands about in slow gesticulations as he whispered, pausing now and then to gaze skyward and clasp his hands slowly together beneath his chin. The man probably was readying a competing sermon, Spider supposed. "Would you reckon it sinful if we just gave those two cutlasses and let them fight?"

"Ha!" Odin quickly swallowed a bit of fish. "Don't matter what you and I reckon, Spider John, and I'll wager the Almighty laughs at these two bastards every day."

Spider watched Fox. The man's gaze lifted from his Bible, sought among the lines and sheets for the answer to some philosophical question, then went back to the Good Book.

Fox's brief upward glance and the Reverend Down's pacing were about as much action as Spider had seen on *Redemption*'s weather deck in the last quarter hour or so. Men sat, ate, and muttered among themselves. Hadley had paced the deck quite a bit earlier, lost in thought and peering at the hatch that led to the guest quarters below. Now he sat alone with his thoughts, perched on a spar just above the main course.

Abigail Brentwood had not come up from her cabin below since she and the flame-haired woman, Anne McCormac, had cleaned up the captain and bound him within his shroud. Hob had gathered spare tackle to insert within the sheets to provide weight that would carry the captain below. He had taken advantage of the moment to learn Anne's name, but he had not learned much else. He'd asked about her husband, and he received naught but a playful scowl in return.

The thought of Anne McCormac reminded Spider of something.

"Hob, after you tried to meet the lass with the red hair, did you ever go back to collect the guns?"

"What? Oh, aye, from target practice. I did. I know my duty."

"Did you get them all back?"

"No, got five, one short."

"Hmm."

"Sam Smoke said one of the lads dropped one overboard, didn't expect the kick and it popped right out of his grip."

"Sam said that, he did?"

"Aye."

"Any of the lads that were shooting own up to losing a gun?"

"No, but ... well ... I did not ask. I didn't wish to get some fool lashed for losing a gun."

"Aye, Hob." Spider wiped a bit of fish from his lip. "Aye. No need to cause a fellow trouble."

Spider glanced at Odin. "That bastard Smoke is probably armed now. That might have been his aim all along with the stupid shooting, to get his hands on a gun."

"Aye." Odin nodded.

Spider winked at Hob. "I think a few more of the ship's guns need to disappear. Balls and powder, too."

"Aye," Hob said, grinning. "I know right where they are."

"You think Smoke shot Brentwood?" Odin's leathery face screwed up tight, as though he was thinking hard.

"I don't see how," Spider sighed. "Cabin was locked up from inside. Still, if that son of a bitch walked away from the shooting with a gun, I want one, too." It was worth the risk. With luck, Mister Wright would be too busy with sailing the ship, burying the captain at sea, and courting Abigail Brentwood to notice a few missing pistols, a bit of gunpowder, and some shot.

"Same goes for me," Odin said. "I want a gun. Maybe two. And I have my cutlass, too."

"I am not surprised." Spider shook his head. "I told you not to bring that."

"I don't listen to half of what anyone says, Spider John."

"Maybe the shot came from the quarterdeck above? Through the grating?" Hob scratched his chin.

"Doubtful," Spider answered. "The preachers were up there, remember? And both were standing at the rail when the shot was fired. They'd have seen a killer."

"Maybe they are the killers."

"I do not think they could agree on anything, let alone on plotting a murder, Hob." Spider flicked the boy's ear. "Besides, judging from the way the blood was strewn about, and the wound, and the spot in the bulkhead where the ball struck, the shot was at a level. Not from above."

"What about Hadley?" Hob's whisper was low and conspiratorial. He pointed aloft where the former slave sat.

"What about him?"

"He loves Miss Brentwood, Spider John. He truly does." Hob wiped his lips. "You see it in his eyes, and he follows her like a puppy. But her father wasn't about to let her be with a slave."

"Former slave," Spider reminded him.

"Former, then. Still, if the cap'n stood between Hadley and the woman he loves, maybe he decided to kill him."

Spider pondered. "No. Hadley would slice you or me deep if we hurt the girl, but I don't see him killing the cap'n. I just don't. And he ain't magic or nothing, couldn't walk through locked doors or anything. I think you're daft, Hob."

"A man will do crazy things for love, Spider John. He surely will. And he didn't need to walk through walls. Maybe he had a key."

Spider raised his head sharply. "A key?"

"Right, a key," Hob said. "Remember Mister Wright lost a key? He had to hack through the door with an axe because his key was missing."

"Hmm," Spider said. "Indeed, you are remembering it right, Hobgoblin. Well done."

Hob's face beamed like the sun.

"I still do not think Hadley so evil as to kill a man," Spider continued. Hob and Odin rolled their eyes and shrugged.

Spider looked across the deck at the crew and passengers. Nicholas Wright was currently in the midst of one of his numerous trips below to check on Miss Brentwood's welfare, allowing the nervous men to settle down a bit without their new captain about.

Sam Smoke stood atop the forecastle, fouling the air around him with his ever-present pipe, and grinning as though he had just shared a joke with Lucifer.

Anne was now on the poop, staring out to sea and seemingly lost in thought, unaware of Hob's steady gaze upon her back.

Everyone else either sat quietly, eating their Sunday meal or playing at dice or sewing up holes in shirts and britches. With every soul aboard lost in his or her own thoughts, the now clear-headed Spider finally had a chance to discuss his suspicions with Hob and Odin.

"However it was done," he said, "I think the girl was right. Her father was shot dead by someone else. There were clues."

"What clues?" Hob was all attention now.

"I should have smelled gunpowder," Spider said. "Anyone who went in there should have smelled gunpowder. So why didn't we?"

"Not a whiff of powder at all?" Odin's eyebrows arched, and the motion stretched his facial scars in a way that made them even more horrid. Spider, for a moment, wondered if perhaps the blade or cannon-ball that had carried away Odin's right eye might have done the poor soul a favor if it had ripped away the right eyebrow as well. Perched as it was above Odin's wretched scars, it seemed like a hairy worm about to burrow into rotting meat.

"None," Spider said.

"Well, the grating was uncovered," Hob said. "So it went out that way, likely."

Spider shook his head. "No, it would not have cleared that quickly, not with everything else shut tight. I tell you, we were hacked through that door moments after the shot, too. Cabin was all closed up. The air should have been thick with the smoke."

"So a shot from the stern gallery, then," Hob said. "The gun and the killer outside in the breeze, he fires his shot and the smoke flies away on the wind. Then he closes it up and goes on his way."

"A bit quieter, boy," Spider admonished before setting aside his empty bowl, picking up his burning pipe and drawing deeply. "God, I love a good pipe after a good meal," he said. He let a heavy cloud of smoke out on the breeze and paid special attention to the lingering scent. "Your idea is sound, Hob, provided I can figure out how a man could fire a shot from the stern gallery, close up the doors, and then latch them on the inside while he is outside. That's the rub, there. They were latched, I tell you, from inside."

"Maybe there is a hole he shot through? Or he squeezed a gun between the slats?"

"No, boy," Spider said. "I checked it all myself, before we ever sailed. Solid doors. I looked them over while we were in there, too. No holes that I could see, and I am a carpenter. That's something I'd notice. And the slats open just enough for some air, but you couldn't shove a gun barrel between them. And besides, those open and shut from the inside and were latched tight."

"Don't see anyone wanting to kill the sad bastard," Odin said. "What would be the reason for it?"

"That I cannot say," Spider answered. "We've all seen a lot of killing"—and he looked about to make sure no one else had heard that, then cursed himself for speaking it aloud—"but we always knew the why of it. This, I do not understand at all. The cap'n was well liked. A good man."

"I bet it was Sam Smoke," Odin growled.

"Possibly," Spider said. "He's a killer if I ever saw one, and I have seen plenty. But what does he gain by the cap'n's death? Why would he do it?"

"Just because it is the very kind of thing that amuses him," Odin answered tersely. "Scum like that don't need no other reason."

"Perhaps he did have a reason," Spider pondered. He inhaled deeply from the pipe, thought hard for a couple of heartbeats, then blew a stream of smoke. "This here pretty ship used to belong to pirates, aye?"

"Aye," Hob answered, his eyes widening. "You think Sam Smoke is here looking for something hidden aboard? A treasure map? Or a chest of gold?"

Spider smacked the lad on the side of the head. "Be calm, Hob-goblin. I never saw a pirate mark on a map where his treasure was hid. Hell, every pirate I ever knew spent the loot as fast as he stole it. And even if a man hides some of it away against a brighter day—a brighter day that don't ever come for pirates, mind you—a clever man hides his treasure where he can find it again, without a goddamned map. No sense leaving a trail for someone else. But maybe there is something hid aboard, from the ship's past, or perhaps Smoke just thinks that to be true."

"Aye," Hob said, eyebrows scrunched in thought. "So not a map, then, but maybe Sam Smoke is looking for something else."

The notion intrigued Spider, but the more he thought about it, the more unlikely it seemed. "I think not, Hob. I looked over very bit of lumber in this vessel before she sailed. Hell, you were right there with me, when I could get you to work. I can't think of a good hidey-hole that we could have missed. If something was hid aboard, by thunder, we ought to have found it."

"Maybe it is among the cargo; perhaps one of those barrels is full of gold instead of rum or molasses, and Smoke knows it!"

Spider had a reply, but it was cut short by a commotion on the deck.

"Thieves!" Lazare, the cook, strode into sight after ducking beneath a boom. He wielded a wooden ladle as though he would club someone. "Scoundrel! Which of you stole it? Admit your crime!"

Hob laughed, for the man's face was a bright red visible even in the lowering light. Odin chuckled, and whispered, "The man's food is worth stealing, ha!"

"We've a more serious crime to tend to," Spider said, leaning forward. Hob and Odin leaned toward him. "Imagine it this way, perhaps. A man, whoever he is, wants to kill the cap'n. He gets in the cabin, say, from the stern gallery, perhaps a bit of fancy climbing out on the hull, down from the poop. Probably on a rope. He'd have to go in that way, would he not? Or else be seen going in? We were all outside the cabin there, waiting for a sermon. Anyone entering through the doors would have been seen. Did you see anyone go in?"

Spider looked at Hob, then Odin. Both shook their heads.

"Right. Neither did I." Spider sucked hard on the pipe; it helped to calm his mind. "And besides that, the cabin doors were locked from within. We know that, too. Very well, then, our acrobatic fellow climbs about, finds his way onto the stern gallery . . ."

"Maybe even hid there all night," Hob surmised. "Waiting for the cap'n to throw it open in the morning."

"Maybe," Spider said. "Maybe." He tried to recall whether anyone had been missing from the Bible gathering but could not come up with a name. Wright had gone through the roll, nearly eighty souls, and no one had failed to respond.

Odin scoffed. "Climbing and sneaking. That's a lot of work to kill a man."

"Aye," Spider said. "But these ain't pirates. Walking in and simply killing the man, and not caring who knows it, ain't their nature."

Odin scooped up another gob of ackee on his knife and swallowed it. "Smoke's a pirate."

"Aye," Spider said. "And he wasn't in sight when the shot was fired, either, now that I think on it. He'd been there before but walked away." Spider tried to reckon whether the man could have gotten to the stern gallery in time to have fired that shot.

"I still bet he did it," Hob said. "He is damned good with a gun, and if you are correct he got his hands on one after the shooting match. If it was a tricky shot through the slats, or some other strange trick, he's the one for it."

"Sam has a fancy for your redheaded lady, too, he does," Odin chided. "Wants to bend her over a barrel, same as you, Hob."

"Quiet," Spider said. "We ain't sailing under goddamned foul-mouthed Barlow anymore, you fucking buffle-headed lobcocks."

Odin and Hob stared at him, stung by the insult at first but gradually grinning.

"Well, then," Spider said. "Our man works his way to the stern gallery, awaits his moment, fires the shot, closes it all up some way we haven't reckoned on yet . . ." Spider inhaled again from the pipe. "Then, he knows he's got to get away, or hide. We're all going to be on him in a heartbeat, see? He's got to have his escape planned."

"I did not steal your fucking bread!" It was Holst, a hulking German forecastle hand who possibly could lift an anvil without anyone's aid, roaring at Lazare. "I do not even like your fucking bread! It is too much air, I say!"

"I've seen you eat half a loaf at a sitting!" Lazare lifted the ladle.

"He is going to strike," Hob said.

"Holst will break his neck," Odin replied.

Spider said nothing. His mind was turning on an idea.

"I eat what is set before me!" Holst shoved the cook, who landed on his ass. "My mother taught me to never waste food, even if the food is waste!"

"Jesus!" Hob laughed like a barking seal.

"Belay this now," said Wright, who had appeared seemingly from nowhere. "What the bloody hell are you men at?"

Lazare rose quickly. "Another theft, sir. A loaf, a special one, that I wished to give to the poor miss to lift her spirits."

"And he accuses me," Holst said, bowing to the sailing master. "I do not even like his food. It is like shit in a bowl."

"You eat it well enough!" Lazare rushed the man, ladle uplifted, but Wright grabbed him from behind, spun him around, and shook him like a dusty blanket.

"No choice!" Holst bellowed. "No choice but to eat your puffed-up airy bread and weak sauces, made for babies and kittens, not men! I..."

"Settle yourself," said the sailing master—captain, Spider reminded himself—"or I will order you flogged. Both of you."

That sobered Lazare. "Aye, sir. I am sorry. Forgive me."

"I am sorry, sir," Holst said. "But, if he is to be flogged, I will volunteer."

Wright, still holding onto the cook, turned to Holst with a glare that said the man had better start taking matters seriously. "Will you answer his charge?"

Holst inhaled deeply and ran a hand through his thick blond hair. "I eat readily enough, sir. My mother taught me never to waste food, no matter if it tastes like weasel soaked in piss—"

"Cretin!" Lazare tried to free himself from Wright's grasp but could not.

"If I stole this man's food, sir," Holst said, "it would be only to spare some other poor damned soul from eating it."

Wright seemed to fight a battle within himself, Spider thought, but managed not to laugh. "Lazare," he finally said. "I do not believe Mister Holst stole your loaf. However," he added quickly before Lazare could shout again, "I do not doubt that someone aboard has helped himself to more than his share of your fine food. We shall find the thief in time, but in faith I do not believe Holst is the culprit."

"Thank you, sir," Holst said.

Lazare settled himself. "Very well. Forgive me, sir. It was a special loaf, as I say, and the young miss would have loved it, I am certain."

"We will find your thief," Wright said, waving the man off. Lazare went away, and Holst returned to his place along the starboard rail and shrugged at his friends. Wright wandered over toward the bulkhead where a few men played at dice.

"Well, then," Spider said, once Hob and Odin stopped laughing. "Our killer, as I said, makes his way into the cabin by way of the stern gallery. Bespeaks a certain nimbleness, I would say. Once the deed is done, though, how is he to escape? He might climb back out the way he came in, but by thunder, how would he latch the doors from the inside? Tell me, how?"

Hob scratched his head. Odin shook his.

"No way to do it," Spider said. "I know those doors well, mind you. One needed rehung, and both needed paint. The latch is solid. If you are out on the stern gallery, you can shut the doors, but you cannot latch them from outside. Impossible."

"So then, Cap'n Brentwood killed himself." Hob spread his hands wide.

"No," Spider said. "I think not. I think the killer shot the cap'n, then closed off the stern gallery and hid himself within the cabin. It is the only thing that fits, as far as I can see it."

"Closed off the gallery? Why?" Odin grabbed Spider's pipe, sucked at it deeply, then gave it back.

"He wanted it to look like the cap'n had taken his own life, see? He wrote a note, he did, and left the gun there." Spider drew at the pipe. "If the gallery doors are open, it leaves room for doubt. We might wonder if someone climbed in there and killed him, then escaped by the same route. See? No. So he shoots from the stern gallery, the smoke floats out on the wind; it was a good breeze, remember? He closes off the stern gallery, latches it tight, so we will think no one came that way, and he hides in the cabin while we hack our way inside. It is crowded, confused, we are all in shock, and the killer, bold as you may ever see, walks right out among the crowd, hidden in plain sight, as you might say."

Hob and Odin stared at him. "That is the most preposterous god-damned thing I ever heard in my life," Odin finally said. "And I saw Blackbeard piss on a shark."

"Let us hear your idea, then," Spider said.

"The cap'n, sad and missing his wife, locked up his cabin and shot himself in the goddamned head," Odin said.

"And wrote a note first," Hob said. "He wrote a note, right?"

"Hmmph," Spider said. "Well, then. Yes. There was a note. I don't read, but I have seen a lot of writing. It was but a few words, written by a shaking hand."

"My hand would shake if I was about to put a gun to my head," Hob said.

"Aye," Spider replied. "But such a crazy scrawl, I wonder if his daughter could look at it and recognize her father's hand?"

"Do you want to ask her to do that?" Hob shook his head.

"She's got the backbone of a fighter in her," Spider said after a moment's consideration. "Yes, by thunder. She wants to know the truth. I believe she would look at it."

"Where is the note?" Odin stabbed at the air with a long finger.

"Cap'n Wright read it after we all burst in and later showed it to the lieutenant," Spider said. "I reckon Cap'n Wright handed it over to the navy, so it could be part of some official inquiry."

"Well, I will just swim over to yonder frigate and fetch it back," Odin said. "The two of you do something to draw the navy's attention while I sneak about and get it."

They all stared at one another, shaking their heads.

"So," Spider said after a few seconds, "that clue is forever out of reach."

Hob and Odin nodded.

Spider puffed at his pipe and watched Wright roll the bones with his men and then kick a barrel as they all cried out in triumph.

"Where would your killer hide?" Odin asked after a few heartbeats. "There was no place inside that cabin where a man might hide himself."

"Under the desk," Hob ventured.

Spider pointed his pipe stem at Hob. "Not a big desk. I doubt a man could fit in that space, in any case. But," he said, glancing across the deck at Holst, "I begin to have a notion."

Spider sucked hard at the pipe, alternating his glance between Odin and Hob.

"Goddamn it, Spider John, what is this bloody notion of yours?" Hob's hands were flung wide, his eyebrows raised and his eyes wide.

"Let me ask you this, gentlemen," Spider said. "Are we well fed?"

"What?" That was from Odin.

"Do we eat well?" Spider blew out a big cloud of smoke. "Our provisions. Generous, do you think?"

"Aye," Hob said, twisting his face as though considering the question hurt. "Not long out of port and some of the fish still fresh. Lazare knows his trade, too, no matter what Holst may say. I don't think I have ever had such good food on a ship." He wiped a finger across the bottom of his bowl and sucked the juice off it, as if to illustrate the point.

"Better than salt pork and weevil bread, for certain," Odin chimed in.

"So then," Spider said, "who is it that steals the cook's food? We eat well, he cooks plenty, so who steals it?"

Hob shrugged. "I don't know."

Spider grinned. "Our thief is someone who can't line up for meals," he said. "Someone not of our crew, and not a passenger, not a paid passenger, anyway."

"A stowaway." Odin reached for the pipe, and Spider gave it to him.

"Aye," Spider said, "one desperate to sail to Boston, I think, and one who does not hold our cap'n in high esteem. One who might hide in tight places—might still be hiding—where another man might not fit. I believe I know where to find him. You two keep an eye on the cabin, make sure no one comes out. He'll likely stay hid in there until dark. I can't get in there now with everyone about. So you keep a weather eye."

"And what will you be doing, Spider John?"

"I am going to talk with Mister Chambers, Hob. He was aloft when the cap'n was shot, if I recall the roll properly, and he might have seen something. You can see a great deal from up there."

9

Spider found Edward Chambers atop the forecastle. The man was eating his dumplings and fish, his gnarled and calloused hand clutching a knife he used to spear the morsels. He had one of those faces that wore a permanent scowl, and sun and salt air had rendered it hard and dark. A gold earring, shining bright against the tanned skin, was the only bright thing about him.

Chambers was alone, leaning against the rail. Spider strode toward him, peered across the sea, and sighed deeply. "Better view up top, I dare say."

Chambers grunted. "Main t'gallant, aye, full and by or haulin' winds, better than scrapin' with holystone." He swallowed the bite of fish he'd talked around and snatched another morsel.

"You have a great view from up there. You were up there this morning, weren't you?"

The only reply was a pause in chewing and a hard stare, as though Spider had asked Chambers if his mother liked to blow sailors. After an excruciating wait, Chambers swallowed his food. "What the bloody hell is it to you?"

Spider grinned and held his hands up in supplication. "I am just trying to have a friendly talk."

"I have friendly talks with my foretop mates," Chambers said. "I don't bloody know you."

"I am John Coombs, ship's carpenter."

"I know that much," Chambers growled. "Don't know why you think I need to answer fool questions."

Spider, taken aback, smiled in an effort to salvage the situation. "I am just jealous, is all. You were in the lookout this morning, with a view of the sea and the sunrise that anyone on God's earth would envy."

The creases around Chambers's permanent scowl deepened to such a degree that Spider wondered if sunshine could ever reach into their depths. "Yes," he finally said after long thought. "The view is fine. That is why we post the lookouts up there, aye. Is that all you need to know? Go hand over fist and take a peep yourself, next time."

Spider nodded and glanced out over the ocean. He counted ten breaths, pondered whether there was any point at all in interviewing such a deeply suspicious man, then decided a deep and direct thrust might yield more than any number of circumspect questions. "Did you see anything strange when the cap'n died? Anyone dangling a rope from the poop deck or climbing about on the hull, maybe toward the stern gallery, or any such thing?"

Spider peered directly into Chambers's cold gray eyes and had to blink when the man spat fish and dumplings in his face.

"Stow that! I did not see any such goddamned thing!" Chambers growled. "And I will not tolerate your foolishness any longer. Poke your nose elsewhere or I'll cut it off you." He hurled his almost empty bowl overboard and stalked off. Chambers did not bother with the ladder. He leapt directly from the forecastle to the weather deck.

"Well, then," Spider said to the empty space Chambers had vacated. "I suppose I shall leave you be."

Spider wiped food from his beard and flipped bits of it into the sea. He looked next for Thomas Ames, who had been at the helm when the fatal shot was fired.

There he was, sitting plump on the ratlines between the mainmast shrouds. His cheeks were red with wind or grog, and he squinted into an empty leather jack inverted above his head while his tongue dangled below it in hopes of one more precious drop.

Spider hoped that meant his luck might change. A drinking man is a talking man, and he had at least exchanged pleasantries a time or two with Ames while *Redemption* was being fitted for her northward journey.

"Ho," Spider said. "I think you got it all, mate."

Ames sighed and lowered the jack. "Seems so." The man, still squinting, looked at Spider.

Spider climbed up beside Ames. The hull kicked up salty, cooling spray around them. "Damn sorry thing about cap'n," Spider ventured.

Ames belched. "Aye." The fumes from the man's breath promised an easier interview than the Chambers ordeal.

"You were up on the tiller, weren't you? Must have been a hell of a thing, that shot sounded right below you."

Eyes widening, Ames nodded. "It was. Frightening loud."

"Did you take a look below?"

"What?"

"Over the taffrail, down to the stern gallery. Thought maybe you saw something."

The scarlet cheeks darkened. "Saw what?"

"I don't know, maybe someone down there."

"Outside the cap'n's cabin?"

"Yes." Spider made it a conspiratorial whisper. "You heard the girl, right? She doesn't think her father took his own life."

The man's eyes went wider still, and he took up whispering, too. "Murder?"

"Maybe. Look." Spider turned his head to look back over his shoulder. The fluyt widened below the weather deck, so that an object dropped straight down over the gunwale would glance off the hull before bouncing into the sea. For a nimble killer, that would be an advantage. "A little rope hung or dangled in the right spots, it would not be so difficult to climb. Pop out of a porthole, work over to the stern gallery, fire a shot . . ."

Ames shook his head slowly. His jaw quivered. "Who would do that? Who hated the cap'n enough to do that?"

"I don't know," Spider answered. "Maybe I am wrong. But it could be done. You were up on the poop when it happened. Did you hear anything other than a shot? Someone scrambling around? Cabin doors opening and closing? Cap'n talking to someone?"

Ames just kept shaking his head, and his ruddy cheeks were now pale. "No. Who would hate the cap'n enough to do that? Who?"

He dropped to the weather deck, his drinking vessel falling from his hands. "No." He ran off, shaking his head, leaving the empty jack behind. He looked to and fro and a couple of times paused to stare confusedly at Spider.

Spider scratched his chin, then swung down from the ratlines. There had been one other fellow up by the tiller at the time of the murder. Nicholas Wright had gone up there, only to rush down immediately upon hearing the deadly shot. Wright was carrying much weight on his shoulders now, so Spider decided to wait before asking him if he had seen or heard anything suspicious. For now, the light was low and the shadows were long. It was time for Spider to hunt for clues.

Abigail Brentwood stood in his path. "A moment, sir?"

Spider nodded and shuffled his feet.

"Your young friend, Hob, tells me there was a murder aboard your last vessel."

Why the hell would Hob talk about that damned journey? "Hob told you things, miss?" Spider stood closer, so he could whisper. She noticed his unease and lowered her own voice.

"He was trying to ease my mind, I believe," she said. "You know I do not think my father took his own life." She almost choked on the words. "Hob tells me a man got killed on a ship you and he sailed on and that you quite cleverly figured it all out."

"I think Hob likes to embellish . . ."

"He said you were quite clever, that if anyone could determine just how my father was murdered, it would be you." Her eyes were wide, staring, pleading.

"Miss Brentwood, I do not confirm anything Hob might have told you, but I already have reason to trust you are correct about your father."

She clasped her hands together. "I knew it."

"I will try to reckon it all out. It had to be a tricky . . ." Her lips on his cheek halted his thoughts.

"Thank you, John." She swirled away.

Spider touched his just-kissed cheek. *I reckon I had better solve this thing, then.*

10

"I fucking say German cheese is better than French cheese! Ha!"

It was not exactly the kind of clever distraction Spider had asked for, once he'd finished berating Hob for talking too much to pretty ladies, but Odin's loud declaration drew the attention of *Redemption*'s crew.

"German? The French make food into fucking art, you old bastard! And I thought you didn't like Germans." Hob's speech was unnatural, halting, as though he was rummaging about in a sack for each word. His wild gestures seemed equally odd, and he smacked his hand against a mainsail stay so hard Spider suspected the boy would have a welt. Hob would never be an actor. No matter, so long as everyone paid attention to Odin and Hob and not to Spider.

Still running the awkward interviews with Chambers and Ames through his mind, Spider glanced about, assured himself no one was paying attention to him, then slipped into the captain's cabin. Shattered wood, still hanging from the hinges, tore at his sleeve as he passed through the entrance. He would have to tend to that later.

The captain's quarters had been scrubbed clean with vinegar, and Mister Wright had removed the ship's log, important charts, and any other papers of consequence to his own quarters belowdecks, saying he could not bear to use the captain's quarters himself, though he now had the right.

The captain, wrapped in sailcloth doused in vinegar in a rather vain attempt to mask the death odor in the tropical heat, was in his hammock on the starboard side of the cabin.

The sunlight was very low now, but Spider had dared not take a lantern within, for he wished to draw no attention to himself. As carpenter, though, he had done much work in here, restoring the doors and putting a smooth finish on the captain's desk. Spider knew this chamber well, and low light would give him little trouble.

Blood-red sunlight oozed between the slats in the stern gallery doors, spilling across the room and painting orange streaks on the bulkheads. Spider could see no holes in the doors, or anywhere else, that someone could shoot through, and the slats themselves would not open wide enough to admit a gun. They opened just enough to allow some light and air, but the spaces between were narrow to keep out sea and salt. Spider could not imagine anyone, not even Sam Smoke, shooting a ball between them without leaving a mess.

The gallery doors were latched tight now, but that meant nothing. Abigail and Anne had been in to tend to the body, and crewmen had been in to scrub the blood, brains, bone, and hair from the walls, and those fellows had certainly opened the cabin to the sea air. But Spider was damned certain the doors had been closed tight and latched when they had all rushed in immediately after the shooting, and that was the key point.

Spider opened the stern gallery doors, allowing sunset light and sea breeze into the cabin.

He glanced at the captain's remains. They had cleaned him up, but even so blood had seeped through the cloth around his head. That would get a fresh wrap in the morning when the captain's body would be consigned to the deep. Spider muttered a silent prayer, then went on with his work.

Spider closed his eyes and remembered the splatters of blood everywhere. The captain must have been standing and must have spun in his death throes. Blood had flown in all directions. Spider could almost see it—the gun against the head, the shot, the swirling tumble to the deck, the blood flinging everywhere.

If he was murdered, Spider thought, *the killer must have been sprayed with gore. There is no way around that fact.*

Spider opened his eyes and crossed toward the door, where he'd seen the hole in the bulkhead. He dug with his knife and fished out the bloody, misshapen ball. He glanced at the grating above, the spot where the captain had been found, and then at the ball. There was no way the shot could have come from above, unless someone had devised a way for a ball to change course mid-flight.

Could the hatch have been an escape route? Not with the preachers up there as witnesses, Spider reckoned. And the man at the tiller, above on the poop deck, would have been a likely witness, too. The grating should have been latched down tight from above, as well.

Spider turned and glanced at the shattered cabin door and at its intact mate on the other side of the mizzenmast. Unless the culprit had been able to walk invisibly, like a ghost, the killer could not have left that way without being seen, and if Spider had surmised correctly, the culprit could not go anywhere on board without being immediately recognized and clapped in irons.

So Spider leaned harder toward another possibility, that the killer had hidden within the cabin and escaped later. There was one other option, however.

Perhaps the bastard is still in here.

Had the cabin been empty for even a moment since the captain's death, giving the killer a chance to exit by way of the stern gallery? Possibly, but it would not have been an easy escape.

Spider stared at the wardrobe along the port bulkhead. It would be a squeeze, what with the captain's coats and shirts and britches hanging within, but a man might hide there. Spider gripped his French throwing knife, ready to stab if necessary, and flung the wardrobe open.

It held nothing but clothes and small chests stacked below those, leaving no room for anyone to hide within.

Spider sighed quietly. There still was one more place to look.

He turned to the great case clock. When the thing had been brought aboard, Spider had suggested wrapping the gorgeous creation in sailcloth to protect it from salt air and spray during the voyage, but Captain Brentwood had insisted the clock could give him little joy if its beauty was hidden. *That*, Spider thought, *is not the attitude of a man about to kill himself, now is it?*

So there the clock stood, all of its splendid woodwork and carvings there to see.

In five steps, Spider closed the distance. He held the knife at ready.

A great hart at the top of the case stared back at him, a thin rope wrapped around its body and lashing the clock to the bulkhead as a guard against the rolling of the ship. The clock was likewise bound at its feet, but the main body of the case itself was not bound by the ropes and could still be opened.

Spider examined the door that opened on the works, or rather, the place where the works would be had they not been removed and stored away. A window showed the empty space within, but it did not expose the bottom of the case. Oak panels hid whatever might be down there, and so that was where the killer had to be.

An ordinary man could not have curled into such a tiny space of concealment, Spider knew. But the man he sought could.

Knife raised in his right hand, Spider took a deep breath, held it, then opened the door with his left hand.

Little Bob Higgins was not hiding within the empty case clock.

"Fuck and bugger," Spider whispered, returning the knife to his belt. He spun around slowly but could not discern any other place within the cabin where Little Bob might be hiding.

"Damn."

Spider pondered. He went toward the stern gallery, intending to step outside, but a fucking gull squawked and Spider froze.

A dozen or so of the damn things floated behind *Redemption*, hovering over the ship's wake for reasons only birds knew. That didn't bother Spider too much; he was used to seeing birds gather around ships. But one of the gulls—all claws and beak and beady eyes—perched on the rail, and Spider could not step out on the stern gallery as long as it was there. He could not bring himself to approach that unholy combination of speed and weapons.

"Damn," he muttered. Instinct told him to shout at the gull, but he did not want anyone on the ship to know he was snooping around in here. Nor did he want to abandon his investigation just because of a fucking bird. He knew his fear of the feathered beasts was irrational— but that did not make it go away.

He considered just stepping out into the open air and shooing the bird with a wave of his arms, but that would mean actually getting close to the damned thing. There was no way to know how a bird would react to a man rushing at it, and Spider suddenly imagined himself cringing on the deck with bleeding holes where his eyes used to be while the gull carried the blood-soaked orbs to show off to its friends.

Spider took three deep breaths. Captain Brentwood had been murdered. Of that, Spider was certain. Gull or no gull, Spider had promised the man's daughter he would try to figure out who had done it. The daughter needed that.

Her face appeared in his mind suddenly, and guilt stabbed at him. *Em is waiting in Nantucket,* he reminded himself. *Solve the murder for this girl because you said you would. No other reason.*

Spider inhaled sharply. He looked about, rummaged through the captain's desk, and found a granite paperweight. He nodded, turned to face the gull, and hurled the stone as hard as he could.

His aim with a paperweight was not so true as his aim with a knife, but it was good enough. The bird, untouched, lifted into the air with a shrill, mocking cry and joined its brothers and sisters hanging in the wind.

Spider paused to close the desk drawer and spotted the captain's key ring. He recognized the cabin key, for Captain Brentwood had entrusted it to him briefly during the renovations. The sight of that key brought Wright's missing key back into Spider's mind. As far as he knew, Wright's key was the only other one that could open the captain's quarters—and that key was missing.

"Damn," Spider muttered. *Even with a key to lock the door behind him, the killer could not have gone out that way. We all were on the bloody deck, right outside the cabin. If the killer was not hiding in this cabin, the stern gallery had to have been the means of escape. So how had the doors been latched?*

Spider stepped outside onto the gallery. *Such a fine place to be*, he thought, *once it is bloody free of gulls*. It was built for a captain's pleasure. He could sit upon one of the built-in oak benches, glass of wine or a burning pipe in hand, or both, and look out over the sea, watching *Redemption*'s wake trail off into the distance.

Spider looked upward, toward the poop deck. Could a man dangle on a rope from there to reach this spot? Yes. And the housing that contained the rudder's workings, which ran down the stern of the ship and partially divided the stern gallery, would have made the task easier.

It was not difficult at all to imagine a man in good condition climbing down from above, although how such a thing could escape the helmsman's notice Spider could not fathom. Ames might have been paid off, of course, in return for silence. A killer might have explained it all away as a lark, or even a bit of theft. Perhaps he had claimed to be raiding the captain's liquor. Ames might have been willing to share in that.

But *Redemption*'s men were not pirates, and it seemed unlikely a man would remain quiet about such an escapade once the captain died. Perhaps the helmsman was part of a conspiracy? Spider did not know Ames well but thought him too plump for a sailor and too slow-witted for a companion. And he certainly had seemed genuinely shocked at the suggestion of murder.

The killer need not have used the poop deck to gain access, though. With clever use of rope, a man might have traversed the bowed hull and reached the gallery that way. It would have required some sneaky advance work, but it could have been done. Little Bob had been thought to be back in Port Royal, and so no one aboard expected him to be attending duties anywhere or anytime. He might have found time to rig a hand line from a porthole to the gallery.

Spider had easily convinced himself Little Bob was hiding below, somewhere, so as to reach New England. His pleas to the captain had seemed desperate, and the cook's missing food and booze most likely were sustaining the stowaway. Little Bob was a layabout and a complainer, but he was accustomed to working in the trees and could make his way along shrouds or ratlines as well as any other sailor. With everyone's attention on the Bible reading, Bob could have kept quiet, scrambled out through a porthole, made it to the stern gallery, and avenged himself on the captain who had ordered him off the ship.

The scheme fit together rather well, Spider thought, if he could only work out how the little bugger had escaped the captain's quarters afterward.

Spider looked around in the fading light but saw nothing that explained that mystery. He could swear the gulls were laughing at him.

He closed the gallery doors while remaining outside and tried to figure out how someone could have latched them while standing out here in the salt-tinged air. He tried it himself, using his throwing knife as a tool, but the blade was too thick to slip between the doors. He considered whether he could do it with a nail or some other tool. *Redemption* had as fine a kit of tools as Spider had ever worked with. His mind ran through the tools he had aboard, trying to think of one that might suffice to slip between the doors and bend toward the latch.

He could think of nothing that would do the job. If he wanted such a tool, he would have to create it himself. And the person performing this miracle, even if he had a proper tool, would have done so blindly, unable to see the arrangement of hook and bolt inside the chamber. There simply was no way to see adequately through the doors, even with the slats opened as they were now. The essential bits and pieces were out of sight.

If the goddamned thing could be latched from out here, Spider was not clever enough to think of a way to do it. *Who could—damn*, he thought. *Rufus Fox might be the very man to devise such a tool.* He had built that keyboard contraption for Miss Brentwood, full of tricky moving parts. And he did small work, too, with clocks and watches. Perhaps Fox had a small tool that could slip between doors and bend around and lift a latch. Or perhaps he had created such a device.

But why would Rufus Fox kill the captain? They were friends, or so said Fox and the captain's daughter. Spider could think of no motive. And Fox had been right there, peering down from the quarterdeck, when the fatal shot was fired. He could not have done the deed.

Spider's original notion still held up. He was sure Little Bob had done this bloody thing, even if he could not determine precisely how the slaying and escape were accomplished.

"Fuck and bugger." Spider growled his frustration at the seabirds, then went back into the cabin.

He nodded briefly at the captain's wrapped form, then held his nose against the unpleasant odor. "I will figure this all out, sir," he whispered. "You deserve a measure of justice. I'll just find the tiny son of a bitch and thrash the truth out of him."

He peered out of the cabin entrance and saw that he had an easy escape if he hurried. He stepped out quickly and headed toward the foremast, where Hob and Odin were waiting.

"Well?" Odin handed Spider a jack of grog, their daily ration.

"I was wrong," Spider answered after draining the drink. "I thought he had to be in there, somewhere, but he is not. He must have gotten out, but only God and the devil know how."

"You are sure Bob is aboard, though."

"Yes, Hob. Did you get us some guns?"

"Did you think I was going to wait?" The boy grinned. "I have already loaded them."

"Fetch them. And grab some lanterns. We are going below to find the fucking little bastard."

11

The three hunters had decided to take separate areas of the ship, for *Redemption* had plenty of places in her spacious holds where a man could hide, especially a man as small as Little Bob Higgins.

Spider had taken the main cargo hold, on the theory that a wretch such as Bob could not resist the temptation to pop the bung from one of the many rum casks stowed away there. Odin was somewhere in the damp bowels of the orlop, having quipped, "Best place to find a rat, ha!" Hob was exploring the passenger deck, thinking perhaps Bob had occupied an empty berth. Spider had argued that Little Bob was not likely so stupid as to hide so close to other people, but Hob had persisted, insisting that "he is that bloody goddamned stupid, Spider John." In the end, Spider had agreed that if anyone was so stupid, surely it was that "shit-licking lobcock Bob."

After that, the hunters had gone their separate ways. Spider moved slowly now in the darkness, one hand holding a lantern, and the other a flintlock. Holding the pistol and recalling Hob's joy in handing it over, Spider couldn't help but reflect on how eager the young man was to see some action. *Wish I could keep him out of this*, Spider thought before wondering if he was trying to be a father to Hob because he couldn't be a parent to his own son. Not a fun thought, that.

Spider eyed a hogshead of rum and put his nose almost upon it. The liquor seeped into the wood, and after a time the aroma fought its way out, filling the hold with an enticing, boozy scent. Spider took a deep whiff. But this was no time to drink, he reminded himself. He was looking for a killer. But damn, did he want a drink.

Spider inspected the gun in his hand one more time. It was ready. He hoped he was, too, and uttered a brief, barely audible prayer.

Redemption listed toward port and rocked a good deal on the swells, so Spider proceeded slowly. He held the lantern, nearly shut so as to emit only a thin beam, as far from himself as he could. The light made him a target in the dark, and for all he knew Little Bob had a gun, too, so Spider kept the light off to the side, away from his head, chest, and belly. If Bob aimed at the lantern, he would miss Spider. That was, he would miss if the damned ball went where Bob aimed. No guarantee of that on solid ground, let alone on a moving vessel. Pistols were so unreliable. Spider's gun hand went toward his belt, and a thumb knuckle tapped the throwing knife tucked there. Reassured, Spider pressed onward.

Sweat trickled down Spider's brow. He had his hair bound in a kerchief, but tension had soaked the damned thing and now the salty fluid stung at his eyes. He brushed it away with a sleeve, using the gun hand, so as not to wave the lantern in front of his face.

Spider paused, leaning against a stack of barrels lashed to the bulkhead, trying to adjust his vision to the blackness around him. The smell of wet wood predominated, but plenty of rum scent oozed through oak barrels, for rum was *Redemption's* principal cargo. Spider inhaled deeply and slowly and wondered if the fumes alone might relax him a bit.

As near as he could tell, the answer to that question was no.

He took another step forward, peering into the nooks and crannies between barrels and crates, scanning the dust and mouse shit on the deck to see if any had been swept aside by human steps. He hunted with his ears, too, listening for the sound of breathing or snoring or eating. He heard a rat scuffling about somewhere.

Spider tried to ignore the rum's siren song, to filter it out in his mind so he might detect any stench of piss or sweat. He thought he could just make out the latter, but that might be his own foul smell. He was sweaty and tired and miserable, but he had work to do.

Spider crept forward cautiously and immediately halted. A thump, followed by a twittering mousy sound, echoed in the hold. He could not make out the direction from which it came. It could have originated anywhere. Spider spun quickly, then looked up.

That last decision probably saved his life.

Little Bob plunged from the top of a barrel stack, and the reflection from a dirk exploded in the lantern's beam. Spider stepped back just soon enough to keep the arcing knife from cutting anything. Little Bob hit the deck awkwardly, with a thud and a stumble and a "damn and blast!"

The wildly swinging lantern beam was inconveniently aimed, so Spider kicked in the direction of that voice and smiled after his boot heel connected solidly with what he surmised to be Bob's jaw. Little Bob fell with a heavy thud, followed by a soft, sharp clatter that Spider hoped was the sound of the bastard's teeth rolling on the deck, but it could have been just a scurrying rat.

A swing of the lantern revealed Little Bob, crouching and bleeding profusely from the mouth. Spider stomped, driving his heel into Bob's ribs. Certain now where his quarry was despite the veering lantern beam, Spider kicked thrice until Little Bob huffed a wet, weak gasp. Then Spider stepped back. "I've a gun, Bob, and I shall use it if need be. And hell, maybe even if I do not need to."

Bob's only answer was a dejected groan.

Spider tucked the gun into his belt, next to the French throwing knife, then opened the lantern wider. Each move was that of a man who had fought many times, and the gun was back in Spider's hand before Bob could even think of an attack.

"I am going to kill you, slow," Bob muttered.

"Not today." Spider wiggled the gun. "And not any day if you make me nervous. I do not need much of an excuse to paint the bulkheads with your blood, Bob. I truly do not."

Bob wiped blood from his lips and chin, and a couple of fresh gaps told Spider he'd kicked out at least a pair of teeth. An ugly gash creased the man's forehead, and he struggled to breathe. He stank, too, as would any man hidden below for several days.

Little Bob's knife seemed to have vanished somewhere in the darkness.

"Will you come above peacefully and answer for your crimes,

Bob?" Spider backed away a step. "Or should I just shoot you in your ugly face now and save everyone a lot of bother?"

"I will surrender," Bob said softly. "I will implore for mercy."

"You will find none of that," Spider said. "Rope for you, I wager. You might later wish you had taken a quick ball in the brain. Come."

Bob rose, shaking and unsteady, but he complied. As Bob climbed the ladder, Spider poked the gun at Bob's rear end. "Try a surprise jump again, Bob, and I will put a ball right up your arse. This close, you'll get powder burnt, too, I reckon."

"I hate you, you fucking bugger." But Bob pulled no tricks, and soon they were on the weather deck, where a fresh Caribbean breeze cooled their skin and carried away the worst of Bob's stench.

It was almost as dark here as it had been below, for thick clouds veiled the moon.

"Rouse Cap'n Wright," Spider said loudly after forcing Bob to kneel. A few hands blinked, and there were several refrains of "I'll be buggered" and "It's fucking Little Bob," but a couple of fellows went forward in search of Wright.

"Wait," Bob said, his eyebrows arched and his wide eyes trying to project an apology. "I do not . . ."

"Quiet," Spider said, aiming the gun at Bob's head. "I do not like you, Bob, never did, and I might just shoot you to watch your head burst like a fucking pumpkin."

Bob actually growled, like a frightened dog, but he said no more.

"What is this?" Wright asked upon his arrival a few moments later. His shirt was untucked, and he rubbed his eyes hard. He clearly needed sleep, and Spider hoped bringing the killer to justice would ease the man's mind. "Little Bob Higgins? Son of a bitch. Little Bob, what the bloody hell do you do here on my ship?"

Bob seemed confused but managed to answer. "Sir, please, I stowed away. I need to get to Boston, I say, in any way possible. My sister, sir, she is bad ill. Damn and blast, sir, I love her, and I have got to see her before she's gone." His words whistled a bit through the gaps in his teeth left by Spider's boot, and he spoke in awkward gasps. Spider grinned savagely, proud of his work.

"Feel no pity, sir," Spider said. "He killed the cap'n."

"What?" Wright's eyes went wide, and he inhaled sharply. He noticed the gun in Spider's hand, and Spider tucked the weapon into his belt.

"What?" Bob's jaw, still dripping blood, quaked. "I did not fucking kill anyone!"

"He killed the cap'n," Spider repeated.

Wright shook his head slowly, as if stunned. Hadley emerged from the men crowding around and placed his hand on the hilt of his work knife. Spider gave him a hard look, and Hadley halted. But the young man's eyes burned. He nodded at Spider, then aimed his eyes at Bob.

"I reckoned Little Bob was on board, sir, because Lazare's food got stolen. Made me think we had a stowaway, and Bob seemed desperate before, so I figured the stowaway might be him. And Bob hated the cap'n, right? Here's how he done it. Little bastard climbed in through the stern gallery, shot the cap'n in the head, hid in the goddamned case clock, and then climbed out again when he could. I think that's how it happened, anyway, but I don't have it all reckoned out yet. It had to be something like that, though. Had to be."

Spider stared at Bob. "Maybe we can beat the details out of Bob. I reckon we'll have plenty of volunteers for that."

"If the cap'n is dead, that is right well with me," Bob spat. "Good! Damn and blast the bugger! But I did not kill him. Tell me who did and I will shake the man's hand. But I did not kill him!"

"You cur," Wright growled through clenched teeth. Then he slapped Bob backhanded. Another tooth sailed off to rattle across the deck, a thick gob of blood and spit splattering in its wake.

"I did not kill him!" Bob tried to rise, only to be knocked down by another vicious blow from Wright. This one would leave a black eye, no doubt. But Bob, frantic, tried to rise again. He fell, weakened by Wright's blows. "I stowed away! I stole food! But I did not kill the bugger!"

"You hated him," Spider said.

"You swore revenge," Wright said.

Bob shook his head. "I never . . ."

"Everyone else aboard is accounted for," Spider said. "We were all waiting to get a Bible lesson, right? We were all gathered for the reading, except a few men aloft and Ames on the tiller. But no one missed you at the Bible reading, Bob, because no one thought you were on the damned ship. And you, you tiny fuck, are the only person aboard who could have hidden in that clock."

Wright looked at Spider with a new respect. "Very clever," the master said. "Very well done, John."

"Cap'n wasn't a man to kill himself," Spider continued. "Bob scribbled that damned note and placed the gun in the cap'n's dead hand."

"Undoubtedly," Wright said, shaking his head slowly. "Goddamn."

Whispers rushed among the assembled hands, and Spider saw many men nodding. No one aboard liked Little Bob Higgins, and they were ready to believe the worst of him.

"Williams. Johnston. You men take this wretch, bind him up, stow him in the orlop, and stand guard over him until relieved," Wright ordered. "I want him bound so tight that breathing hurts. And if he resists, put a goddamned knife deep in his throat."

"Aye, sir."

As those hands dragged Bob away to his fate and Wright went to the rail to stare off into space across the dark ocean, Hob appeared and tugged at Spider's sleeve. "Spider, I don't think Little Bob killed him."

Spider, still caught up in the drama and rather proud of himself, had not even noticed the boy's approach. "Of course he did." Spider admonished Hob with a finger. "Little Bob is the only one who'd have been able to pull it off. No one else could have hidden in there."

"Well, I heard someone else all but confess," Hob said.

"What?"

"Little Bob didn't kill Cap'n Brentwood," Hob said. "Anne McCormac did."

"Ha!" Odin stepped forward and continued in a harsh whisper. "No. I do not think so. I found something very interesting, and by God, I can tell you it wasn't the red-haired woman, nor was it your fucking Little Bob, that killed the cap'n."

12

"**F**uck and bugger, boy, what in bloody hell do you know?"
They had moved to the main cargo hold, Spider practically dragging Hob, and they all stood now not far from where Spider had fought with Little Bob. Spider had wanted to get away from the gossip and speculations that reigned upon the main deck and in the crew quarters. No one was sleeping, and there had been no chance to hear Hob's tale up top, not with men asking Spider again and again how Bob had pulled off his crime and how the ship's carpenter had sorted it all out.

So they gathered here now by lantern light in the wee hours, where the only companions were rats, rum barrels, crates of goods, and the slush of ocean against the hull. And, of course, the seductive aroma of rum.

"Anne McCormac killed Cap'n Brentwood." Hob drew a deep breath. "I heard her say it."

"Damn!" Spider thought hard. "Are you certain, Hob?"

"It is the truest thing I have ever said." The lad attempted a courtly bow.

Damn, Spider thought. *If Hob is right, I have managed no more than to accuse an innocent man of murder.* Spider did not like Little Bob Higgins, but he did not want to see him hang if he had not murdered the captain.

Spider took a deep draw from his pipe. Odin, seated on the deck with his knees drawn up to his appalling face, tried to take a swig from a flask, then turned it upside down and sighed loudly when nothing spilled from it.

"Spider."

"Sorry."

Hob sighed. "Might I get on with it?"

"Yes, damn it, Hobgoblin, tell us."

Hob inhaled sharply, swelling his chest and rubbing his hands together in front of his face. "There I was, on the passenger deck, looking into the unassigned berths," he began. "I saw no signs of Little Bob, of course, and now we know why. I listened at all the doors, too. I could hear Miss Brentwood crying to break your heart, and the Reverend Down snoring. Mister Fox was asleep in his berth as well, but Sam Smoke's berth was empty. I took an opportunity." Hob reached into his shirt and brought out a small pouch heavy with the scent of tobacco. He tossed it to Spider. "You go through your ration so quickly, thought you might like some of Sam Smoke's stuff."

"Thanks," Spider said. He took a deep, appreciative whiff. "Did he have any rum or whiskey?"

"No."

"Go on."

Hob opened his mouth to speak, but a thud from above interrupted him. All three men looked up, Hob and Odin drawing pistols and Spider whipping out his throwing knife. Thomas the cat peered down at them from atop a crate.

"Goddamned cat," Spider said. "Go catch a rat."

"He misses the cap'n, I reckon," Hob said. "Poor thing."

Spider tucked his knife away. "How in the bloody hell did that cat follow us from our old ship to here?"

"He got off *Austen Castle* and found Odin," Hob said.

"Can we talk about the killing?" Odin spat.

Thomas dropped from the crate, with an agility rather surprising in a cat so fat.

"Odin kept feeding him," Hob said. "They are quite chummy."

"He's just a mangy cat," Odin muttered, his lone eye narrowed in a scowl.

"Fierce, hellfire-spitting Odin, friend to felines." Spider shook his head slowly, unable to suppress a laugh.

"I am saving Thomas to eat. Might eat you and Hob, too, if need be!"

They all laughed, then realized they were making more noise than was wise. After they quieted, Thomas curled up beside Odin, and Hob continued his report.

"As I was looking about I could hear the lady, Anne, humming to herself, in her own bunk."

"And you tried to get yourself a peep, ha!"

"I did not, Odin," Hob said, but even in the uncertain lantern light his face seemed to flush. "I went to creep out of there, all quiet, and then I heard someone coming down the ladder. It was Sam Smoke."

Spider and Odin leaned forward. Hob blinked.

"As I had his tobacco in hand, I thought it best to hide."

"Wise, wise," Spider said.

"So I hopped into an empty berth, happened to be next to hers . . ."

"Of course it did." Odin scratched his ugly scar.

"Aye. And I heard Sam approach and he walked right into her berth. Did not knock, did not speak, just walked right in."

"Maybe he was expected," Spider pondered.

"I do not think so," Hob said. "I heard her gasp, and I heard him laugh. I put my ear up against the bulkhead. They were being quiet, but I heard her plainly tell him to get out. He laughed again and told her, 'Drop the knife, Anne.'"

"Did she stab him?" Odin's eyebrows arched, and he grinned in hope.

"No. She asked him what he was doing, and he said he had come to ask her the same, said he never expected to see her in these waters again."

Spider sucked on the pipe until it glowed. "And what did she say to that?"

"Said her unfinished business was none of his goddamned affair and to leave her be or she'd decorate her fancy hat with his balls."

"Rough talk from a fair woman," Spider said.

"The talk got rougher," Hob replied. "Their voices got even lower, and I did not hear all, but I heard enough."

Spider leaned toward him. "What did you hear, lad? Little Bob's life might depend on it."

Hob snorted, and snot flew from his nose. He swiped a sleeve across his face. "Little Bob? They can hang Little Bob three times, and I'll watch every time, gladly. I do not care a rat's balls' worth what happens to him."

"Damn, boy, what did you hear?"

"I heard Sam say, 'You came to kill him, didn't you?' And Anne said, 'You goddamned know I did, and good riddance, too!'"

"Bugger," Spider muttered. "Why would she kill Cap'n Brentwood? What's the connection there?"

"I do not know," Hob said. "She told Sam she had no problem killing him, meaning Sam, too, and he'd better get the bloody fuck out of her berth. He laughed, but he left. He went on to his own berth. I waited until I heard him shut it; then I crawled on out of there, quiet as a mouse."

"Well done, boy." Spider waved his pipe about as he tried to sort it all out. "So, do we tell Mister Wright maybe Little Bob didn't kill the cap'n? 'How do you know that?' he'll ask. 'Why, we been spying on the paying passengers,' is that what we say? And if she did kill him, exactly how did she do it?"

"She vanished before the Bible reading," Hob said. "I recall that, because I was watching her."

"You do watch her closely, don't you?"

Hob shrugged. "A sight to see, she is."

"Yes," Spider agreed. "She's a fine sight. And maybe a murderer."

"Aye," Hob said. "Not so fine now, I reckon." He dropped his gaze to his feet and muttered something Spider could not discern.

"So, assume it was her and not Little Bob. She ain't big, but she could not have hidden in the case clock; I don't see how she could. And there was no place else, really, for her to hide. Maybe she could climb in through the stern gallery, she don't seem all that dainty after all, but how could she shoot him and then latch those doors behind her? How could anyone possibly do that?"

"Witchcraft."

Spider turned toward Odin. In the lantern light, the man's eye was as bright as wet, white marble under a strong noon sun. "What?"

"Witchcraft, maybe. She's a woman. Maybe she's a witch."

Spider gulped. His own grandmother had been executed years ago when the madness of Salem spread to other communities. He never believed she was a witch, and his mother had denied it vehemently his whole life, and that had made him wonder if perhaps all the hangings had been naught but fear cooking and bubbling within a community until it boiled over. Maybe all of those women were innocent. Anyway, his own past had taught him to be skeptical of witch claims. He shook his head.

"Let us not speak of such," he said. "I think witchcraft is nonsense, and words like that make men mad, and we need to keep our heads here. Besides, if she's a witch, why kill him with a gun?"

"Maybe she made him do it," Hob surmised. "Goddamned cursed him, maybe, and compelled him to kill himself."

"I think maybe all women are witches," Odin mused. "It's the only thing that makes sense, if you've known some women. But I do not think she killed the cap'n. Ha! I truly do not! Don't you want to know what I found, Spider John?"

"Bugger." Spider hung his head. "You said you found something, and I forgot. What was it you found?"

"This," Odin answered. He unfolded his heavily calloused hand to reveal a key.

"That is the cap'n's cabin key," Spider said. "I am sure of it. Where did you find it?"

Odin leered. "Before I went to the orlop, I peeped about in the fo'csle. Rummaged in some chests. I found this little gem in Hadley's trunk."

"No," Spider said.

"Aye, hidden in the bottom under his clothes. I grabbed the key out of there because the boy don't own nothing but them clothes, so why does he have a key? You sure it is for the cap'n's door, Spider?"

"Well," Spider answered. "It looks to be. The lock is still intact. I will check this key against that, but . . . I had that key in my hands a couple of times whilst getting *Redemption* in top form, and I think this is the correct key."

"So Hadley killed him, not Anne?" Hob seemed relieved.

Spider shook his head. "She might have killed him. You are correct, Hob, she did walk away from the Bible reading. I don't know where she was when the shot was fired. And I would rather think it was her, not Hadley. I just can't believe it was Hadley."

"Ha! Why?"

"Because Cap'n Brentwood's death would hurt Abigail Brentwood, Odin." Spider shook his head. "Hadley just would not hurt her. He would not."

Odin scowled. "You put too much faith in people, Spider John."

Spider sucked deeply on the pipe, pondering. "Probably. What do we tell Wright? Let us keep this key to ourselves, I think." He removed the leather cord carrying Em's pendant from around his neck and added the key to it. "Hadley would not get fair consideration, I do not believe. Black men never do. And I think him innocent."

Hob spoke up. "Even if it was Hadley or Anne, can we wait until Bob is hung, and then tell Wright? Thomas would like that, I should think." The cat leapt into Hob's arms.

"Lord, help me," Spider muttered, making his way to the ladder.

13

*E*ven as he climbed, Spider tried to imagine flame-haired Anne killing the captain. He did not want her to be the killer. He wanted her to be beautiful and mysterious and flirtatious. He wanted her to be a pleasant distraction on this voyage, maybe even a bit of a dalliance to ease his separation from Em. He did not want her to be a ruthless killer.

It had been much easier to envision Little Bob doing the bloody deed.

Anne had been on the crowded deck only moments before the fatal shot was heard, so she would have possessed very little time for the kind of tricky maneuvering necessary. Could she have rigged some sort of line ahead of time and swung over to the stern gallery while everyone else was on deck? It seemed unlikely, but it seemed a better bet than cauldrons and spells and black candles full of human marrow.

Still, what Hob had heard in the berths below was damning, and the wench's eyes seemed to say she was capable of anything.

A grand theory rattled in Spider's head, one in which Anne sneaks away from the Bible gathering, climbs up to the poop deck, and bribes the helmsman with a bit of coin or a dram of liquor or a toss of her hips. *I'm going to see the cap'n,* she says with a wink, *for a bit of fun. Keep your mouth shut, and you might have a bit of fun, too.* Then she slides down a rope from the poop deck, shoots the man from the stern gallery, closes the doors . . .

Not bloody likely at all, Spider decided.

Could Anne have hidden in plain sight? Ducked aside from the cabin door, then joined the crowd when everyone rushed in to see what had happened?

She was a stunning woman and tended to draw men's eyes. But there was a boldness about her, a confidence.

Spider paused on the ladder. Anne McCormac had vanished from the crowd before the shot. So had Sam Smoke. Could one of them have snuck into the captain's quarters, snuffed out his life, scrawled the note, and hidden near one of the doors? It had taken Nicholas Wright four strong cracks with an axe to burst through the portside cabin door. Perhaps the killer had stood by the starboard door, obscured by the mizzenmast rising through the deck, while Wright fought through the sturdy oak on the portside. Once they were through the door, all eyes were on the dead man. The killer might have stepped away from the shadows and joined the crowd. Would anyone have really noticed?

Jesus, could it really be that simple?

No. Anne would have been noticed, Spider was certain, and he was equally certain she had not been among those in the initial rush to see what had happened to Captain Brentwood. Could she have disguised her fine dress, perhaps dressed as a seaman with a scarf and hat to tuck up the long, flaming red locks? Stood there brazenly as just one of the crew, and then stepped out in the confusion to don her dress over the sailor's shirt and britches?

She had been bold when confronted by Sam Smoke, if Hob's account was accurate, but was she bold enough to stand in the room while the crew discovered the body? And could she have changed apparel so quickly?

Spider smacked his forehead. The killer must have changed clothes because the captain's blood had flown everywhere. The killer would have been splattered with it. No one in the cabin had been covered in blood. The killer must have doffed the bloodied clothing, perhaps tossed it overboard from the stern gallery.

What of Sam Smoke? That bastard could not escape the tobacco reek that followed him everywhere. Spider had not smelled Smoke's pipe in the captain's quarters.

That realization brought Spider once again to wondering why he had not smelled gunpowder and to supposing the shot must have been fired from outside on the stern gallery. It had to be that, or else all the rum had addled his sense of smell—but he had not had trouble discerning the lovely scent of Abigail Brentwood's hair, nor the luring aroma of the rum he'd stolen. No. His nose still worked. The shot had to have come from the stern gallery.

So then, why did Hadley have a key?

It was all enough to make his head spin and make him want more rum.

"What the hell do you wait for, Spider?"

It was Hob, awaiting a chance to climb out of the hold himself.

"I was thinking, Hob," Spider growled, "something you would not know about since it doesn't involve your whore pipe."

Spider resumed climbing and ascended into the fresh dawn air. A boat from HMS *Southampton* likely was on its way now to collect the prisoner Little Bob Higgins, and it would be a fine thing because Spider was now convinced once again that Bob had to have done the deed, whatever Hob might have overheard. Anne or Smoke would have been noticed, and everyone else was on the damned deck when the shot was fired. Bob had to be the murderer.

An image of the key Odin found in Hadley's chest flashed in his mind. That image did not fit with Spider's neat summation. Spider scowled at the image. Gnashed his teeth at it. Chased it off.

Spider tried to think of a good excuse to be out of sight when the navy boat arrived at *Redemption*. The presence of navy men aboard the fluyt would be unsettling, and Spider had no intention of reliving the experience of guarding the captain's body while a king's officer stood near enough to smell him. He would find a place to hide until it was over. The crew would pay respects to the captain and send his body into the deep. Wright would then hand over Little Bob, the navy men would take their prisoner and stow him in a brig until it was time to hang him, and that would be that. *Redemption* would continue on her way to Boston, so close to Nantucket that Spider imagined he would be able to smell Em's sandalwood perfume from the pier.

An image of Em, naked, awaiting him, smiling at him, filled his mind. He fought it off.

Spider glanced over the port rail. For a moment, his mind still on home, he thought how lovely it would be to see some fin whales break the surface and toss up some spray. There were no whales here, though, not in this bright sun-swept sea, so different from the leaden, cold northern seas. He realized he was sleepy and his mind was wandering, and he forced his thoughts to snap back to the present.

Southampton was not there.

Spider worked his way around the ship's boat lashed on its mount, ducked a boom, and strolled across the tilted deck toward the starboard rail. There was no sign of the naval frigate there, either. Nor could he see the East Indiamen.

"I am damned," Spider said to Odin and Hob, who had followed behind him. "Get on up top, lads, and have a look. See if our escort, hell, our whole fucking convoy, is out there. And," he added, scratching his beard, "keep a weather eye for goddamned Ned Low, too."

Spider headed toward the prow, for ponderous *Redemption* always brought up the convoy's rear, and it was a safe bet that the other vessels were well ahead of the fluyt. "Pardon," he said after nearly knocking over a seaman who was securing a foresail stay. Spider clambered out onto the bowsprit, nearly tumbling into the sea as he worked his way around the ropes, and peered ahead once he had managed to secure himself.

He saw nothing but open water.

The convoy was gone.

Spider looked aloft. Odin was there on the foremast. The one-eyed man looked at Spider and shrugged.

"Jesus," Spider muttered, reaching for the pendant under his shirt. "Where the hell is our escort?"

That was when he noticed the rising sun was aft.

"This just got much, much worse." Spider spat into the sea.

Redemption was coursing west, not north. They were headed west into island-rich pirate waters, not north toward Boston and Emma and little Johnny.

Nicholas Wright was trying to prove something to a woman.

And Spider's dream of home sank beneath the waves.

14

"*L*uff and touch her, Mister Gangley." Wright peered aloft. Even at a distance and in the dim morning light, Spider could see the bags under the man's normally bright eyes and could tell the new captain was fighting a yawn. *No wonder*, Spider thought. *Goddamned lovesick bugger has been up all night thinking of ways to keep me from getting home to Em and little Johnny.*

Spider watched the man from a vantage just before the forecastle. Others watched him, too. Whispers and nervous glances worked their way through the crew.

Wright stood aft, on the quarterdeck and above the cabin where Captain Brentwood was wrapped in his shroud. Wright called out his orders and fought sleepiness but did not seem to notice the worried hands around him.

"Goddamned fool of a lobcock," Spider muttered.

Shadows from the masts and sails spilled over the forecastle. "Goddamn," Spider whispered again.

"What is it?"

Spider turned toward Hob rather fiercely. "I thought I told you to go up and have a look!"

Hob gulped. "You looked haunted. I was worried." The boy ran to a foremast ratline and started to ascend. Spider chased after him.

"I am sorry, Hob. I am. We slipped away from the frigate and the rest in the night, and if I am not mistaken, we are headed toward that island the cap'n so loved, there to bury him. I think our new cap'n Wright is eager to prove his worth to Miss Brentwood, whether the rest of us get buggered by it or not."

"Truly?" The boy halted his climb and seemed pleased.

"This is not a good thing, Hob." Spider lowered his voice to a whisper barely audible under the flapping of sails and humming of taut stays. "This is flirting with the devil's wind. Hell, not flirting. Sailing right along with it, letting it drive us to goddamned perdition. We are headed into a string of isles, boy. Pirate waters. Ned Low might be hiding somewhere among those isles right now, do you hear?"

"Yes, I hear, and I have been in pirate waters before, as you well know, Spider John."

"Look at this vessel, boy. Do you see a single gun mounted? Do we even have a long nine stored below? No, we do not. And we've got a pirate aboard in Sam Smoke, and a murderer, and . . ."

"Mister Wright loves Abigail Brentwood," Hob said. "But she don't love him, it seems. He will do anything to win her. Wouldn't you do anything for your Em?"

Spider's jaw opened, but no words came out.

"I think it's a good thing Mister Wright has done. A brave thing. And if we have to outwit some pirates and do a little fighting, well, I am not a coward and neither are you." Hob continued his ascent but stopped after a moment. "If you love a woman, you dare anything, right? Would you not?"

Spider didn't answer. He watched the lad climb higher and higher, until he was out of sight, hidden by the swelling sails. "You don't have anyone waiting for you," Spider said softly, now that Hob was beyond earshot.

Spider, sullen, headed aft. Wright had descended from the quarter-deck, and it was all Spider could do to keep himself from striding across the weather deck and slapping the son of a bitch.

"What have you done, sir?" Spider asked, close enough to assure his words were not overheard. If there was a chance to talk Wright out of this rash course, that chance would be spoiled if Spider embarrassed the captain in front of his crew.

Wright leaned in close. "I have done what I had to do. She would go alone if she could, to see her father laid to rest. She cannot, so I will . . . we will do it for her."

The captain noticed men trying to eavesdrop and raised his voice. "Is there a man aboard who did not love the captain? Is there a man aboard who wants to see that girl watch her father's remains buried at some lonely spot at sea?"

He was answered with silence.

"We will slip into the bay at Eden Isle. We will conduct our business and honor our deceased friend and captain. And we will depart with haste. In and out, quick as may be. The navy has decimated the pirates, lads. There are few left. Our odds of running into any of them are quite low. We should be brave enough to risk it for our captain and for his daughter. Now, pass the bread and grog and let us be about our work."

Heads nodded, a few sighs rose, and the words "aye, aye" were heard here and there, though Spider thought they lacked conviction. Then the men parted to make way for a newcomer.

Abigail had ascended from the passenger berths, the mysterious Anne in her wake. Both marched straight toward Wright. Hadley followed at a distance.

"Sir." Abigail aimed the word like a dagger, and Wright turned slowly to face her. "I am told we have diverted our course?" She stared, her arms crossed. Anne glanced over the rails to port and starboard. Spider gave Abigail and Wright a bit of leeway, pretending to be on his way somewhere.

"Abby." Wright ran a hand through his disheveled hair. "Yes. Your father will be laid to rest in a place of his own choosing, not in the midst of a lonely sea." Wright noticed Hadley eavesdropping. "You have duties, do you not?"

"Aye."

"See to them."

"Aye." Hadley moved forward reluctantly.

"You fool," Abigail said. Anne caught Spider paying close attention, so he wandered farther away—but not too far. He busied himself checking the fit of a hatch cover and the sturdiness of the coaming, then spotted the wreckage of the captain's door, still clinging awkwardly to the doorframe. The wood shards had been swept from the deck, but the shattered wood and broken hinges hanging there were things Spider should have attended to. Everyone on *Redemption* was distracted, and Spider counted himself lucky Captain Wright hadn't slapped him for neglect of duty.

He suddenly recalled something else he was neglecting. He had the key Odin had discovered in Hadley's trunk. Spider was determined to see if the key and lock were mates. He prayed they were not.

The voices nearby rose in volume, and Spider realized he could eavesdrop while doing his duty. He began examining the shattered remains. The broken wood was useless for anything save the cook's fire or perhaps a bit of whittling, but he could salvage the hinges. Spider also hoped to save the intricate carvings that trimmed the top of the door. That was the work of an artist, and he could not let that simply die. He regretted not having his tools with him, but he wanted to listen and so did not go fetch them. He tore away what he could with his hands and eavesdropped.

"Gallantry is not for the navy alone, Abby," Wright said. "I am doing this for you."

"It is a sweet gesture, but a foolish one," she answered. "You heard what Lieutenant Price said. . . ."

"Lieutenant Price," Wright snapped back. "You were ready to sail into peril with him, weren't you?"

"Well," Abigail said, shaking her head slowly, peering at Anne, then looking back at Wright. "Well, the lieutenant has trained fighters and big, bloody damned guns, does he not?"

"Abigail!" Wright seemed shocked.

She stared at Wright for several long seconds, unapologetic about her use of sailorly language. Wright stared back aghast, as though the universe had just spun down a maelstrom.

Anne covered a smile with a kerchief pulled from somewhere within her blouse. Spider tried to remember he had work to do, but his fingers strayed to Em's pendant hanging from his neck and the key next to it. "Betwattled bastard," Spider whispered, glaring at Wright. Spider inhaled deeply and pondered whether he could seize the damned ship himself and set her course for Boston. Odin would help him, he was certain. Hob, too. *The little shit would love to be a goddamned mutineer.*

Spider would have lopped off another finger for a bottle of kill-devil at that moment.

"Enough!" Wright's voice exploded like a cannon shot.

Redemption's hands, some eating hot morning bread or drinking their grog rations, suddenly found something else to arrest their attention.

"It's done," Wright said. "Consider it a service to your father if you do not appreciate it yourself. But truth is, I did it for you, not for him."

"This is a dangerous course," Abigail said. She turned to walk toward the bow. Anne followed, caught up quickly, and placed an arm around the girl's shoulder. Spider watched them go and thought he detected the outline of a flintlock tucked beneath Anne's dress, at the small of her back.

"What the bloody hell goes on here?" Spider whispered to himself.

"Fetch me a compass," Wright called, noting the hands staring at him. "We've a fine wind, lads; let us use her, and we'll bid the captain farewell soon enough, then on to Boston. Topgallants! Studding sails!"

Spider gathered the good trim from the shattered cabin door into his arms, glanced at the hinges, and determined to return with tools to collect them. Then he headed toward the lumber hold and climbed down.

Once the trim had been stowed safely away, he retrieved the chunk of timber that bore the captain's lock. He freed the key from his neck. He had only faint sunlight streaming down into the hold to see by, and in it he half convinced himself the key looked different from the one he remembered. But when he placed the key into the lock, it was a perfect fit.

"Hadley," Spider whispered, "why the hell did you have this?"

He threw the lock into the tool chest with a curse, fit the cord around his neck, and hurried up the ladder to the weather deck. Lazare stood amidships, bucket and ladle in hand. Spider strode toward him with purpose. A variety of pewter and wooden cups filled a net slung across the cook's back, and Spider fished one out.

Spider held out the cup, and Lazare ladled in some grog, a mixture of rum and water that Spider considered a waste of good liquor, but it was the best he could do at the moment, and, by thunder, he needed a goddamned drink.

Spider swallowed his ration in a rush and snarled savagely at Lazare. "Another."

"No, sir," Lazare said. "We have our rations."

Spider leaned forward and pitched his voice in a low, menacing growl. "I spent the night in the hold, dodging rats and searching for a killer. And now I see our goddamned besotted captain has steered us away from the naval escort meant to blast the fucking hell out of any pirates who might think our cargo ought to be theirs. So unless you can turn this goddamned ship north right now, Lazare, you had better fill my cup again."

Lazare filled it, Spider drained it, and Lazare filled it once more. During the entire operation, Lazare did not look Spider in the eyes again.

15

"You're swayin' more than the damned ship," Odin said.

Redemption had just come about on the southwesterly tack and was settling into the gentle wind. Watches had just changed, the sun was lowering, and Odin had dropped from a ratline to land in front of Spider. Once the cabin door had been repaired and other chores were finished, Spider had found a flask on a hammock in the forecastle and traded good tobacco for it. The flask, half empty now of the good whiskey it contained, was tucked into his belt and hidden under his shirt. The captain was distracted, and discipline was lax aboard the ship now, but it still would not do to be caught with strong drink on deck.

"I have acquired a few drams," Spider quietly told the one-eyed sailor. "I am headed to the bowsprit to think. Join me, and I will share."

"Ha! I will, but I must thrash a ninny first. Clod nearly cost me a good sheet today for want of a good knot, and he'll either learn to tie a goddamned knot or learn what I can do with a good knot lashed across his back."

The old pirate wandered away, and Spider continued forward. All about him, whether they were starting their watch or taking their rest, men glanced out to sea in search of pirates or, perhaps, a miraculous appearance of the navy frigate. It was out there somewhere, probably to the north and east. Many aboard seemed to think *Southampton* would come searching for them immediately and would appear any moment riding over a distant swell, full canvas mounted and all gun ports open.

Spider found himself gazing into the distance, too, but he did not expect to see the frigate. *Southampton* had other ships to worry about, and if a fool merchant captain decided to veer away from the frigate's protective guns, well, so be it. *Southampton* would guard those smart enough to stay with her, and let *Redemption's* lovesick captain endure the consequences of his mistake.

There was the matter of Abigail Brentwood, though. Lieutenant Price had seemed smitten with her. Was he smitten enough to convince his captain that his duty as an Englishman, by God, was to race to the young lady's aid? Would *Southampton's* captain be swayed by such an appeal?

Spider didn't think so, nor did he truly believe Price would suggest such a course. He had scant direct knowledge of navy captains, but he had sailed with many men who had served in His Majesty's Navy. The image of a naval captain that had emerged from many grog-fueled discussions in the forecastle was that of a rigid sort, who would do what his orders told him to do, and to hell with any circumstances that might arise and indicate he ought to do otherwise. *Southampton's* captain had a mission to escort a merchant convoy to Boston, and that was what he most likely would do. A merchantman straying off into pirate seas? The Admiralty could not have envisioned that, and so its orders certainly did not cover that contingency. *Southampton* probably continued northward.

Meanwhile, *Redemption* sailed on the devil's wind.

Spider was glad the workday was done, but the melancholy strains from a well-scraped fiddle somewhere in the forecastle seemed the perfect accompaniment to his worries. He'd thought the whiskey might help ease his mind. Instead, it seemed to usher in an ungodly clarity. He was on a ship plying outlaw waters and, for all he knew, rushing straight into the grasp of that goddamned fiend Ned Low. Em and little Johnny seemed like ghosts, something he'd heard of but could not quite believe in. He wondered if he would ever see them, and the doubt gnawed at him.

He had concocted a simple plan. He would climb out on the bowsprit, his favorite thinking spot aboard any vessel. There, dangling his feet over the ocean and listening to the water swish past *Redemption's* bow, he would slowly sip the whiskey away, buying silence from witnesses with a swig or two. He would drink until he could forget his troubles, at least for a while, or until the whiskey was gone.

A jarring tug at his elbow stopped him, and he turned to face the Reverend Abraham Down.

"Are we truly headed into pirate waters? I have heard the talk." The man's jaws kept working even after he'd finished his sentence, and he clutched a leather-bound Bible against his chest as though it might try to get away.

"Judging by my past luck," Spider answered, "I expect we shall run into pirates, hurricanes, sea monsters, and the bloody goddamned ghost of fucking Blackbeard."

The reverend stepped backward and ducked as though Spider had swung a blade at him. "Blasphemy will profit you not," Down said after an awkward moment. "Fear the Lord, carpenter, fear the Lord, and embrace him as he would embrace you. Your trade was his, you know. He was a carpenter. Embrace him. Then you shall have no need to fear pirates!"

"Your knees are shaking, Reverend." Spider turned, leaving the sputtering Reverend Down behind him.

Spider ascended the ladder, climbed atop the forecastle, took two steps—and saw Anne McCormac staring off across the ocean. His first thought was that she just might be the most alluring woman he'd ever seen. His second thought was that, according to Hob, she just might have killed Captain Brentwood. His third thought was the memory that he had previously noticed what seemed to be a gun hidden at the small of her back beneath the gray dress.

He was still trying to decide whether to speak to her when she turned to face him.

Once he'd pondered the wind-swept red hair and piercing green eyes, Spider realized she had spoken to him. "John Coombs, is that right? Ship's carpenter?"

The accent was as Irish as it was devastating.

"Yes," he answered. "John Coombs."

"I am Anne McCormac," she said. "Pleased to meet you."

"Aye." Spider nodded. He was fairly certain courtesy required more than that, but he'd not the slightest idea what else to say. He guessed her age at anywhere from nineteen to twenty-five. The wedding band caught sunlight as she brushed back her hair.

"Did you know our captain well?" She turned back to stare across the sea. In the distance to the north lay dark gray lines that were islands. The last time Spider had seen these isles, he had been a pirate, sailing under the bloody black flag of Bent Thomas aboard *Lamia*. Her question reminded him that there was a dead man aboard, slain by an unknown agent, and that Hob had heard this woman say she had come to kill someone. Spider swallowed, joined her at the rail, and inhaled deeply. If he could not aim *Redemption* toward his beloved, perhaps he could solve the puzzle of how a ship's captain had been murdered in his locked quarters and keep his promise to Abigail Brentwood.

"I signed on for this voyage," he said, "and that was my first experience of Cap'n Brentwood. He treated me fair, though, and I liked him. And he was proud of this ship, too, a rare beauty, he called her."

"She is that," Anne said. Her gaze was not on the islands, as Spider had first surmised. Her lovely eyes went left and right, as though she was looking for a ship.

"Looking for pirates, I suppose," Spider said and instantly regretted it. But she seemed amused, not frightened.

"I am, indeed, John." She smiled wickedly.

"You do not seem afraid."

She turned the sparkling green eyes on him. "I do not frighten easily, sir."

"Is that because you've a gun tucked beneath that pretty dress?"

She tilted her head and smiled. "You notice things, don't you?"

"It has kept me alive."

"I have a gun, yes," she whispered. "And a couple of knives, if you must know, but if you notice those you are looking far too closely." She winked.

Good Lord, Spider thought, *what a dangerous creature she is*. He was now ready to believe she had killed the captain and was plotting to kill everyone else.

"It seems, um, not ladylike, I guess," he replied after an uncomfortable pause.

"I am a woman, traveling alone, in a ship full of men," she told him. "I notice the hungry gazes, John. Even if there was no possibility of pirates, even if we yet sailed under the protective wing of the Royal Navy, I would keep my blades and pistol at the ready. I am the last woman you want to trifle with."

She had said it all very quietly and had not stopped smiling for even a moment. Anyone looking at them from a distance might have supposed they were discussing the wind or the gulls.

She is deadly as a copperhead, Spider decided.

He was still looking for a graceful way to end the conversation when her eyes looked past him and narrowed, and the smile vanished behind tightly drawn lips. The thick scent of tobacco drifted between Spider and the woman, and he did not need to turn around to discern that Sam Smoke had approached. Spider spun slowly, eyes fixed on the man's leering gaze.

"Ma'am," Smoke said, doffing the wide-brimmed hat and allowing a cloud of smoke to rise from the pipe tightly clenched in his teeth.

"I have told you, I have no interest in speaking with you," she said.

"But I have interest in speaking with you." Smoke returned the hat to his head and bowed slightly.

Spider stepped between them. "It would be best, I think, if you fouled the air on some other part of the ship."

Sam Smoke stared at Spider as though he had just noticed his presence. "I do not believe I sought your opinion, carpenter. I am a paying passenger aboard this ship, I'll remind you."

"Passengers, crew, they all bleed the same," Spider said. Whiskey essence rose in his head, and his fingers rested on the hilt of the knife in his belt. Truth was, he was so angry that life with Em had been snatched away that he was spoiling for a fight. *Draw a blade,* he thought. *Show me a gun. I will gut you like a fucking tuna.*

"We should spill some blood and compare." Smoke pushed his shirt aside to show that he, too, had a knife. Then he leaned forward, grinning. "You have spent some time on the account," he whispered. "Pirating. I see it in your eyes. The way you look about you. The way you always seem to know exactly where your knife is."

Behind Smoke, with a belaying pin in his hand, Odin waited for a signal. Spider grinned and pointed. "One advantage of being in a crew. I don't fight alone."

Smoke turned slowly, saw Odin, then faced Spider again. "It might take more than the two of you."

"The three of us," Anne McCormac said. "And you bloody well know that."

Behind Smoke, Odin laughed quietly, no doubt relieved that even at close quarters, Smoke did not recognize the hideously scarred face as that of a former shipmate.

"Find somewhere else to be," Spider said. "Or swim."

Smoke sucked hard at the pipe, removed it from his jaws, and blew a foul cloud. Saying nothing, but fixing each of them with an icy stare, he departed, humming along with the fiddler's tune.

"God, I hate him," Anne said.

Spider looked at her. "How do you know him?"

She smiled. "I don't think I want to tell you. Good evening, gentlemen."

She departed with a swirl of her skirt and a jasmine scent that filled the wind.

"I want her," Odin said. "Ha!"

"You may have to fight Hob," Spider said, whipping out his flask and taking a fast swig, then handing it to Odin. In his mind, though, he added a sentence: *We may have to fight everyone.*

16

"Mister Coombs," the lilting voice said. "I did not have an opportunity to thank you."

Night had fallen, and a low moon and diamond stars provided but dim light at the bowsprit. Spider could not make out the pale blue of Abigail Brentwood's eyes. He could imagine them, though. Spider stifled a laugh and was proud of himself; despite the whiskey, he had remembered he was known aboard *Redemption* as John Coombs, not Spider John Rush.

Spider sucked at his pipe, then climbed down from the bowsprit to join the girl. Rufus Fox was with her, following at a respectable distance, and Hadley watched from the top of the ladder leading up atop the forecastle. The young man seemed unconcerned that Spider had noticed him. Spider watched him intently, thinking of the key Odin had found.

Spider exhaled a cloud of smoke into the ocean breeze. "What have you to thank me for, Miss Brentwood?"

"You brought my father's killer to justice," she said, pushing a bit of wind-swept hair away from her face. "And now I know my father did not . . . did not . . ."

She began sobbing into a kerchief, and Fox stepped forward to put a protective arm around her shoulder. "Now then, Abby, dear. Be still. Be assured your father is beyond the pain of his loss."

"But why should that miserable little man kill him?" At least, that was what Spider thought she said. It was difficult to discern amid the nose-blowing and deep inhalations. Hadley climbed up onto the deck and paced, his gaze glued on Abigail.

"The Lord's ways are not ours," Fox said quietly. "And it is the Lord's place to judge, not ours. Your father's sense of loss was great, child, and he was weary of this world. Perhaps, even so meager and mean a man as Bob Higgins served the Lord's purpose, giving your father the peace he could not, dared not, give himself."

The slap cracked like lightning in the darkness, and Fox's gasp was almost as sharp. "I will not hear this!" Abigail said, staring at her hand as though it had decided to smack Rufus Fox all on its own. "I will not hear of forgiving that mongrel bastard! And I will not hear of how it is somehow the Lord's mercy that my father is dead!"

"Child, I . . ."

"Please be so good as to leave," she said, turning her back to Fox. The man stood silently for a few seconds, and Abigail, apparently sensing him there, continued. "You have been good to us. I know you were my father's friend."

She turned to face him. "And I know you are trying to help me cope. In time, I shall appreciate it. But tonight . . ."

Fox bowed. "I understand. I shall always . . . always . . . be available for you. You must know that."

"I do."

Fox glanced up at Spider, nodded his farewell, and turned to go. Hadley stepped aside to allow Fox passage, and the man descended and strode aft, toward the sounds of a fiddler scratching out a bouncy Sligo tune and the clomping of dancing feet.

"He is a good man, that Fox," Spider said. Hadley winced slightly.

"I know," Abigail replied. "But for all his desire to help me, you actually have given me more comfort." She turned to face him. "You have given me justice. Thanks to you, I know my father did not . . . put the gun to his head. I mean, I always knew it, or . . . wanted to believe it, I suppose. But now I know it, for certain. That is a comfort. A great comfort, and I mean to thank you for it. Hob was correct. You are quite clever at such puzzles. I . . ."

Spider could not help but smile; the girl had made a real effort to say all that without choking up and had damned near done it. If Hob had any goddamned sense, he'd be chasing this lass, not that red-haired she-devil.

"Well," Spider said, "I don't suppose the world will miss Little Bob much when he swings." He decided not to mention that perhaps Abigail's friend, Anne McCormac, had done the deed. Or Sam Smoke. Or some other bloody bastard. Abigail needed to get on with her life, and if swinging for the captain's murder was the only real good Bob did in this life, so be it. He wondered what Rufus Fox would say about that?

Abigail turned her pretty eyes to starboard and peered across the dark sea. "Are there really pirates out there? One hears that so many have been hanged and that the navy has so purged their ranks that there is little to fear. But I can feel the fear on this ship growing, like weeds."

"Aye," Spider said. "All the great bloody bastards... pardon, miss... all the most famous pirates are hanged or fled. Bart Roberts, Ed Teach—your Blackbeard, you know—Calico Jack, all gone. But..."

He was not certain what to say. He had no wish to cause her fright, but she was a brave lass and he had no wish to coddle her either.

"Please, Mister Coombs, continue."

He smiled at her and made up his mind. "Well, then, all the great and famed pirates are gone, I am certain. But the sea is wide and the ranks of pirates quite vast. I have no doubt that there be some still who think reaving upon the sea is the way to independence, and preying upon the wealthy is no more than justice, as it were, restoring a balance, if you will."

She grinned. "You make no sense, sir. You almost sound as though you are excusing their deeds."

"Blame the whiskey," he answered. *God, she is beautiful.* "Do not tell Mister Wright about the drink, please."

"He and I are not speaking," she told him, tilting her head downward for just a moment before fixing her eyes on Spider once again. "I think him a fool for leaving the escort behind."

"Aye," Spider said. "It was not the wisest thing he might have done."

"For certain."

"I think he did it out of love, though," Spider said. "I hope you know that."

Spider found he could not handle her gaze and looked away. "Very well, we shall discuss pirates. There is a man, perhaps out there somewhere"—he pointed out to sea—"named Ned Low. He is aptly named, as low as a man can get. A goddamned serpent, by reputation, and I have heard tell of some of his bloody work from a man I've come to trust and who was there to see it himself. I do not mean to frighten you, but you should know. He is rumored to be close by, perhaps in these very waters. There was much gossip before we left Port Royal."

She swallowed hard. "I see."

"It would not do for him to take you," Spider said. "He would ... would..."

She lowered her head. "I understand."

No, he thought, *you do not. You would be passed around, as men might pass around a jug of beer. And the moment you fought too hard, drew blood with your nails, or broke skin with your teeth, you would be killed.*

"Have you any weapon?"

She suddenly stood at attention. "No. Do I need one?"

"If Ned Low should cross our path, yes." He stared at her hard. "You and Mrs. McCormac, you have become friends?"

"Why, yes, I should like to think so. She has been most consoling."

Spider nodded. "Talk to her. She is a strong woman, and I think she might just be able to provide you means to protect yourself and some advice as to how you can do so."

Abigail's smile erupted. "Are you joking?"

"No, miss," Spider said. "I cannot vouch for her purity and goodness, but I am quite certain that if she deems you a friend, she will fight to protect you, and I am also certain she can, by God, tell you how to kill a man. Should the need arise."

Miss Brentwood's eyebrows arched, and her eyes widened. She stared at him for a few moments, and then her gaze went from starboard to port and back again. "I do not know what to make of you, Mister Coombs."

"John," he said. "Spider John, actually." *Well, then*, he immediately thought, *that was a bloody goddamned whiskey-soaked mistake.*

She actually laughed. "What an atrocious and horrid name!"

He thought for a second about telling her the usual lie, that he was so named because of his prowess at climbing the ratlines and not because of any tendency to eat spiders just to horrify his sister when he was a boy. In the end, he decided not to explain. "I suppose it is."

Spider's eyes caught a mean look from Hadley.

"You are quite worried, are you not?" She whispered it.

"It could be very, very bad, yes," Spider said, lowering his voice. "If it does turn for the worse, stay close to Anne, or me, or even Hob. He can fight, trust me. So can Odin."

"Oh, my, the frightening fellow with one eye? I am quite certain that he truly is a pirate!"

Spider let that remark pass. "He is crazy, but he is pure bloody hell in a fight."

Spider then leaned close and whispered, "And Hadley, there by the ladder, would fight off all the spawns of hell for you. I am certain of that."

She nodded slightly and seemed lost in thought. Then she said, "You seem well acquainted with violence, John. And with pirates."

"The sea can be a rough place, miss, and I have been on it a long time now."

"Surely you are not so much older than I am." She lowered her eyes.

"Some years age you more than others, I think."

She looked up at him. They stared at each other for a few heartbeats, and he struggled for a moment to remember Em's sweet face. Then Abigail curtsied. "Thank you, Spider John."

"Most welcome, Miss Brentwood. And just John, if you please. Not everyone knows Spider. Now get a gun. Anne will show you how to use it."

She saluted. "Aye, sir." Then she turned, perfume swirling in her wake. Hadley moved to follow, as though he were on a towline.

Spider stared out to sea and hoped to God he would see no pirates.

17

*A*bigail Brentwood had not yet descended the ladder leading down from the forecastle deck before a ruckus erupted amidships. The fiddler halted his rendition of "Blackbird" abruptly, the dancers all stopped at once, and cries of alarm rose into the moonlight.

"Damn and blast! Damn and blast, I say!"

Spider recognized the goddamned voice instantly and dropped the pipe he was filling. Racing past Abigail, he whispered, "Go forward, now, and be alert. Hadley, you stay with her."

Hadley nodded.

Abigail ignored Spider's instructions and instead moved away from the ladder to a spot near the foremast. From there, she peered below and chewed on a knuckle. Hadley, his gaze on the ruckus on the weather deck, drew his work knife.

"Good Lord, this is bad," Spider muttered.

Spider could scarcely believe what was happening.

The sailors had gathered in two groups between the ship's boat, mounted in its berth, and the port rail. Between those two groups stood Little Bob Higgins, a primed flintlock in his right hand and a lantern in his left. "Think I will swing?" Bob bellowed in a voice powerful for so small a man. "Think I will swing on the gallows? Damn and blast the lot of ye!"

Bob swung the gun menacingly back and forth between the two sets of sailors who blocked his way, and though he was vastly outnumbered, no one wanted to take a ball at close range. A few had drawn their work knives and clutched them at the ready, and a couple of fellows had snatched up belaying pins, but no one made a move.

How the bloody hell did he escape? Spider inhaled deeply, looking for a chance to act.

Redemption rocked on the ocean swells as everyone waited for the drama to unfold.

"I did not kill your precious fucking captain!" Bob wiped his sweaty brow with the back of his gun hand, and a couple of intrepid fellows stepped toward him, but the gun was back on the level in an eye blink. "I can't believe you would think that. I can't believe all this trouble because I swatted a goddamned cat."

A sailor took a short step toward Bob, hands raised. "Now, Bob, let us . . ."

Bob aimed at the man's head. "I will shoot you, Joe; don't think I won't."

Everyone froze. The swaying, bobbing ship and the fluttering of sails and flags were the only things in motion. Time seemed halted.

Bob was the first to end the strange interlude. He pivoted, arms wide, gun and lantern at a level. The moving lantern tossed shadows up onto the sails and filled them with orange glow at odds with the frosty moonlight. The ever-changing nature of the light made a knife throw impossible, and Spider cursed. He eyed a foremast backstay, thought he could reach it, saw a good spot below, and leapt from the forecastle. He snatched at the rope and made a nimble swing. Mid-plunge, he saw Bob's gun arm take aim at him, but the shot never came.

Spider landed in a crouch on the deck with the others and drew his knife.

"What are you waiting for, lads?" Bob growled. "I need some assistance."

In answer, Ames stepped forth and drew a pistol that had been hidden behind his back. Chambers did likewise. They drew closer to Bob and menaced the surrounding sailors.

Good Lord Almighty, Spider thought, *Little Bob has friends. No wonder those fellows didn't like my questions. They probably had been stealing food for the little muckworm.*

"Here is how it will be," Bob said, drooling and sweating, rotating slowly while trying to keep his gaze on all hands. Ames and Chambers mimicked him, taking up stations to either side of Bob. "I will not go to the gallows. I will not. I would rather die here now killing a few of you bastards than submit to that."

"Fucking stupid fool," Spider muttered. He shouldered his way through the crowd and gulped. He stared into Bob's mad eyes and recognized the fear blazing there. Spider knew exactly how Bob felt; fear of the hangman had haunted Spider most of his adult life. A man that afraid might do anything.

"What the hell goes on here?" The voice, loud and strong, came from aft, and men made way for Captain Wright. The former master strode forth like a general. "You shall stop this at once and await a fair hearing from the Admiralty, Bob. And Ames, Chambers, drop your guns now."

"A fair hearing from the bloody Admiralty?" Bob aimed the gun at Wright's face, and the officer wisely halted. "Me? When did the Admiralty ever care for the likes of me?"

"You have numbers against you, Bob, and you cannot shoot more than one of us." Wright drew himself up like a statue. "Fire at me, and you had best hope it kills me of a sudden, because if it does not I will snap your puny neck before I bleed to death."

Spider raised his throwing knife.

"Better a quick death in a fight than waiting and waiting and waiting for the hangman," Bob said. "But there is another way, and no one has to die."

"Heed the Lord, sinners!" The Reverend Down had climbed atop the ship's boat and now peered down upon the crowd with wide eyes. Heads in the crowd swiveled back and forth between this interruption and the drama on the deck. The Reverend Down raised his Bible high. "Think of the perdition that awaits! Think of the salvation that might be yours instead!"

Rufus Fox clambered up behind the preacher. "Yes, fellows. Guns and blades and violence are not the answer. Let us talk, come to a reasonable conclusion."

Wright shrugged. "I am in no mood to bargain with a murderer." He glared at Bob.

"I am no murderer!" Bob shouted so loudly he shook, and it was a bloody miracle the gun did not go off. Chambers and Ames, both shaking with nerves, each took a nervous step away from him.

"I am no murderer!" Bob's jaw quivered.

Damn, Spider thought. *I hate the son of a bitch, but I think I believe him.*

"Do this," Bob said, swinging the pistol around quickly to stave off any surprise pounce, then leveling it again at Wright. He nodded toward the ship's boat, mounted there amidships. "Hoist this over the side," he said. "Give me some water and food, and I'll take my leave with my true mates here." He nodded toward Ames and Chambers. "Such as want to can come with us. You all know Wright's leading you into pirate waters, right? Maybe right into the bloody reach of goddamned Ned Low?"

A chorus of grumbles rose, and Spider wondered just how many men might take Bob up on his offer. As he scanned the crowd, he noticed Anne McCormac on a ratline by the mainmast, wide green eyes catching the light from Bob's lantern. She had stationed herself well, so that she could see above the men, and her stance convinced Spider she was hiding a cutlass or gun behind her skirt.

"Be still," Wright said. "I know what . . ."

"Damn and blast ye, man, close your mouth!" Bob again wiped sweat away but had the pistol aimed before anyone could react. "I will take my chances at sea, and I dare say a few hands will go with me."

The gathered crewmen shuffled and jostled one another, and Bob kept up his weird back-and-forth, with the lantern acting almost as a lighthouse. Spider clutched his knife and cursed. A throw would be too risky.

"Aye," one unknown man said quietly. "I will go with you, Bob."

A few scattered echoes among the men followed.

"Would you take that bet, Mister Wright?" Spider turned toward the source of those words and saw Sam Smoke emerge from the crowd.

The usual fog of tobacco smoke accompanied him, but it did not hide the cold, hard glare of his eyes. The man smiled wildly, the pipe jutting like a bowsprit from his teeth. "Survival in a boat in these waters? Pirate waters, I hear?"

Wright spared a quick, irritated glance toward Smoke. "I would not. And neither should any of you. You hear? It is a foolish notion. Bob's no navigator; he'll get you lost on the sea."

"The boat will serve us; we can reach civilized lands, damn and blast! We can reach the Turks, or Nassau, or Jamaica!"

"You will not take my boat," Wright said.

"I say otherwise," Bob said, grinning. "Think you can survive a ball in your brain, Wright? Do you?"

"Men," Wright said, eyes locked on Bob. "On my word, we rush this bastard. If he fires at me, so be it. You take him down anyway. And cut his throat."

Anne McCormac smiled and licked her lips, and Spider could swear her gaze was climbing from Wright's boots to his ass.

"To hell with you!" Bob aimed, sighted, and closed one eye.

"Now!" Wright rushed forward. No one else did.

Spider lifted the knife over his shoulder.

Bob's forearm tensed.

A streak of yellow-and-white hissing fury launched itself from somewhere and into Bob's face. Bob's flintlock sparked and roared.

His scream was unintelligible and almost lost in the cat's angry yowling. The errant pistol ball shattered the fiddle's neck, and the instrument uttered a sad, discordant death cry before clattering to the deck. The fiddler himself, miraculously, seemed unharmed.

"Goddamn cat!" Bob spun wildly, the lantern's light streaking like crazy lightning, as Thomas clawed his adversary's face. Bob climbed atop a tool chest by the rail in a desperate attempt to escape his tormentor. Bob fell, and the lantern burst against the chest in an eruption of flame.

Thomas dashed away, with something Spider thought might be Bob's eye glinting in his fangs. Bob screamed and slapped at the burning whale oil that clung to his sleeves and britches.

Spider suddenly remembered the other two armed men. He spun toward Ames and raised his knife, but before he could throw, a cry from above drew everyone's attention.

"*Redemption*!" Hob arced on a rope from the mainmast, his heels driving toward Ames.

"Idiot boy!" Spider held his knife in check.

Ames lifted his pistol toward Hob and fired just before the lad's boots hit him like a battering ram. Hob's heels caught Ames square in the chest, while the lead ball zipped through a sail, leaving a tiny hole. Ames slammed into the rail with a gusher of breath, and his smoking gun clattered to the deck. Before Ames could catch his wind, Hob had a pistol tucked right under the man's chin.

"I shall blow a hole through your skull, man, from chin to crown," Hob said. "Damn me if I won't."

Spider turned toward the spot where he'd last seen Chambers, but Wright, bathed in orange from the firelight on the tool chest and deck, blocked his vision. That same light revealed Sam Smoke, diving toward Chambers. Smoke's shoulder took Chambers right in the gut, and the men toppled. Spider lost sight of them as crewmen scurried across the deck, some to get out of harm's way, others to get a better view.

"Fire! Buckets! Now!" Wright's commands drew instant action, for fire on a sailing vessel was the last goddamned thing anyone wanted. Men rushed to fetch pails of water. Others ripped off their own shirts and batted at the flaming deck. Some swatted at Bob, who rose screaming and burning atop the tool chest.

Redemption was heeled slightly to port, though, and Bob lost his balance. He lurched toward the rail and ended up with his head and shoulders hanging over the sea. He surely was about to go overboard.

Spider dropped his throwing knife, dove at Bob's burning legs, and kept the son of a bitch from going into the deep. Sailcloth and shirts flailed them both, and buckets of water drenched them as they lay in a heap next to the rail.

"Silence!" Wright fought his way through the hands, shoving men aside as easily as he tossed dice. Bob wailed, and once the moonlight caught the man's face Spider knew why. His right eye was gone, and the black-and-red burns on his forehead still smoked despite the drenching. In what seemed an odd bit of undeserved mercy, the fire had staunched the bleeding, but Bob would spend what little life he had left looking much like the hideous Odin.

Spider rolled away from Bob and sat with his back against the rail. He eyed the assembled crowd, noted Hob still had his man under control, then saw Smoke crouching over Chambers. Smoke's hands were clamped on the man's neck, and Chambers alternatively pounded the weather deck and clawed at Smoke's fingers. Smoke ignored the man's futile resistance and grinned savagely as Chambers fought for breath. The man's gun lay nearby until a deck hand snatched it up.

Bob groaned, looked as though he would move to help his friends, and then Wright kicked him in the face, spattering hot blood and oil on Spider's chin. "I said silence! And you, Mister Lawrence! You have subdued the man, so desist. We will turn these men over to the navy when we can. Alive!"

Smoke, leering, grinned at Wright. He waited at least five heartbeats before he released his grip on Chambers's neck, and the man sucked in air like a bellows.

Bob remained as silent as he could, but the pain was too much. The man's pathetic whimper snatched at Spider's soul.

"Are you burned, John?"

"No, sir," Spider answered Wright. "I think not, anyway." Spider stood. His shirt would need mending, and it smelled of burnt wood and oil, but his skin seemed intact and he felt no sting from salt water digging into cuts or burns.

"Good. You are a brave man, John. That was well done." Wright dug a boot toe into Bob's side. "And you, you had better hope you see the Admiralty, because I have a mind to cut your intestines out of you and watch you eat them!"

A quiet chuckle followed, and Spider saw Smoke's eyes. He looked as though he really liked Wright's suggestion.

Wright pointed at two men. "Go below, see what has happened to the guards. And you"—he pointed at Hob and two others—"bind this burnt bastard up so tight that he can scarce breathe. And get him and his friends below, and see that they all stay there. I will send guards to relieve you."

"Aye, aye, sir!" Hob grinned and waved his gun theatrically. "This way, you son of a whore! Did you see me, John?"

"Yes, Hob, I saw. That was foolish, boy."

"I got him, I did," Hob growled.

The prisoners were escorted below.

Spider saw Abigail Brentwood passing by. "Are you well, Miss Brentwood? No injuries from a stray ball or . . . ?"

She answered him with a glare of contempt. "He killed my father, and you . . . you saved his life."

She spun away and vanished before Spider could find any words to answer her. Hadley followed her.

"Do not let her dismay you, friend John." Fox rushed to his side. "It was the Lord's work you just did, even if Bob is a murderer, and the girl will come to understand that."

"I hope it may be so," Spider answered.

"Rely upon it. It is the Lord's place to decide life and death, and ours to offer one another every chance of mercy and forgiveness. Even for such as Little Bob. The girl will see the good in your deed. Miss Brentwood has a tender heart, and though it is hurting grievously now, it will lead her to see you favorably again. I am quite certain of it."

"I hate to see her suffer," Spider said.

"Indeed. But I do not think she broods the way her father did," Fox answered. "He held his feelings in, gave them no vent, and the sadness ate at him from within once his dear wife passed. He wore a brave face around his daughter, mind you, and would rather have suffered boils than let his crew see him dejected, but he was not a happy man."

"I got that sense," Spider replied. "Do you think it merciful, then, that he has gone on to join his wife?"

Fox drew a deep breath. "I do not know, John. Merciful for him, perhaps, but not for others. He no longer suffers, of course, but his girl, and his friends . . ."

"Aye." Spider nodded but kept his gaze on Fox.

"Miss Brentwood is young, and resilient, and not so much like her father," the man said after a few moments as the ship kicked up spray around them. "She will recover, may even fall in love"—he grinned, for only a heartbeat—"and she will certainly forgive you, John, for saving Little Bob. I know she will. She has a pure soul."

Fox's gaze lowered to the deck. "She will not, of course, forgive Little Bob."

The man's earnest expression raised a thought in Spider's mind. "You think a wretched soul like Bob might yet find his way to heaven?"

"I think we all have equal opportunity for that just reward, God being Lord of us all, and merciful beyond our worth. At least, it is to be hoped. Yes. Even such as Little Bob might find grace, if given ample time to ask for it. Time that he has, now, thanks to you."

"Grace? Even if he killed a man?" Spider shook his head slowly.

Fox looked skyward. "We all fall short, carpenter. Each and every one of us. Let us hope and pray that he"—and Fox pointed to the sky—"can forgive us our worst trespasses."

"I am wondering now if I was wrong," Spider said. "Bob's a wretch, but he seemed in earnest when he said he didn't kill Cap'n Brentwood."

"Do you mean to say he is innocent?" Fox looked perplexed, then continued the conversation in hushed tones. "Who else might have done the deed?"

"When you were on the quarterdeck, and the shot was fired, you and the Reverend Down peered through the grating. I remember looking up and you were there."

"Yes." Fox wrung his hands briefly, then put them behind his back.

"When you looked down, at first, what did you see?"

The man's head worked slowly back and forth. "Just the captain, there on the deck, gun in his hand."

"No one moving about?"

"No."

"And did you get there quickly?"

"As soon as we heard the shot," Fox said. "Well, there was a confused moment, the Reverend Down and I staring at one another wondering what had happened; then we rushed, simultaneously as I recall it, to look into the cabin below. And we saw the poor man."

"No one else was in there?"

"No."

"Then do you suppose Bob had time to shoot the cap'n, scrawl a note, and hide before you looked down?"

"I . . . I suppose not." Fox's lips tightened. He shook his head vigorously. "Perhaps Bob shot him from a place of concealment."

"And then crept out of hiding to write that note?" Spider wagged a finger. "And then hid again before you looked? That all seems unlikely. Cap'n is hardly going to stand there while Little Bob writes a note. That had to come after the slaying."

"Well, then," Fox said after a pause, "that puts us back to a self-inflicted death, then, as it seemed from the beginning. Poor Abigail. She will not take this well."

An idea popped into Spider's head, and he decided to make a direct thrust. "Was the grating latched down?"

"Excuse me, John?"

"The grating, the one you peered through. Was it latched down tight?"

"It was. I remember because for a frantic moment I considered lifting the grate and leaping into the cabin in hopes of a rescue. Then Mister Wright burst through the door. But, yes, the grating was latched tightly."

"So no one got out that way."

"Well, no," Fox said, confused. "And the Reverend Down and I would have seen them anyway."

"Aye," Spider said. "I am thinking on it too hard."

"And we would have seen if anyone had fired a gun from above," Fox added, nodding. "Surely, we would have."

"I do not think the shot came from above," Spider said, "not unless someone could make a lead ball change its course. Impossible, that."

Fox, eyebrows working up and down and eyes squinting above the potato nose, finally shrugged. "Yes. Impossible. So, will you tell Nicholas about all this, then, that you think Little Bob is innocent?"

"I need to think on it more," Spider answered. "We can't turn Bob and his friends over to the navy right now anyway, and I kind of like having Little Bob tied up, killer or no."

Fox turned his face toward Spider and smiled. "Those points all seem well considered." He clapped a hand on Spider's shoulder. "I do know this. If Little Bob has not yet sought the Lord's forgiveness, for whatever crimes he may have done, he has time yet to do so. Thanks to you. It would have been a sorrowful thing had he fallen overboard, unredeemed. You did well, Spider John."

Spider's eyes widened. He and Hob and Odin had tried hard to avoid that nickname aboard *Redemption*. Spider John Rush was a wanted pirate.

"Forgive me," Fox said. "Do you find the appellation distasteful? I overheard young Hob call you that at some point. I do not mean to offend, or be overly familiar."

"It is well," Spider stammered. "Do not trouble yourself over it. It is merely a name my friends tease me with. I ate spiders as a lad, to make my sister scream. I don't much care for the name."

"Forgive me, John. I did not mean to offend."

"Forgiven, sir." Spider nodded, and Fox departed.

Moments later, Odin approached Spider. "Why the bloody hell did you not let that son of a bitch Bob go overboard? He killed the cap'n, and no one aboard likes his ugly arse anyway!"

"I do not think he killed Cap'n Brentwood," Spider said. "His voice had the ring of truth to it."

"You should not trust that little bugger. There's a fair number of us jealous of Thomas getting to claw that man's eye. I might kiss the furry little shit! And catch him a fresh fish! No one likes Bob, and the world would not miss him."

Spider groaned. "Bob is in this predicament because of me, Odin. Because I said he killed the cap'n. And, damn me, I am not so sure now that he did. If I had let him go overboard, it would have been as though I had knifed him, or shot him."

"If you had done either, a lot of us would envy you. Ha! You dropped this." Odin handed Spider the French throwing knife. "No one would care if you had stabbed him dead."

"I would care. Thanks for fetching the knife. I love this knife."

"Caring is going to get you killed one day."

"What happened to Bob's guards? Do you know?"

Odin laughed. "Aye. His guards were clubbed and hog-tied, probably by Bob's friends, Ames and Chambers."

"Ah." Spider scratched his head.

"Seems those two buggers knew Bob was aboard the whole time, too, to hear them talk," Odin said. "Helped him get back aboard, stole him food. They were begging for mercy all the way down to their chains, the bastards."

Spider nodded and snapped his fingers, earning a nod from Odin. "That's why they went all odd when I asked them questions. I wanted to know if they had seen anything suspicious, like ropes dangling down the hull or anything. They probably snuck food to Bob that way, maybe."

Odin shrugged. "So maybe some people like Little Bob after all. Seems Bob convinced those two bastards that taking the boat and rowing to Nassau was a better thing than waiting for Wright to sail us into goddamned Ned Low's bloody clutches. Hell, they may be right. But their mutiny failed, and those boys are in irons now."

Spider sighed. "I just want to get home to Em, and my boy, with a wee bit of my soul intact. That is truly all I desire in life, Odin."

"I know," Odin said. "A soul is a tricksy goddamned thing. Glad I lost mine to the devil a long time ago. I don't need to worry on it anymore. God help you, though. Ha!"

"Fox called me Spider John," Spider whispered. "How might he know that?"

"We have been careful, I swear," Odin answered.

"I know," Spider said. "I know."

18

"You think Anne had a sword?" Hob's eyebrows arched.

Hob, Odin, and Spider sat on the forecastle under a moon-washed sky, eating snapper and curry rolled into bread and washing it down with an extra ration of grog. Wright had ordered the repast in hopes of easing tension aboard *Redemption*, and Spider had noted the increasing use of the word "captain" when referring to their former sailing master. The trio spoke in hushed tones, for even though it was long past time for the day watch to have bunked in the forecastle or berth deck, no one wanted to sleep. They wanted to get drunk, scan the horizon for pirate sails, and turn about and head for Boston or Jamaica—anyplace but pirate waters.

"A sword, or a gun. Yes, Hob," Spider John said. "I am certain of it."

"Why?" The boy did not wish to believe anything bad about Anne.

Spider sighed. "The way she held her right arm behind her body, the way her muscles tensed." He paused to take a bite of his meal as a pair of hands passed by after setting a jib, and watched them head down the ladder. "One learns a thing or two on the devil's wind. And I have reason to believe she has a few other weapons tucked away as well."

"I'll search her, ha!"

Hob shot Odin a wicked glance, then turned back to Spider. "So now you think she did kill the cap'n?"

"I don't know. I don't know."

Bright moon painted the sea, and in the northern distance he could just make out the dark outline of an island. It was not the one they sought—Eden Isle, as Captain Wright called it, saying the name had been given by Captain Brentwood himself—but it made Spider think of their destination just the same. They might reach the isle tomorrow, Captain Wright had said, if the fair winds and calm seas continued. Many of the hands took that as a positive sign, thinking that maybe they could rush in, bury the captain at sea under a fine eulogy from Fox, and then ride the winds on to Boston as swiftly as possible.

Spider had his doubts about all that.

"Damned good fish," Odin said. "And damned good grog. Bugger those preachers." The Reverend Down and Rufus Fox both had objected to the extra measure of alcohol, fearing what it might fuel among an already tense crew, but Wright had insisted sailing men needed to unwind, and that sailing men knew best how to do it. Spider had applauded that decision.

"Well, if it wasn't Little Bob that killed him, as you say now, then who?" Hob handed over the rest of his grog to Spider, who had finished his own rather quickly.

"Thankee," Spider said quietly. "I don't know. Little Bob, slippery piss pot that he is, seemed to be truthful when he had us under the gun. I think the shit would have bragged about killing the cap'n, had he done it. He sure as hell wanted to kill him, but the more I think on it, I wonder how he might've snuck up from below and hidden inside that damned clock. Hiding in the clock, yes, easy for such a little bugger, but getting from his hidey-hole belowdecks and into the cabin, without us seeing him or Thomas guttin' him? I don't think so."

"And we heard that shot, and hands rushed right in," Odin said. "Even if he hid in the clock, he wasn't there when you looked, and how the hell could he have snuck back below? Broad daylight and him so small? Anyone would recognize him."

"Right," Spider said after draining Hob's grog.

"Maybe he had help," Hob said.

"Maybe. But I doubt it. As Odin said, no one really likes Bob. A couple o' twits in fear of pirates might help him break captivity if they thought it would help them escape, too, but no one aboard is going to help Little Bob Higgins murder a good cap'n."

"I think it was Sam Smoke," Odin said.

"Do you think he could have snuck in there, killed Cap'n Brentwood, hid for a moment, and then joined the rest of us unnoticed?" Spider shook his head. "Not with that pipe reek. I love a good pipe—fuck, I lost mine—but that man smells of all the brimstone in hell. We'd have smelled him in that close cabin soon as we entered. Which reminds me, we should have smelled the powder from the gun, too. Fuck and bugger."

"So, Anne?"

"No," Spider said. "Bold enough, I think, but too womanly. Somebody would have noticed her, I think, even if she had dressed as a man. And not even a few heartbeats before the shot, she'd been swirling about the deck all pretty as you please, dressed for a Bible reading. And that still leaves us with the gunpowder problem. I'm wondering how the doors got closed from outside but locked from inside, if the killer went out that way. They had to have been open when the shot was fired; that's the only way I can figure the gun smoke might've been blown out before we rushed in—but they were closed and goddamned locked by the time Wright hacked his way through the door."

"So," Hob said. "Do you think Anne is the killer? Or not the killer?"

"I am fairly certain she is a killer, but not so certain she killed Cap'n Brentwood, if you take my meaning, Hobgoblin. I'd give her leeway."

Hob hung his head and ran a hand through his blond hair. He said nothing.

"So the cap'n killed himself after all, then," Odin chimed in, "or some clever son of a bitch snuck in there, shot him dead, scrawled that note, and left by way of the stern gallery, then locked the damned doors and clambered up a rope like a monkey. Ha! Fucking Blackbeard could not have accomplished all that!"

"A moment ago you were thinking Sam Smoke did," Spider reminded him.

"Sam Smoke likes to kill men just for joy. I think he did it, hid by the mizzenmast, joined the rest after they rushed in—all eyes on the corpse, right? No one looking back behind them. Not so mysterious, and he is just the man for such a job."

"But the reek of him," Spider said.

"Stern gallery is open when he shoots," Odin said. "Blows away pipe reek and gun reek. He wants it to look like cap'n took his own life, so he closes up and locks it while Wright waits for an axe and hews his way in. Ha!"

"Why does he do all this?" Spider lifted Hob's cup to his lips, realized it was empty, and handed it to the boy.

"I tell you, Samuel Smoke does not need a reason to kill a man. Or a woman, or a dog."

Spider thought hard. "I don't know. Did anyone see him go into the cap'n's quarters?"

Hob and Odin shook their heads.

"We were standing right in front of those doors," Spider reminded them. "We should have seen anyone going in."

"So the killer was already in there," Odin suggested after a long silence.

"Or a ghost," Hob said.

"Or the cap'n killed himself," Odin answered.

"Or a ghost," Hob repeated.

"Fuck and bugger." Spider inhaled deeply, sorely wishing it had been through a pipe.

19

"**W**e've been roused, Spider."

Spider opened an eye, cautiously, as Hob swung his hammock. Sunlight poured into the forecastle. The other hands apparently all had departed, and the watch coming off duty had not yet come to hunker down. Spider yawned. God, how he had needed that sleep. Short as it was, it did him some good. A pipe, a tot of rum, and he'd be ready to go.

He swung his feet to the deck. "Aye, Hob, thanks."

"This is for you," Hob said, holding forth a clay pipe as though it were a fresh mincemeat pie.

"Did you peer into my head and see my very thoughts, lad? Look in through my ear while I was sleeping?"

"You always want a pipe in the morning, Spider."

"Well, then, where did you find this?"

"I traded for it." His gaze wandered as he said it.

"Yes. A trade. I get the pipe, and the fellow who owned it gets to wonder where his pipe went."

"That is how it goes," Hob said, laughing.

"Little bastard." Spider broke off the end of the stem—indented with the previous owner's bite marks—and fetched his tobacco from beneath the shirt he'd used as a pillow. "Off to work, then."

Upset as he was about the ship's diversion, Spider was determined to see to his duties. Sitting and fretting would not get him to Nantucket any sooner, and working with his hands often cleared his mind. Maybe he'd think of something. A bite of hardtack, a swig of grog, and a head full of tobacco later, Spider was inspecting the boat, masts, decks, and more for any damage that might have occurred during the previous night's fracas.

A small portion of the deck was blackened from burning oil, but the crew had doused the flames quickly and the damage was superficial. The boat was intact, too. Spider crossed to starboard and found no significant damage there. The tool chest lid would need to be replaced, though.

Lazare tended a fire box on the deck with one hand and sprinkled salt onto a bucket of fish fillets with the other. Spider crouched beside the sea cook to light his pipe again, then rose. His gaze found the horizon. He made out an island far to the north, one of the many cays dotting this stretch between the Turks and Nassau. The island they sought was one of those, but apparently not this one, for they were sailing away from it. Captain Wright was giving it much leeway, but Spider reckoned he'd have been wiser to avoid coming within sight of it.

"You worried about something, Mister Coombs?"

Spider glanced to his left. "No, Hadley. I am just waking up slowly today."

Hadley nodded but looked as though he did not believe Spider.

Nor should he have, for Spider was plenty worried. It was not at all uncommon for pirates to use these islands as rendezvous points, or places to careen hulls, repair masts, divide spoils, or simply rest and get drunk for a few days. Hell, he may have set foot on this one himself once or twice, although he could not discern any particular landmarks.

The islands made good cover for pirate ambushes. A man on a high point with a spyglass could see far-off prey and signal a swift sloop— or several sloops—hidden in a convenient bay or on the other side of the isle. *Redemption* was far off from this island but not far enough for comfort. She was a fluyt and not a fast ship, and the pirates would know that. *Redemption*, by passing within sight, had already taken a huge risk. Spider inhaled deeply, searched the sea for sails, and exhaled a great cloud of smoke.

Looking aloft, he noted that Captain Wright had set full sail, and because the ship's current tack was falling away from the island, those sails presented a highly visible profile. Anyone high up on that island was certain to spy them. At least there was a lookout posted to the crow's nest, and with any luck *Redemption* would spot any pursuit in time to make preparations—whatever the hell those may be. *Redemption* had no ship's guns and few trained fighters. As far as Spider knew, the only men aboard who had ever been in a fight were himself, Odin, and Hob. And Sam Smoke, of course, but there was no trusting that son of a bitch.

Spider turned toward the quarterdeck. He would carry his concerns to the captain, quietly so as to not make the hands more nervous than they already were.

"A word, John?"

Rufus Fox approached, sections of a broken fiddle in each hand. The fragments were joined only by a tangle of slack strings.

"Hello, sir."

Fox held the broken instrument higher, showing how the pistol ball had torn the maple neck from the spruce body. "I am afraid it was never a superlative violin to begin with, and salt and sun have not been gentle to it, but a man named Allard is in the hold crying over its loss," Fox said. "Absolutely bawling. Music is such a solace in difficult times, I suppose."

"Aye."

"The tuning pegs survived, as did the strings, by the grace of God, but this neck must be replaced. I believe I can do the work, but I wonder if you've some good wood that might serve."

Spider peered at the broken mess. "I think you might need to be a sorcerer to fix this. But I applaud you for trying. Indeed, I even have some maple stowed."

"Wonderful!" Fox's voice fluttered like a slightly slack sail, and his gaze wandered to sea.

"Watching for pirates?" Sam Smoke, trailing a cloud as he walked past them, grinned as though he shared a secret with the devil. He chuckled softly and did not wait for an answer.

"May God forgive me, but I detest that man," Fox said. "The way he leers at Miss Brentwood. It is revolting."

"Indeed," Spider agreed. He paused a moment, wondered, then decided to take a sounding. "Are you sweet on the girl, Mister Fox?"

The potato nose reddened a bit, as did the cheeks below the man's widened eyes. "What? No, sir. No. Why, she's not half my age."

"I just wondered. You seem protective of her, is all."

Fox grinned awkwardly and looked about at everything but Spider's eyes. "She is a fine girl, and I suppose she sees me as something of an uncle, or rather, I should say, I see her as a niece. Yes, that's all it is." He nodded sharply, smiled, and met Spider's gaze at last.

"Well, then," Spider said with a nod, "forgive me for thinking otherwise."

"Are you . . . sweet on the lass, John?"

"I have someone at home." Spider felt a pang and gulped. "I think Miss Brentwood might be a bit above my reach, in any case. Don't think she's meant for a sailor's wife."

Fox grinned. "Perhaps." The man glanced across the waves. "Do you think there are sea robbers about?"

Spider sighed. He liked Rufus Fox, and did not wish to lie, but he did not wish to frighten the man either. He felt a bit like a ship he'd heard a tale about, caught between a man-eating monster and ship-bashing rocks. Spider drew deeply from the pipe, exhaled slowly, then decided an honest answer was best. "I think it could be the case. Certainly, these waters are known pirate haunts." He pointed west. "Not far that way is Nassau. Woodes Rogers, governor there, has hunted down or chased away a great many pirates, so you might think yourself safe. But he could not have hung or cowed them all, and word back in Port Royal was that Rogers has gone back to England. That news alone is enough, probably, to bring some men out of hiding and back on the account."

"I see," Fox said, eyes lowering.

"And there are few better places to hide than these islands. Indeed, I was on my way to urge our cap'n to not draw so near them. Ships can slip right out from behind them, and pirates pick vessels much swifter than this massive . . ."

"Good Lord, then," Fox said, looking a bit green. "I shall not detain you."

"I will have my mate fetch you some nice maple soon as may be," Spider replied before dashing off.

He found Captain Wright on the quarterdeck. "Come about, north by northwest. Smartly there," the man hollered, sparking responses from the helm and the men aloft, before turning to acknowledge Spider's presence with a weary sigh. "What is it, carpenter?"

"Forgive me, Cap'n," Spider said, not wishing to embarrass the commander. A quick glance confirmed the island still was within sight, so coming about now would only keep *Redemption* within view. "It would be best to continue away, beyond sight of the island, and make our course more southerly."

Wright turned his broad shoulders. Captains could be temperamental beasts, and Spider wondered whether he might receive an earbursting bellow or a backhand across the face. All he got was a calm response. "I am listening, Mister Coombs."

Spider released the breath he had been holding and explained his concerns about an ambush. He spoke almost in a whisper to avoid spreading worries. Wright gave him full attention.

"And how do you know so much about pirate ways, John Coombs?"

"Survived an attack once, just plain luck," Spider answered.

He and the captain locked eyes for a few seconds. "You saved Little Bob, though I and everyone else aboard might have preferred you hadn't," Wright said, brushing long hair from his eyes. "I do not suppose that was the action of a pirate."

Spider forced himself not to turn his eyes from the captain's.

"I shall do as you suggest, carpenter."

"Aye, sir."

Captain Wright looked aloft. "Was that smartly done, men? Are we Frenchmen? Can we come about no more sailorly than the bloody French? I believe we shall practice this until it is done to my satisfaction! South by southwest, lubbers!"

With that, Wright gave commands to set *Redemption* on her

former course, away from the island, and Spider left his side, scanning the sea and hoping nothing pounced at them.

He saw no sails and pulled free Em's pendant to kiss it. Their luck seemed to be holding.

For now.

20

Captain Wright rapidly descended on a ratline and dropped the last seven feet, landing in a crouch and a loud thunk that startled people nearby.

"Eden Isle, by God!"

Anne, who had been strolling amidships and staring off at the early-evening sea, hustled toward the bow in a swirl of skirts and red hair. Sam Smoke, for once without a pipe clenched in his yellow teeth, trailed her, a few feet behind. The man pulled the pipe from the band in his wide-brimmed hat and the tobacco pouch from his belt without once taking his gaze off Anne's slender figure.

Hob watched her, too. The boy sat atop the forecastle, gazing at Anne as she climbed the ladder. The woman noticed Hob and smiled, and the boy's face beamed like the sun.

Jesus, Spider thought. *That is not what we fucking need right now.*

Abigail Brentwood, who had been alternatively weeping silently and playing at her makeshift keyboard, became suddenly still before finally shaking her head and inhaling sharply.

Rufus Fox turned toward the captain so quickly that he nearly lost his balance on the swaying deck; only an assist from the Reverend Down saved him. Down seemed ridiculously pleased with himself. "Lean on me, sir, but lean not on your own understanding," he said wryly.

Fox smiled. "I do not pretend to understand so much, Reverend, nor do I suppose you understand as much as you believe." He pulled his arm gently from Down's grasp. "I do thank you for preventing my physical stumble, if not my perceived theological ones."

The reverend's face reddened a bit, and his jaw worked in search of a rejoinder, but he remained silent. Both men turned their attention to trying to spy the island Captain Wright had mentioned.

Wright rose from his crouch, pointed theatrically toward the lowering sun, and smiled. "The captain's island, Eden, he called it, and by God there he shall rest in blessed peace."

Miss Brentwood placed Fox's keyboard contraption on the deck and rose from the chest she sat on. Her gaze followed Wright's pointing finger.

Spider looked, too. It was just a smudge on the horizon, waiting for the sun to drop behind it. As *Redemption* climbed the swells, the island seemed to grow, stretching like a fin whale just breaking the surface. As the ship settled into the troughs, the isle almost vanished.

Abigail Brentwood stepped toward Wright. "Is it really so different from the other islands we've seen?"

The captain, taken aback only a heartbeat by her willingness to talk to him, smiled.

"Assuredly," he said. "Green and lush as Ireland, your father called it. On the far side of it, there's a cove, nice and deep, and the hills rise all around it. We'll set him there, in the cove, exactly where he would want to be." The man's chin quaked with emotion, and even in the dimming light Spider could see tears welling in his eyes.

"It is a dangerous path you've led us on, Nicholas," Abigail said, her head bent. "I am not so certain my father would have approved. He'd have had you remain with the convoy to keep his passengers and crew safe. I am certain of that."

"He is your father, girl," Wright said, choking. "I would do right by him, for his sake and for yours."

She looked up at him. "I know."

For a moment, Spider thought Wright might wrap her in his arms, but he did not.

The two of them stared at each other for several heartbeats.

"You are a fool, Nicholas Wright," she said. "But I understand why you've done this, and I do appreciate it."

"Abby," Wright said, reaching for her hands.

"No." She stepped back. "Please."

"Aye," Wright said, then headed aft, calling orders. "We'll reduce sail, lads, and sail in by morning light. Luff and touch her, if you please."

Abigail's gaze followed Wright.

Spider suddenly felt as though he was intruding on a private moment, even though he was across the deck by the port rail. He crossed the deck, nodded at Abigail while avoiding a meeting of eyes—he still felt the sting of her earlier rebuke—and turned his attention to the distant island. He narrowed his eyelids and looked for a speck of bright fire, or a plume of telltale smoke, or a bit of sail on the horizon. He scanned the low hills, looking for a reflection of sunlight on a spyglass. He saw none of those things and sighed in relief.

With any luck, they would work their way into the cove in the morning, bid Captain Brentwood a final farewell, and then head north. *Redemption* was well provisioned, and there should be no need to stay at the island longer than it took to say a few prayers and relinquish the captain's body to the sea. No one, thus far, had mentioned going ashore and digging a grave, and Spider had mentally rehearsed a long and windy speech in the event someone did suggest such a fool thing. Captain Brentwood was a seaman, Spider would say. He should be buried at sea, not in the damned sand, not on a damned hill. *And, by the way*, he would add with a wagging finger, *these are pirate waters. We'd best be off as soon as may be. Unless you want your throats slit, by thunder.*

It had taken longer to arrive here than the new captain had anticipated, but that was because Wright had heeded Spider's warning and held to a more southerly course, and for that, Spider was grateful. He realized, too, that trying to duck into the cove by night would be a fool's mission, no matter how much of a hurry they might be in to perform their task and be on their way. By night, they might run aground on a reef or even on a shipwreck. Plenty of vessels had met their doom in these waters. Captain Wright had made the correct decision in this instance.

Spider pulled the heart pendant from beneath his dingy shirt.

Sweat and salt air had stiffened the leather cord, and it was frayed in spots. He would have to replace it soon.

He began a prayer in his mind, but it turned into a message to his beloved. *Soon, Em, dear. Soon. We have to lay a good man to rest first. Then we'll turn for Boston. We'll leave these waters behind us, and I'll get back to you soon as may be. And I won't go wayfaring again.*

He tucked the charm back out of sight and realized he could no longer feel the rum working in his head. That wouldn't do, he thought. It was going to be a long night. He was going to need more rum.

He headed toward the galley. His thoughts, once again turned toward the captain's murder, raged like a storm. Someone aboard this ship had murdered the man, and the mystery of it nagged Spider's mind like a splinter you could feel but not quite find. He had missed something. He was sure of it. And he felt he owed it to the daughter to figure out what the bloody hell that was. He closed his eyes and saw her face in his mind, imploring him to bring her father's killer to justice. A man couldn't ignore that.

Spider opened his eyes to find Odin suddenly at his side. "I know what you are thinking, Spider."

"Do you, now?"

"More rum. Ha!" Odin clapped his hands together. "Do you suppose . . . ?" he said, then tucked at Spider's sleeve and stopped him short. "Do you suppose, perhaps, you have been drinking a might too much too often?"

"I suppose no such bloody damned thing." Spider resumed his march toward the galley.

"These may be bad waters, Spider," Odin urged in a tense whisper almost in Spider's ear. "We've had a murder. We have Sam Smoke aboard. We may be fetching up into the same waters as goddamned Ned Low and Wicked Pete Reese. Maybe soaking your brains in rum isn't the best thing to do right now."

Spider glared at Odin's ungodly ugly face. "You know, Odin, I smell a wee bit of rum on your breath, I do."

"Aye." Odin chortled a moment and even danced something that vaguely resembled a jig for a couple of heartbeats. "No one is looking to me to lead nothing! I'll just cut down any man who stands before me, whether that be the sensible thing or no. But you, that boy Hob looks up to you, and I've known you to use your brains a time or two. We kind of rely on you to do the thinking. So maybe . . ."

Spider leaned into Odin's face. "This ship is supposed to carry me to my lass and my boy, and it is carrying me everywhere else instead. Hob is supposed to listen to my advice, and he's gawking at that gun-toting bitch Anne instead. You are supposed to be my devil-may-care boon companion, and you are lecturing me instead. By God, man, I need a drink and I mean to have one. Maybe two. Maybe three!"

Odin spat on the deck and turned his lone eye on Spider. "Well, hell, I've lived longer than I had any goddamned right to already. And so have you! So no loss, I guess, if we get drunk and die in a fight. I feel right damned bad for young Hob, though."

Odin headed toward the forecastle, cackling and dancing that damned almost-jig every third or fourth step.

Spider headed to the galley. *Now I really need a drink*, he thought. *And one after that.*

21

"**S**on of a bitch."

It was just a glint of light, tiny, there on the northernmost of the two green hills that rose to either side of a sweet little cove on Eden Isle. It was morning, and the ship had slipped around to the island's west side in search of Captain Brentwood's beloved cove. The low hills blocked the sunlight, but something on top of one of them had caught a sunbeam and flashed—just one, brief flash.

In Spider's mind, however, that small glimmer was the spark that could blow his future into splinters and smoke.

It had to be a signal. It just had to be.

Redemption was slowly heading into the cove, after making slow loops in the deeper waters to the south overnight. Spider had climbed the mainmast, despite his throbbing head, and endured the swaying that even a gentle sea imparted to the heights of a tall ship. He had perched there on a topgallant beam for more than an hour now, his pipe extinguished and his eyes watery from staring. He'd spied for sails, or smoke, or a boat on the beach—or a glint of light such as the one he'd just seen. The waters around *Redemption* seemed empty, and there was no sign of habitation ashore, nor was there any vessel in the cove. But that light up above meant someone was on that damned island.

If that someone had signaled a ship somewhere, to the north or east, hiding beyond those hills and the two slender arms of land that embraced the cove, *Redemption* could be sailing right into a trap. Once in the cove, a vessel with guns could easily bar the way out. *Redemption* would be caught tight, like a seal in a shark's maw. And if that pouncing ship were commanded by the likes of Ned Low . . .

Spider cursed again and swung himself onto a ratline. He looked below for Captain Wright. He had thought to find him at the bow, looking ahead of the ship as it entered the cove and perhaps discussing Captain Brentwood's funeral ceremony with Rufus Fox and the Reverend Down. The theologians hunkered atop the forecastle, peering into a Bible and, for once, nodding together in seeming agreement. Captain Wright, however, was not with them, nor was he anywhere to be seen forward.

Spider climbed a bit lower and searched aft. *Redemption* had reduced sail as she eased her way into the cove, so there were fewer obstructions to vision than would have been the case were the ship plying the sea at full speed. It took only a moment to spot the captain, pacing rapidly and gazing over the rail to port, then starboard, and back.

Spider descended swiftly, like his namesake, and that was not good for his rum-soaked head. Odin's words rang in his mind, and once he reached the deck Spider took two uncertain steps before he felt in command of his own body again.

"Hob!" Spider turned slowly, looking for the boy. "Hob!"

"Here I am, John." Spider rushed to him. The boy was wearing the closest thing he had to a clean shirt; they were planning to lay Captain Brentwood to rest this day, and many of the crewmen were stitching holes in shirts or drying clothes on lines stretched amidships.

Spider pulled Hob aside to a spot by the ship's boat and took a quick look about him to make sure no one was paying attention. "I think we are headed for trouble, boy."

"If you mean a bit of bright light on the hill, I dare say you are right."

"You saw it, too?"

"Aye."

"Good lad." Spider ran a hand across his face, wiping away the sweat dripping from his brow. "I am going to try to get Cap'n Wright to turn this bloody vessel around, but he is sotted with love for that girl and may not listen to me, so . . ."

The gravity of the situation seized Spider's mind, and the pause irritated Hob. "So, Spider?"

"So if he won't turn about," Spider whispered now, "we are going to take the bloody goddamned ship and turn it about ourselves!"

"Mutineers!" Hob sounded as though it would be a dream fulfilled.

"Yes, by God, but be bloody quiet about it! Go fetch us guns and ammo, fast, but quiet. And find Odin and tell him what we are about. You and Odin and me are likely the only ones aboard this damned ship that have ever been in a fight."

"Sam Smoke has, you know," Hob reminded him.

"Aye," Spider said, "but if lead flies I may damn well shoot him first. Can't trust him, son."

"Indeed." Hob nodded.

"I'm headed to the cap'n. Go!"

"Aye!" Hob ran off.

Spider worked his way aft, toward the quarterdeck. His search was brief, for Captain Wright was descending the port-side ladder. "Cap'n, sir, a word, please?"

The captain nodded.

Spider rushed to Wright's side. "We've got to come about, sir, get away from this island," Spider said in a hushed, but urgent, tone. "I saw a light atop the hill, sir. I think it was someone signaling."

"Signaling? Signaling us?"

"No, sir, signaling pirates. Maybe a ship in hiding beyond that isle, waiting for us to draw too near so they can pounce like an eel."

Wright turned to look at the hilltop. "I see nothing."

"They won't risk more signals than they need, sir. I saw it because I was watching for it, and I watched a long time. And I am not alone in seeing it. At least one other did, too."

"Is that so? Then we must be quick, perform our duty to the late captain, and be off."

"No, sir," Spider urged. "We must dispatch the cap'n's remains here, in sight of his isle but no closer, and do it while we veer off. It may be too late already, sir, and we've women aboard. Think of them."

"Abigail," Wright whispered.

Spider nodded. His relief wilted an instant later, though, when he noticed *Redemption* already was slipping into the deep cove's entrance. And hope died when he saw the dirty sails of a schooner emerge from behind the island, to the north.

The interloper was a crowded vessel, and Spider could make out guns and swords waving above her crew. He could see at least four guns mounted on her deck. Those would fire four-pound balls, probably, or perhaps loads of devastating grapeshot that would scatter and rip the hell out of sails and bodies. Spider had no doubt those guns were already loaded, waiting for the spark.

"Fuck and bugger," Spider muttered. "Cap'n Wright, look!"

"Panic is unbecoming in a sailor." The mocking words rode an odorous cloud. Sam Smoke had joined the conversation.

"Being wary and being panicked ain't the same thing," Spider said, but he noted his clenched jaw and a slight shake of his knees. He knew how to fight, and fight well, but he didn't want to do it.

Sam Smoke approached and stood next to Spider. "I know that ship, Captain Wright. Know her captain, rather well. We've nothing to fear from them. Indeed, I think it a lucky meeting. It will be a joyous reunion for me, and I shall introduce the rest of *Redemption*'s company to new friends." A heavy undercurrent of menace chilled any warmth his actual words might otherwise have conveyed.

"I am not so confident," Wright said. He rubbed his chin roughly with his right hand while his left made a fist low by his hip. "I think the carpenter might be wise. I was a fool to try this. A fool. We will have to make a run for it."

Spider clapped his hands together in a loud smack. "Aye, Cap'n, and prepare some pistols in case we are chased."

Sam Smoke's pipe flared violently as the foul man stepped backward, and a second later Spider felt a small, metal cylinder poked behind his right ear. "Now, then," Smoke said. "Let us all be silent, like a grave, or you will find out just how silent a grave truly is. I swear it."

"Nicholas?" That came from Abigail, who had ducked under a boom and shoved aside someone's hanging wet shirt. She was approaching in haste, clutching at her long black skirt. She was attired in a white blouse and wearing her hair long and tied back, prepared to bid her father farewell. Beautiful as she was, the sight froze Spider's blood. If the spy on the hill saw a woman aboard . . .

"Stay away, girl," Spider said. He reached for the knife on his belt but stopped when Smoke increased the pressure on the gun. Spider held his hands out to either side where Smoke could see them.

Spider noted Hadley, lurking near Abigail as always. "Hadley, lad, get her away from here. Now."

Hadley took her arm, but Abigail shrugged him off. "I need to know what is happening here." Hadley, seeming torn between desire to protect the girl and heed her wishes, stepped back, confused.

"You had best heed the carpenter's words, pretty girl," Smoke said. The man was behind him, so Spider could not see the leer, but he could certainly hear it. "Your lover captain has some important decisions to make, and unless he does exactly as I say, lead balls are likely to fly through pretty little heads."

"You will not hurt her," Wright growled.

"I will do anything I please," Smoke said, "and neither you nor God nor the devil is going to stop me."

Abigail froze.

Hadley drew his dirk.

Wright seethed.

Spider's gaze cast about, looking for some means of turning things to his advantage. What he saw was more trouble.

The schooner was flying a flag now. A black flag, with a blood-red skeleton upon it.

Spider had never seen that flag, but he'd heard of it. Everyone who sailed these bloody waters had heard of it.

It was Ned Low's flag.

22

A half dozen calculations swirled in Spider John's mind.

First, could he shake off last night's rum quickly enough to be of any bloody use to anyone in this dire situation? Aye. A pistol pressed to his head seemed to have sobered him up pretty goddamned fast.

Second, could he knock aside that gun and slam a fist into Sam Smoke's leering face fast enough to avoid being shot dead? No. That was not going to happen. Sam Smoke was not some virgin to violence; Spider could not see him, but he was certain the man had either another gun or a knife in his other hand by now. Any sudden move on Spider's part was going to get him killed.

Third, how much time did *Redemption* have before the pirate schooner could set up its blockade? None, Spider decided. Ned Low's vessel was still some distance away and was as much dependent on the wind as any other ship. That wind was light now and out of the southwest. The schooner was beating against that wind, and white water breaking on reefs told Spider there was yet much maneuvering to do on the pirates' part before the schooner would come about to close off any escape from the cove.

But none of that mattered. *Redemption* was already in the cove and would have to beat its way out against that same wind, which, for her, was partially blocked by land now. *Redemption* was sturdy as a boulder but slow as a pig running in deep tar. And her crewmen were not thinking of sails and lines. They were watching the drama, and freeing work knives, and wondering who the hell here might die. Even if Wright commanded them to bring the bloody ship about right now, they would respond slowly, their minds as much on the danger aboard as on the peril across the waters.

Even if *Redemption* did somehow miraculously get out of the cove, say by some favorable trick of the wind gifted to her by a loving God, she still would not outrun that schooner. It mattered not at all what the wind did. *Redemption* was already at Ned Low's mercy.

So Spider tossed that hope aside, licked the salty sweat from the corner of his dry mouth, and moved on to his fourth calculation. How soon might Hob and Odin come to his rescue? Would they see what was happening in time to do something? Or did Sam Smoke have allies aboard who already held Odin and Hob—and anyone else who might thwart them—at bay?

"What is your game, Sam?" Spider put a hint of conspiracy into his voice. "Might be one where you could use a steady hand? I am quick and able in a fight." *And I can't bloody wait to show you, you son of a bitch.*

"You ready to join ranks with me now that you realize who has the weather gauge here, John?" Smoke laughed. "I haven't thought of you and me on friendly terms, and I think I like you right here, with my gun pressed on your skull."

"You know the value of a good fighter, Sam. I am not, to be sure, happy about the idea of linking my fate to yours, but I see it as a better prospect than being your enemy."

"I think we shall keep matters just as they are."

Even as he played for time, Spider moved on to his fifth calculation: If Sam Smoke was not working this scheme alone, who might his henchmen be? Or was it a henchwoman? Sure, Hob had overheard Smoke and the mysterious Anne exchange harsh words, but they obviously knew one another, and Spider had known pirates and thieves to fight among themselves, yet still work together for a common cause. Was Anne working with Smoke, perhaps to capture *Redemption* and hand it over to Ned Low? Or was Anne playing Smoke like a fish, using him to some purpose of her own?

Spider had to wonder who else among the crew might be working with Smoke, for this current situation seemed a bold play for a solitary brigand. The men Spider could see out of the corners of his eyes were motionless and silent, watching the drama but taking no apparent part. Were they with Wright, or were they with Sam Smoke? Or would they simply try to stay uncommitted until this all played out?

Then there was the last calculation. How long would Wright endure Smoke's threat to Abigail before he did some goddamned stupid thing? And if Wright did act, could Spider take advantage of the distraction? Spider steeled himself. If Wright sprang and Smoke shot him, Spider would have his knife freed and in Smoke's throat within a heartbeat.

That did not happen, though. Anne intervened.

"I knew it, you salty, scraggly son of a bitch," she said, apparently addressing Smoke, although Spider wondered if perhaps she meant him.

Spider glanced upward; Anne stood on the quarterdeck. The woman must have gone up the starboard ladder, seeking higher ground, while all attention was on the action to port. She had traded the dress for britches and a shirt, and wore a bandolier holding at least three knives and two guns. A few stray red tresses streamed from beneath a wide-brimmed hat, but most of her hair had been tied up in a braid that spilled over her shoulder. She had a sheathed cutlass on her hip and a flintlock pistol in each hand. The guns were aimed at Smoke, or at Spider and Wright. It was difficult to tell, since *Redemption* gently rocked on the water. But one thing was certain. She had chosen a high vantage and could easily keep an eye on the combatants below.

"Good morning, Miss Bonny," Smoke said. If he was intimidated at all, there was no hint of it in his voice.

The name Bonny bounced around in Spider's mind. *Jesus! Anne Bonny!* The woman pirate who reputedly fought as well as any man and better than most. She had sailed and raised hell with Calico Jack Rackham himself. Rumor on the Spanish Main had been that Anne Bonny was in prison, or already hung, but some few held that she had pleaded her belly—gotten pregnant by some prison guard or visiting minister—and so escaped the noose.

Spider formed a seventh calculation. He had assumed things could not get worse, but he had obviously been wrong, and so he began wondering and figuring just what the bloody hell would go wrong next.

"I knew if I followed you, Sam, you would lead me right to that bastard. And I was right," she said, nodding toward the schooner. "He's over there, isn't he?"

"Wicked Pete is over there, indeed," Smoke said, laughing. "Are you going to bounce your delicious tits right up against him, let him grab your pretty arse while you put a knife in his brain? He's a dumb one, Pete. He will fall for your beauty, no doubt."

Well, then, Spider thought, *perhaps Hob had not overheard a confession to the captain's murder during that little spying foray into the guests' quarters. Perhaps he had heard Anne plotting to kill Wicked Pete instead.* Of course, Spider knew, the woman might well have decided to kill one man while on her way to kill another. He didn't much trust Anne Bonny any more than he trusted a goddamned sparrow flitting about his head.

"A knife in the brain, a lead ball, doesn't matter," Anne said. "I will kill him any way I can, and I know a lot of ways. Know this, though. He will see me coming because I will make sure of that, and he will realize in his dying moment that it was me that took his life. Rely on it. You know what the bastard did."

"Aye," Smoke said, leering. "I thought about doing the same myself."

"You are not man enough," Anne scoffed.

Spider heard Smoke's low growl. "I am man enough to do this, bitch."

The gun that was pressed against Spider's ear moved, aiming its deadly ball at Anne Bonny.

Spider freed the knife from his belt.

Smoke's gun erupted in thunder and smoke.

Anne Bonny had hit the deck, and a lead ball splintered the rail where she had stood.

Spider pivoted, his knife arcing toward the red blaze of Smoke's pipe shining inside the blinding cloud of gun and pipe smoke.

The knife caught flesh, slicing through Smoke's neck. Then a gun erupted, and Sam Smoke's skull exploded in a shower of bone and blood.

23

Sam Smoke spun slowly, his eyes wide. He looked as though he was laughing as his flying hat spun in the air like a top before plopping on the weather deck. Then he toppled, blood pouring from his head.

"Ha!"

Spider, who had been in more than one bloody scrape over the years and had been hoping Odin and Hob would spring into action, barely flinched. He calmly wiped gore from his face. Others, though, had dodged for cover behind masts and storage boxes.

Abigail shrieked, ran to Captain Wright, and then recoiled in horror as she noted Smoke's blood splattered across his face and shirt.

"I enjoyed that." Odin, poised on a ratline, had a smoking flintlock extended in his steady right hand, and his lone eye opened wide despite the gunpowder cloud surrounding his face. "I should have done that years ago!" He tossed the expended gun to Hob and pulled another one free from his belt. The cutlass, the very blade Spider had advised Odin to leave in Port Royal, dangled from Odin's belt, and for once Spider was glad the old bastard had refused to heed his advice.

Men peered from their hiding places, but none confronted the hideous piratical figure. Hadley, though, placed himself between Abigail and Odin.

Hob, carrying a bucket of pistols and shot and gunpowder, knew better than to put Odin's hot weapon into his load. He held it in his free hand.

Spider rotated like a dervish, readying his knife for a throw, but no one had made a move to aid or avenge Sam Smoke. Spider turned to the captain, who was embracing Abigail, who apparently had overcome her horror of blood. She clutched at Wright tightly, and tears rolled on her cheeks and fell from her quivering jaw. "What is happening? What is happening?"

"Cap'n," Spider said as calmly as he could while wiping more of Smoke's gore from his face and beard, "we must put Cap'n Brentwood overboard now and pray for him later." He moved toward the rail and pointed. The pirate schooner had begun coming about. There was now nowhere to run that would not be covered by her long guns. "We are trapped, sir."

"Who is this man? Why was he holding a gun to John's head?" Abigail pointed at Sam Smoke. She was shaking like a flag in a hard wind.

"He is a pirate," Spider told her, "Samuel Lawrence, known on the Spanish Main as Sam Smoke. I think he meant to keep us from fighting or fleeing from this neat little trap."

Wright gently freed himself from Abigail's arms and looked at the schooner. He glanced at Smoke and back at the schooner. Then he stared into Abigail's eyes. "We'll run," he said. "We'll run!"

"No," Spider urged. "By God, we will not run."

Wright's eyes widened, and his face flushed. He nearly knocked Spider over as he shoved his face forward. "What did you say?"

"Think not of fleeing, sir," Spider said, stepping back and raising his voice now so others could hear. "We already squandered any time we might have had for that. *Redemption* is a fine ship, sir, but she is slow as a sermon."

Somewhere behind him, the Reverend Down scoffed.

"I remind you who commands here, carpenter." Wright's nostrils flared.

"I know that, sir, forgive me, but . . . our situation is desperate and . . . I know something of pirates and their ways."

"You do, it seems. Just how . . . ?"

"Sir, we have no prayer of outrunning that schooner, nor staying beyond reach of her guns, not if we mounted all the sail our trees can hold, not even if we added stunsails, skysails, and moonrakers." Spider turned slowly, meeting as many eyes as he could. "She'll ride closer to the wind than we can and sail faster. Her guns will be on us like a wolf pack; she'll get within reach, blast us with grape, and even if we have enough timber and canvas left to tack away, she'll just do it again and again until we've got no sail left. It would be folly to run."

Spider drew a deep breath. "Am I right, lads?" He hoped to rally a few voices in support, and indeed Hob tossed out an "amen," but everyone else seemed dubious. Spider considered his next rallying words, then paused a moment, arrested by the sight of Sam Smoke's blood running in rivulets down the surface of the door he had replaced on Captain Brentwood's cabin. The good man's remains, wrapped in thick sail canvas, were still in there. Even as the pirates closed off *Redemption*'s means of escape, even as he steeled himself for battle, Spider's mind filled with the scene of that horrible morning when they found the captain dead. *Blood then, blood now . . .*

The blood flowed slowly down the oak, streaming in lines with the grain of the wood and soaking into it in spots.

Jesus, Spider thought. *How fucking drunk was I that day? What a fool, what a bloody idiot . . .*

"What then do you think, John?" The question came from Rufus Fox. "Must we fight? We have women aboard."

"Look hard at this woman, sir, and you shall see steel in my sword and in my eyes. I can fight, I assure you," Anne said, looking as if she meant it.

"No," Spider said. "No, we must bloody well not fight." He was almost stuttering because his mind was suddenly working on two problems at once. *So that's how the captain was murdered, aye?* He could at least narrow the list of suspects now. He just needed to think, but the pirates' approach left him no goddamned time for that.

A couple of gunshots—blunderbusses, thank God, and not the schooner's long guns—brought Spider back to the moment. A glance showed men aboard the schooner, waving guns and swords. Spider expected that soon they would begin to hum and growl ominously, a tactic designed to instill fear.

He glanced around at *Redemption's* men. They were frightened enough already. *These men will piss themselves once battle is joined*, he thought.

Spider inhaled sharply, then cursed. Two more vessels, a sloop and a brigantine, were coming into view in the schooner's wake. They were farther out but flying black flags. *Redemption* had wandered into serious trouble.

"Lord have mercy. We stand no chance in a battle. None," Spider said. "We have few aboard who have ever been in a real fight, if I am any judge, and every bugger aboard that schooner will be a killer many times over. The same goes for those ships yonder. They will be well armed, and they'll not hesitate to cut throats or shoot us down." *They may bloody well rip us to tatters with grapeshot before they even set foot aboard* Redemption, he thought but did not say.

"Then we will have to negotiate," Wright said, his chest swelling and his voice rising. He looked into the eyes of his crew, his expression firm. "We have goods. We will let them take what they want without a fight, we will see to Captain Brentwood, and go our separate ways."

"Sir," Spider replied, "these bastards know only two kinds of men— men they can use . . . and witnesses. And they will want the whole damned ship, sir, not just her cargo."

Wright and Spider locked eyes.

"There is nothing reasonable about them," Spider said quietly. "And if that be Ned Low pouncing on us . . ."

Anne Bonny weighed in. "Ned and Wicked Pete are seldom far apart."

Whispers and gasps filled the air around them.

"Let us leave the ship," Spider said. "Drop anchor. Then let us get the boat and some supplies overboard before they board us. We cannot take much, for they'll rush if they think we are taking anything valuable. They have a spy on the hill, there, too, so they will know what we are doing."

Spider caught sight of Abigail Brentwood, hair streaming in the wind, and his backbone went cold despite the Caribbean heat. He cursed himself. He had so much going through his mind, but there was no excuse for his slovenly thinking. He should have ordered her below already.

"Miss Brentwood, get out of sight."

"I don't understand." Fear seemed to have erased any lingering anger she might have harbored against Spider. She was confused but attentive.

"Hide, girl! They may have seen you already."

"So..."

"So they may not have seen a woman in some time, and there are places in the world where a pretty girl is considered a valuable commodity."

"Oh," she said quietly. "Oh."

"Get below, dress like a sailor."

She ran off, Hadley trailing, and Spider turned back to the captain. "We'll get Miss Brentwood, the passengers, and as many as want to go ashore out of harm's way. Maybe these pirates will be happy with the ship and cargo and leave us be."

Wright paced, chewed on his lip, and wrung his hands. That seemed to go on forever. Meanwhile, the enemy vessels moved to close off any hope of escape.

Spider sighed and spat on the weather deck. "It is the only way, sir."

"I suppose you are right." Wright sighed deeply. "That island is our best hope. Abby's best hope, anyway. She must go ashore."

"How is this?" Abigail stood nearby, arms wide. The long hair had been cropped short, and she wore britches and a shirt. A smelly wide-brimmed hat that had seen too much salt and sun hid most of her face.

"Good," Spider said. "That was fast."

"Hadley lent me clothes and chopped my hair with an axe."

Spider glanced at Hadley, who now held a knife and a hand axe.

"You've done all you can do," Spider told her, "short of growing a beard."

Wright turned to Abigail. "You will go ashore, Abby?"

She nodded. "We'll be marooned. But that will be better than being taken, I suppose?"

"The island is green," Spider said. "That means freshwater springs. And we can fish; we will take nets. The cove will be teeming with life. We will be fine. And once settled, we can send some lads off in the boat to fetch help. It will be fine."

Wright turned to holler up at the helmsman and the men in the rigging. "Furl sails! We will anchor here." Men rushed to comply. He pointed at a few other seamen. "You lads, help Mister Fox and Reverend Down. Commend the captain to the deep, gentlemen."

Down and Fox nodded. Abigail shook her head in protest.

"And do it quickly," Wright added.

"Nicholas, my father, he . . ."

"He deserves better, I know, Abby. But . . . I have to protect you. I've put you in harm's way. I thought I could protect you. Your father . . ."

Spider cleared his throat. "It is the only way, miss."

She nodded slowly. "Very well," she said. "We shall have a proper ceremony after we go ashore."

"Not we," Wright said.

"What are you saying, Nicholas?"

The splash of an anchor filled the air.

"I am captain now," he said calmly. "I am staying with my ship. Others might, too," he added louder. "If they think it better to join with pirates than to be marooned on an island."

Abigail grabbed Wright's collar. "You fool, do not do this! Father would not ask it of you, nor should anyone!"

"I will be fine," Wright said, "and it is my duty. To *Redemption*, and to you. They will accept me, Abby. I am a navigator and brave enough. And I can protect you, keep them from knowing about you. I vow that much." He punctuated that with a stern glance around.

The man was all puffed up with love and virtue. Spider felt sort of sorry for him.

Redemption settled slowly to a stop as the anchor took hold. The ship turned as the helmsman guided her, and another anchor was dropped aft to hold her in position. Men began freeing the boat, and already some kegs and barrels were being hoisted from the hold.

Spider pulled a belaying pin free from its slot.

"Nicholas, come with us," Abigail pleaded. "Don't be a fool. I am sorry. I do not . . . I never was in love with you, you know that. Even had my father approved, I would not have . . . been yours." She was whispering, aware of all the eyes and ears surrounding them. "But you have nothing to prove to me. I know you to be a good man."

"I shall remain with my command," Wright said.

"No, you will not," Spider said, clubbing the man with the belaying pin. Wright collapsed upon the deck like a dropped sack of grain.

"Get him in the boat," Spider ordered.

Abigail, horrified, stared at Spider.

"He is not dead," Spider told her, reading her expression. "I have just given him a nap. It's a trick I learned, never mind how."

She shook. "I thought you'd killed him, but you . . . This will save his life. We will take him ashore," she said. "He won't have to turn pirate."

"Not if they leave us be," Spider said. "But there is no guarantee of that. We shall have to be swift. See your father into the afterlife, quickly, then fetch your journal and quill." He looked toward the schooner, measuring its progress. "We should have time. I want to leave a message for these bloody bastards. I will need you to write it."

"A message?"

"Aye," he answered. "I hope to convince them they are better off taking the ship we are leaving them and not coming after us on the island. Go now."

"Yes," she answered, running off.

"Anne," Spider said. "Will you go below and fetch any frilly or pretty things you and our lass here have stored there? Sink them. We can't have these lads notice there were women aboard."

"When they discover me, it will be to their very great regret," she said, sounding more Irish than ever. "Some of them, anyway." She vanished.

Men brought forth Captain Brentwood's corpse on a plank and covered with the flag of England. Holystones, normally used for scrubbing the deck, and some spare metal weighted his sailcloth shroud so his body would be carried below. Spider had no doubt Captain Brentwood's soul had already risen above.

Fox and Down prayed as the small group walked to starboard. Abigail Brentwood gasped, ran to her father, kissed the flag draped over him, and wept as his body slid off the plank over the starboard rail. Men folded the flag, sloppily, for their attention was on the pirate vessels.

"We should dump him overboard, too," Odin said, pointing at Sam Smoke.

"No," Spider replied. "I think those bastards on the schooner will be expecting to find Sam, and I don't want to leave them wondering. Leave him where he is."

"Aye," Odin answered. "I like looking at him like this, anyway!"

Spider turned to address the crew. "We can't all go in the boat," he said. "If you can swim, do it. Some of you may even prefer to stay and throw in your lot with pirates. I do not recommend it. I think we will be a short time on the island. We will have food and water. The navy will come looking for us when we do not arrive in Boston, but we can send the boat and fetch help if we do not want to wait for that. But if you prefer piracy, so be it."

"I will stay," Anne said. "I have bloody work to do on that schooner." She led a trio of men carrying a trunk, presumably full of dresses and shawls and pretty hats. That went overboard with a great, heavy splash and sank readily. More holystones for weight, Spider figured.

Spider stared at Anne Bonny. Her eyes were harder than any stone. She was certainly bold. "It is a treacherous way to go, miss, staying aboard."

"I am a hard woman," she said. "There is a man over there, if the word 'man' fits him at all. I will kill him." She smiled. "I will kill him twice if I can."

Her calm certainty chilled Spider. "Is Ned Low really on that ship?"

"Probably," she said. "He is not the one I am after, though. Wicked

Pete Reese is going to die by my hand. The others can live if they leave me be."

Spider wondered if Captain Brentwood had died by her hand. Had she killed him and then manipulated things so as to reach her prey? Could she have done that? Anne Bonny was something of a legend on the Spanish Main, known for fierceness and fighting ability. But was she a schemer?

"Did you kill Captain Brentwood?" Spider hoped to shock her with the blunt question and gauge her reaction. She did not seem surprised at all.

"I kill when I must," she said. "And I had no reason to kill him. Nor can I walk through walls nor cast spells upon men to compel them to do my bidding, despite what you may have heard. Do you think I bewitched him? Made him shoot himself?"

"No," Spider answered while wondering if he was being bewitched right now. Sam Smoke obviously had intended to turn the ship over to Ned Low. Hob's notion that something special was hidden aboard seemed to fit well with that. Anne Bonny was a pirate, as was Sam Smoke. The two of them could have conspired to kill the captain and manipulate matters to lead *Redemption* into Ned Low's hands.

It was the best theory Spider had, but he needed to ask a couple of questions to confirm it.

"You and Smoke had a past, obviously," he said. "Did you ever sail on this ship before? *Redemption* used to be a pirate's vessel, I hear."

Anne sneered. "I am no part of whatever conspiracy you have concocted. I bought passage on this ship because I was following Sam Smoke, and he had already arranged his own passage. I knew him of old, but I never liked him and never trusted him. He is one of Ned's dogs, as is Wicked Pete, and I knew Sam would lead me to my revenge if I stayed on his heels, and I would have trailed him as long as it took. That is all. I had nothing to do with Brentwood's end."

Spider explored her face. She could be lying. She could be telling him the truth. Nothing in her expression indicated she cared at all what Spider thought.

"You should not stay aboard," he said, more in hopes of keeping his suspect close at hand than in any concern for her safety.

"I do as I please, and I will kill Wicked Pete Reese even if it means dying myself." Something brightened in her eyes. "I might have time for some fun before, though. You are not a bad-looking fellow, John."

Spider gulped. Was she trying to distract him or was she serious? That was his brain, though; another part of him was growing interested and did not care if this was a trap. "A bit scruffy, I'd say," he mumbled. "Missing a finger, you know." He raised his hand.

"It is not your finger I want," she said, winking.

Jesus, he thought. *I don't know whether to fuck her or shoot her.*

Spider nodded and turned to find Odin and Hob approaching. The latter was staring at Anne with adoring eyes. That tightened the growing knot in Spider's belly. He'd hoped his dealings with pirates were behind him, but here he was, riding the devil's wind again, looking for ways to avoid a fight, and doubting that was possible. Meanwhile, Hob was making puppy eyes at Anne Bonny.

"What is she laughing about?" Hob pointed toward Anne.

"Nothing," Spider answered. "She is just playing with me. I think." He pondered whether he could somehow contrive a means of knocking her unconscious and dragging her to the island. He could not rule her out as a suspect in the captain's murder. But she was on edge, keen to fight, and armed to the teeth. She probably could kick his arse too, if the legends were worth anything.

Hob waved at Anne and smiled.

Spider ran a hand through his sweaty beard. There was no way he could keep Anne Bonny nearby, he decided. If she turned out to be Captain Brentwood's killer, that crime would simply have to be added to her ledger one day when the law eventually caught up to her again, as it almost certainly would. Spider would have Abigail Brentwood write down his recollections and those of everyone else on board, and he would find a means of providing that testimony to the Admiralty without landing his own neck in a noose. Perhaps, one day, she'd pay.

He glanced at the spot by the rail where Captain Brentwood had been consigned to the waters and where Rufus Fox, the Reverend Down, and Abigail Brentwood still prayed.

Spider sighed deeply and looked at his friends. "Keep working, lads. I think I have something figured out and need to have another look."

Spider ran through the captain's cabin and stepped out onto the stern gallery. He ignored the doors this time and instead inspected the deck below his feet. He found what he expected, a black smudge, rather quickly. A sniff at the stained planks confirmed his suspicion.

"Damn me," he muttered. "Now that was clever. Clever, indeed."

24

"'*D*ear whore-pipe-licking spawn of a shit pile...' Fuck. No. Don't write that."

Abigail stared at Spider with wide eyes and high brows. "No. I most certainly will not write that."

Spider's gaze followed the schooner. "Sorry, miss. We might see action, and that always makes me a bit testy."

"Always? You've faced down pirates before?"

"Aye."

She blinked and assessed him as though seeing him for the first time. "Well, I suppose nervousness means we can make some allowances, but I really don't..."

"No, no. I'll find better words. Let me think. Very well. Let us try this. 'Dear Cap'n. A few of us have gone ashore, where we will never see your faces nor hear you called by any names.'"

"We know their names, I thought," Abigail said. "Wicked Pete something and Ned Low."

"Aye, but they do not need to know we know that. Keep writing and let us pray some fucker over there can read." Abigail scowled at his language again.

"Wicked Pete can read." That was Anne Bonny. "Do not use large words, though. Keep it simple."

Spider pressed onward. "Write this. 'We hope that going ashore demonstrates we have no desire to ever testify in an Admiralty court, or to any other court body, and we have took only enough supplies with us to help us survive until we be found by a friendly vessel, and when you look below you will find ample goods to reward your crew, and you have a fine ship to take with you as well.'"

Abigail sighed. "Slow down, please. I am not accustomed to doing this on a rolling ship." She was using the keyboard Rufus Fox built for her as a lap desk while she sat on a coil of rope. Spider had suggested using the desk in her father's cabin and then instantly regretted the thought when he saw the clouds in her eyes. So here they were now, swaying on anchors in the cove as *Redemption's* men loaded the boat and the schooner zigged and zagged among reefs to cut off all escape. Beyond the schooner, the other two vessels drifted. The pirates were deploying their small fleet well.

"I do not mean to rush, but we might want to be off the ship when the bastards over there come. . . ."

"I know that!" Abigail waved the enormous goose-feather quill at him in admonition, then dipped it into the ink jar. She held the bottle with her left hand and used it to guard one corner of the parchment from the wind while writing with her right hand and securing a bottom corner of the parchment with her forearm—all this while writing words with great loops and whorls that reminded Spider of leaves and petals. It was an awkward task, and Spider could not blame her if she was a bit growly.

Nearby, Hadley paced nervously, weapons still in hand. Tension was everywhere.

"Got your best tools, Spider John." Hob rushed by. Spider noted a pistol tucked into his belt at the small of his back.

"Good, Hob. We'll need sailcloth, too."

"Aye."

Abigail blew across the parchment. "There. I am caught up. Pray continue."

"Aye," Spider said. "Well, then . . ."

"And that last was something of a lengthy sentence, sir. I divided it up, considerably, into separate sentences. It flows much better."

"It ain't a goddamned poem," Spider grumbled, smacking his forehead. "I do not care if it flows, for the love of God." He laughed. "Just write what I say and chop it up and make it pretty as you think best as long as my words get in there."

"Yes," she said, glancing toward the pirate ship. "Continue."

Spider took a deep breath. "'As for this dead man here, he died after a bit of a disagreement with one of our hands over dice. He seemed to know you gents because he said he recognized the flag, so we leave him here to carry our peace message. . . .'"

"How will a dead man carry . . . ?"

"I am going to shove it in his mouth. They will find it. Write. 'So we leave him here to carry our peace message and so you may see to his passing into the next world as you might deem as proper. We wish no confrontation, and . . . and . . . I do not want to say beg. . . .'"

"Implore?"

"Aye, implore. 'We implore you do not come ashore. We will defend ourselves if we must, but trust you will see the wisdom in not taking up arms against us.'"

He paused. And waited as patiently as he could. She scratched out four or five words, dipped the quill in the black walnut ink, then dipped it again. It was like waiting for a goddamned sermon to end.

Finally, after what seemed an eon of scribbling, she looked up. "I have it all."

"Aye, that's good. Hand it here."

"The ink must dry."

"No time. It will have to do."

"No, wait." She corked the ink bottle and reached into the small sack beside her that held her writing tools. After a moment of fishing about, during which Spider was convinced the pirates would try a blast of grapeshot across *Redemption*'s deck even at a distance, she removed another jar. She bit off the cork and sprinkled the jar's contents across the note.

"Are you pouring a beach on it?"

She glared. "A tiny beach, perhaps. The sand blots up where the ink is too thick, keeps it from running all over the letter."

"It does not need to be beautiful."

She blew sand off of the document. "It needs to be legible. Here. Gently."

Spider took it, holding it by the top corners.

"Do not fold it or roll it," Abigail said. "It should dry quickly in this weather, I should think, but best to be cautious."

"Very well," Spider replied. He took the note, knelt by Sam Smoke's bleeding head, and held the letter with one hand while the other propped open the man's jaws.

"Horrid," Abigail muttered.

Spider placed the top edge of the letter into Smoke's mouth, then tipped his lower jaw up until the paper was clenched in his teeth. The jaw, partially broken from the man's fall, fell slack again, and the letter nearly blew away on a breeze.

"Shove it in his arse," Odin suggested.

Abigail sighed. "Such language."

"Honestly," Spider answered, "we have tried to speak more civilized than usual, considering polite company."

She lowered her head, and Spider could not tell if she was concealing a scowl or a laugh.

Odin chuckled. "All the stuff is loaded, by and by."

"Good," Spider said. "Powder?"

"Two small kegs. Not a lot."

"It will work. Now if I can just get this bastard's teeth to clamp properly..."

"Here," Odin said, pulling free one of the whalebone comb pins that kept his lanky hair from flopping in front of his one good eye. "Pin it with this."

"Thanks." Spider pinned the note to Sam's shirt, once he found a spot relatively free of blood. "There, then. Let us get off this bloody ship."

25

*E*ven drifting naked in the cove, wondering if it harbored sharks and dreading the thought that pirates might decide to start pelting them with cannon fire, Spider had to laugh.

Thomas, the chubby ship's cat, sat perched upon the goods loaded into the boat. *I reckon you're going to follow me around forever, hey, cat? And I should have paid you more attention in my rum-soaked haze, I suppose. Another clue I missed.*

Odin swam nearby. Some of *Redemption*'s men, a half dozen, were in the water with them; another dozen, including Hadley, the cook Lazare, and the two theologians, rode in the heavily laden boat with Abigail Brentwood. The rest had stayed aboard *Redemption*, and Spider was not surprised. A sailor's life was a hard one, with little reward, and the promise of supposed freedom lured many into life on the account. It was a false promise, Spider knew, but the fools would have to learn it themselves.

Abigail's disguise was good. Anyone looking at her from a distance would judge her to be just another sailor. That was Spider's hope, anyway. If the spy on the hill had seen the girl on *Redemption* earlier, however, the disguise was for naught.

Next to Abigail was the keyboard, which she had insisted on bringing despite Spider's objections. In her lap was the head of Captain Wright, still sleeping off the knock Spider had given him. Hob swam near the boat, speaking reassurances to Abigail and drawing an unhappy stare from Hadley.

Spider turned around to tread water every ten strokes or so to see the progress made by the pirates. They had not yet started the traditional hazing—the mad howling designed to instill horror in their victims—but they had twice fired a long gun. The balls had fallen far off from *Redemption* and were obviously not meant as an attack. The shots probably had been a signal to whoever was on the hill, or to Ned Low's other ships.

If the shots had been intended to inspire fear, the tactic had worked.

Spider cursed. He had too many things to think about. He forced himself to concentrate on the murder, for he felt he was finally on the right course on that score.

"I think I know how the captain was murdered," Spider said, drawing near to Odin, who was equally naked and drifting near him.

"Do you, now? Sam Smoke, I say."

"No."

"Was it a ghost? Ha!"

"No."

"Suicide, then."

"No."

A shark fin cut the water several dozen yards away and well behind them. It was a small fin, with a black tip, but where there was one shark, there were more. Spider wasn't worried about the sharks he could see. It was the ones he couldn't see that made his spine chill despite the heat.

Spider reminded himself he had never known a blacktip to attack a man, and there wasn't a bloody goddamned thing he could do about it anyway if they decided to feast. He decided to keep his mouth shut about sharks, figuring a commotion would cause more trouble than quietly going ashore.

"If not a ghost, and not himself, then who shot him?" Odin noticed the shark, too, but merely grinned. "Those things taste good. Let's kill one for dinner tonight. Anyway, we were all on deck when he was killed."

"Aye," Spider said. "Or so we thought. But maybe not."

Odin's grin vanished. "What now?"

"I still need to sort it in my head, now that it ain't all soaked with rum. I had drunk too much the night before, and I missed a couple of things, things that I realized when you shot Sam Smoke," Spider admitted. "You keep lecturing me when we are in tight spots, friend. You are right. Booze fogged my head when I needed it most."

"Ha!"

Spider glanced toward the boat. "Did we . . . ?"

"Yes, by God, we grabbed some rum. And wine. And ale."

"Did we bring water?"

"Don't know. Ha!"

Soon they were drawing up on a wet beach. Beyond the water's reach the sand was pristine, blinding white. Spider and Odin joined Hob at the boat, helped pull it up on the sand, and began gathering their clothes and weapons from within it. Abigail averted her eyes, blushing. Thomas leapt off and vanished into the woods that surrounded the clear blue cove.

"Spider's got it all figured out, who killed the cap'n," Odin whispered, tugging on his britches.

"Truly?" Hob turned wide eyes on Spider John. "It was Sam Smoke, right?"

"No," Spider said. He held his knife again in his hand and found that comforting. He tucked a pistol into his belt and thanked Hob with a nod. "I think I know how it was done, but I need to keep thinking to reckon out who did it. But one damned thing I do know. It was not Sam Smoke, damn him."

"Not Sam Smoke?"

"No," Spider said emphatically.

Odin pitched in. "Hob's pretty girl, Anne?"

"Perhaps," Spider said.

"I hope it wasn't her," Hob muttered. "I truly, truly do."

Spider took a peek toward *Redemption*, where Anne Bonny waited to murder someone. How goddamned convenient was it that the fluyt had carried her here, where she apparently wanted to be? Spider was not a big believer in coincidences. "It might have been her, Hob. Maybe. There is a good chance. I need to think, and for that, I need you two to stop pestering me."

"Aye," Hob said with an echo and a laugh from Odin.

"Drag the boat into the woods, gents," Spider said to the company at large, "and get Miss Brentwood hid. We don't want them to see her. Don't want them to see barrels or crates or kegs or anything they might decide is worth coming to get, and we want them to wonder if we're aiming guns at them if they try to come ashore. Anything that makes them think it might be worth the risk is bad; anything that makes them pause or guess is good. Lively, now! Odin, Hob, fetch those powder kegs and my tools."

Odin grinned at Spider. "When the hell did you decide to take command?"

"I am thinking I took command a few days too late."

"Ha!"

Spider watched men carry goods toward the woods. It gave him no small sense of satisfaction to see the crew put his orders into action. They were frightened and nervous, and because of that, they were grateful that someone was taking charge. Spider muttered a brief prayer: *Dear Lord, help me figure out what the hell to do.*

Rufus Fox and the Reverend Down carried Captain Wright between them, each with one of the man's arms draped behind his neck. Abigail Brentwood followed. Hadley stayed within arm's length of her, knife in hand.

Odin and Hob returned, each rolling a powder keg and Hob bearing a small toolbox. Spider pointed out two spots on the beach, told them what he wanted done, and started pulling nails from the box.

Once that operation was complete, the three followed the crew into the woods, moving along a small stream that ran between the hills. Sometimes the terrain forced them to wade, and the stream and the shade combined kept them mercifully cool.

"Look for a spot we can defend," Spider called ahead to Odin, who had taken the lead. The one-eyed man answered with a laugh. Spider hoped Abigail and the others were too far ahead to hear the sarcasm in that laugh.

As they trudged onward, with the cove vanishing from view behind them, Spider ran the suspects in the captain's murder through his mind.

He had already dismissed Sam Smoke as a suspect. So who then? Little Bob?

"Jesus," Spider exclaimed, halting abruptly. "Did anyone free Little Bob and his friends from the hold?"

He got nothing in reply but blank stares and a snort from Odin.

"Son of a bitch," Spider said.

"Pirates will find him," Hob assured him, "and he'll join up. Or they will kill him. Either way, no need for us to care. Little Bob is shit. And the bastards that helped him are shit, too, I say."

Spider rubbed sweat from his beard and wondered if he'd done Bob a favor in saving his life. A tumble overboard might have been better than whatever destiny awaited him at the hands of Ned Low. "Little Bob will have to see to his own fate. So, too, will Ames and Chambers. We have to see to ours."

Once he'd settled his mind on that, Spider ruled Bob out as a suspect in the captain's death. Bob had a motive, sure, because the captain had dismissed him from the ship. But Bob was not the clever sort, and this killing had been done by a clever person. A very clever person.

Spider looked at Rufus Fox. There was a clever man. A tinkerer, a builder. He'd made that clock, and Abigail's keyboard. He might well have plotted this crime, and Fox had been absent at the crucial moment—the *real* crucial moment, not the damned Bible reading—if Spider had parsed things correctly.

Time. Timing was crucial in committing this murder. Timing was key.

But did Fox have a motive? The captain was his friend. But the captain was suffering, mourning, and Fox was a spiritual, philosophical man. Perhaps he'd killed the captain and seen it as an act of mercy. Did he have that kind of grit?

Or did Fox have, perhaps, some other motive? Had the captain been an obstacle to courtship? Fox denied romantic feelings for Abigail, but his actions, and his expression when he looked at the girl, told another tale.

Spider shook his head. He wanted a drink, then remembered how drink had fogged his mind earlier. Somehow, that realization made him want a drink even more.

"Goddamn it," he muttered and determined to focus.

How about Nicholas Wright? Was he clever enough to have pulled off the crime? Spider did not think so. The man seemed unable to think of anything but Abigail Brentwood. He seemed more confused than anything since the murder, and although he had gained command with Captain Brentwood's death, he seemed concerned only with impressing the captain's daughter. A besotted fool, perhaps, but not likely a killer, in Spider's estimation.

Then there was Anne Bonny. She might be capable of anything. Could she have manipulated things to send *Redemption* toward her target? Had she led Nicholas Wright by the pecker and compelled him to do her bidding? She had known Sam Smoke, and that, perhaps, was crucial in committing this crime, too.

What about the Reverend Down? Could the man have been so incensed over the captain's preference for the theology of Rufus Fox that he would kill? That dour bastard would kill anyone if he could convince himself Jesus wanted it done. Spider was certain of that. Still, he doubted the reverend had the skills to have pulled off this crime.

Spider launched spittle into the air and cursed himself. He had an idea in his head, one that nagged at him, but he did not like it. He did not like it at all. And he was twisting things in his mind, tacking one way, then the other, trying to find a course that led anywhere except the conclusion he wanted to avoid.

His gaze fell on Abigail Brentwood and Rufus Fox, followed closely by Hadley, and he cursed softly.

A hand on his shoulder halted Spider's thoughts. "Good climbing tree here, Spider," Hob said. "I will go up and have a look, see what our pirates are about."

"Fine thinking, lad. Go!"

Hob was aloft swiftly. "They have anchored. Blocking the cove. They are sending a boat over to *Redemption*. A half dozen men."

"No more?"

"No more."

"Do you have a good view of the cove?"

"Aye."

"Stay up there. Raise an alarm if they look to come ashore."

Hob acknowledged the order and pulled a gun from his belt.

"You might better use both hands to stay in the tree, Hob."

"I know what I am about, Spider John."

Spider whistled low. "Everyone, hold up." He sighed and drew his gun and knife. There were trees and boulders here for cover and low, thick woods to either side of them. This was as good a spot as any to make a stand, even a futile one.

"If they come ashore looking for us, they most likely will follow our path. Too tough to walk through all that thorny stuff," he said, pointing to the banks as men put down their burdens. "Keep an eye; get your guns loaded if they aren't already. Odin, you are with me. We are going to take care of whoever is up on that hill. The rest of you, watch out, in case the bastards on the hill decide to take care of us. Listen for Hob; he's a good man and knows his way in a fight."

"Thankee, Spider!"

"You can thank me, Hob, by not doing anything rash."

Odin checked his guns, checked the knife and sword in his belt, and took a dirk from another fellow. A crewman brought Spider two more guns, but Spider gave one to Abigail Brentwood. "Aim for their chest or belly," he said. "Let them get close, because you've just got the one shot, and these things are no more reliable than a king's promise. Stick it right in his guts. It's your best bet."

She nodded and eyed the gun. Her jaw was set, and she inhaled sharply. "I know what to do with this," she said after a moment's contemplation. "Anne and I have talked."

Spider pointed to Captain Wright, who had been propped against a tree. "He will wake soon, I think. Wake him if he does not. We will need him if it comes to a fight. Don't let him do anything stupid."

She nodded again.

"His head will likely pound like a heavy surf in a thunder hole."

"I do not know what that means."

"Shores get undercut, tide comes in fills a hole, too much water and not enough hole, sounds like thunder when water gets forced out."

She shook her head.

"No matter. Cap'n's head will hurt, is all. But he is a tough man. He will work through it. And he'll see to your safety." He glanced at Hadley. "And so will that one."

"I know," Miss Brentwood said, nodding.

Spider turned to the one-eyed sailor. "Let's go, Odin."

They departed from the stream's path and climbed the northern-most hill, where Spider had seen the glinting light. They moved as quietly as they could, and Spider once again marveled at how strong and nimble Odin was, despite his age.

"What is your plan?"

Spider shrugged at the question. "Don't know. Might be one man up there, might be a few. Might be headed back to Ned's ship, might be staying on lookout. But I don't want whoever it is finding us before we find them, and I don't want them to spot a woman in our midst and go tell Ned about it."

"So, we kill them." Odin said it calmly, as though he was discussing the furling of a sail or the tying of a proper halyard hitch.

"Aye," Spider answered, though the thought made him sick. He'd dearly hoped that he'd never have to slit a throat again. "We do. I do not see another way. We can't spare a fighting hand to keep guard over a prisoner, if it comes to a tussle. This is war, when you think of it."

They ascended farther, careful to use the numerous gum trees for cover. The slope was gentle, and the summit not even a couple of hundred feet above sea level, but thick underbrush and the need for silence slowed them. They could not move silently, of course, in such a jungle. But Spider felt as though they kept the noise down to not more than a small animal might make. The constant din of birds provided some cover, too, or so he hoped. At least, he told himself that. Part of him wondered if the birds might pounce on them. *Fucking birds.*

Frequent stops to listen for an ambush or free a shirt from clutching thorns slowed them further. They both crouched low and drew guns when something rattled the low tree canopy, only to relax once they realized they had merely flushed a small flock of little yellow-and-black bananaquits. The whole damned island was thick with the birds, which chattered and squawked.

"I'd like to kill some of these fuckers and eat them," Odin whispered tersely.

"I thought you wanted to eat shark."

"I am hungry."

Spider took a deep breath. The flock's interruption had snapped the tension building within him.

"Quiet," he whispered. "We've got bloody work ahead."

26

$\mathcal{M}$oments later, Spider saw Odin freeze. The man's lone eye was fixed on something up the slope, and he crouched behind the cover of a gum tree.

Spider took cover himself before risking a glance through the fronds of a bright green fern. Above them, less than a hundred feet away, a dark-haired man slowly worked his own way down the hill. His hair was long and black, flowing from beneath a dingy white tricorn hat, and his complexion was that of bronze. He carried a blunderbuss in his left hand and used it to slowly push aside leaves and branches. A pair of pistols rode in a holster on his chest. From his belt hung a savagely long knife in a leather sheath, and in his right hand was a small axe, its blade painted in garish red and yellow.

This grim-looking fellow was far more successful in moving quietly through the underbrush than Spider and Odin had been.

If this man isn't an Iroquois, Spider thought, *I am not a carpenter.*

With agonizingly slow motions, Spider tucked away his gun and drew his throwing knife. A glance at Odin assured him his friend had reckoned the same thing, that this was work for blades, not gunpowder. They did not yet know how many men might be on this island, and there was no need to alert any of this stalker's friends that fighting had commenced. Gunplay would be foolish.

Odin held the cutlass low and behind him, lest any stray sunbeam sneak through the tree canopy and flash on the naked steel. His grin was that of a man who loved fighting too goddamned much.

As nearly as Spider could tell, the approaching man had not sensed their presence. If the Iroquois descended in a direct line, he would stumble right upon them. Spider used a few hand signals to convey his plan to Odin, and for once he was grateful for the lessons a pirate life had taught him. Odin crawled slowly to the right while Spider inched his way to the left. They would let the Iroquois move between them, and then they would pounce.

The Iroquois was not in any bloody hurry to die, though. He moved one foot at a time, stepping over downed branches and pausing after setting his foot down. His eyes pivoted back and forth and seemed dreamlike, focused on something beyond this world. The man was close enough now that Spider could see dark streaks smeared on his face, and the man had blackened his lips as well. When he turned his head, always crouching low to avoid inadvertently disturbing a branch, he revealed long bright feathers cascading from the back of his hat. It was like a waterfall made of a rainbow.

He must have a feather from every damned bird on the island, Spider thought. His mind suddenly filled with stories of his youth, about red men and their weird magic, and he hoped the bastard had not acquired the feathers as a means of controlling the damned birds.

At that very moment, every bananaquit on the island went silent.

Spider shut his eyes and fought off the sudden image of swirling feathers and scraping claws and piercing beaks. *Don't unman yourself, Spider John!*

A dozen feet away, the man held his pause longer than usual. He sniffed the air, and his eyes lost their dreamy quality. He propped the butt of his blunderbuss against his thigh and took aim at a target.

Odin.

Spider rose and threw his knife. The blade skewered a streak of black paint across the man's face, an inch or so below the eye Spider had aimed at, just as the gun belched its flame and smoke. Lead balls tore through the underbrush, and birds scattered in a mind-numbing chorus of screeches and screams.

Spider ducked involuntarily.

Odin, however, rushed forward, growling, on course for his target despite the gun's hazy smoke and the obscuring leaves. Spider forced himself to rise and saw the flash of Odin's blade—and an ugly streak of red on the one-eyed man's shirt.

The Iroquois uttered a hideous cry and swung his axe, but it got caught up in a low branch. He clubbed Odin with his gun; whether the blow had landed on Odin's head or shoulder, Spider could not tell. Odin tumbled aside but left his cutlass planted deep in his foe's thigh.

Spider was upon the man a heartbeat later, ducking as the painted axe arced at his neck. His shoulder met the Iroquois in the gut, and he propelled the man backward against a large stone. Wind left the Iroquois in a rush, showering Spider in blood from the man's bleeding cheek. The hilt of Spider's knife stuck out like a yardarm beneath the man's cheekbone. Spider thought to grab it, but Odin's cutlass was a better weapon. Spider snatched it free with a twist that made the Iroquois gasp.

Two quick slashes later, the Iroquois was dead.

"That was all a might louder than we planned," Odin said. "Ha!"

"I thought you were dead." Spider dropped the sword and pulled his knife out of the dead man's face.

"I sailed with Blackbeard, swam with sharks, busted heads in a whorehouse in Tortuga run by a witch," Odin said. "A little hot lead cutting my arm is nothing to worry about." Crimson stains lined a rip in his left sleeve, but his arm was steady, and the blood was not flowing. He had merely been grazed.

Spider breathed hard but managed a grin of sorts. "Is this how you survived all those years as a pirate, Odin? Blind luck?"

"Aye. And by fighting with men who aren't afraid of birds. Ha!" Odin gazed up the hill, smiling weirdly. "Fun, fun," he muttered in a singsong.

Spider glanced at the blunderbuss. "Damn." The stock had broken in the fall, and from the looks of it the damned thing had been cracked a long time and had been just waiting to give way. "This is good, though." He pointed to a wineskin on the dead man's belt. He grabbed it and pulled the cork free with his teeth, sniffed the contents, and was disappointed to find only a little water. He took a quick drink and tossed it toward Odin. Then Spider grabbed the painted axe and tucked it into his belt behind him, placed the throwing knife back into its spot on his belt, and pulled his guns free. "We do not seem to have drawn attention," he said.

"Not that I can tell," Odin replied, setting down one of his guns long enough to finish off the wineskin. "Fucking water. Did you say you knew who killed the cap'n?" He snatched up the dead man's tricorn and set it upon his own head before tucking the dead man's pistols into his own belt. Then he picked up his own gun.

"Aye," Spider said. "I have it down to a couple of suspects, at least. But let us make certain there is no one else up there before we talk about that. I suppose a quiet approach is rather pointless now."

"Aye." Odin picked up his cutlass and tucked it away.

They spread a few yards apart, aiming their guns ahead of them, and worked their way to the summit. As they neared it, odors of urine and shit assaulted them. Once they topped the hill, they found a small lean-to shelter, a fire ring of blackened stones around a mound of ash, and a sharpened stick with a burnt end. A small sack contained cheeses and bread, all of it smelling of mold. A small spyglass stood on its end near the fire ring, like a tiny lighthouse. "Does not look like a camp for more than one man," Spider said.

"Aye." Odin looked over the ocean. "Nice view from here. Don't see any other ships but ours and Ned's."

Spider grabbed the spyglass and took a look. The schooner and its companion vessels commanded the entrance to the cove now, and helpless *Redemption* still rode anchor. A boat was tied to *Redemption*, but no other boats were in transit. There was no sign that the pirates had sent anyone ashore.

"I hope they don't come looking for their hilltop spy," Spider muttered.

"I wouldn't," Odin said. "He doesn't have nothing valuable up here. Not even whiskey. I like this hat, though. Makes me look like a pirate."

Spider wished he could make out what was transpiring on *Redemption*, but he could only determine that people moved about on deck.

He could not discern faces, nor hear voices. That was good, he realized after a moment, for *Redemption* was as close to this spy's nest as she'd ever been, and if he could not make out faces, then perhaps the Iroquois had not been able to do so, either. Maybe the bastard had not known there was a girl and had not signaled that knowledge to anyone peering at him through a spyglass from Ned's ship.

Spider tucked the spyglass into his belt. It was uncomfortable now, what with the addition of the axe and now the spyglass, but it was a damned nice spyglass, and he'd always wanted one. "I think we got lucky, Odin. They may not have figured out about Miss Brentwood, that is, if no one aboard *Redemption* opened his fool mouth. I don't think anyone aboard is mean enough for that, do you?"

"No. Well, Little Bob, maybe. He's shit. Now who killed her father?"

"Let's get back to the others," Spider said. "I will tell you what I think on the way, and you can tell me if drinking too much kill-devil has turned my brain to chowder. If you think me right, we shall have some justice."

27

"Thank God," Rufus Fox exclaimed. "We heard a shot." The man was heating water over a campfire.

"We had a tense moment or two," Spider said. "We don't think anyone else is on the island now. Gather around." He called up into the tall palm. "Any sign of pirates coming ashore?"

"Hell, yes," Hob answered, dropping out of the tree. "Six men, pistols and cutlasses, rowing ashore this bloody instant!"

"Fuck and bugger." Spider wiped sweat from his brow. "I reckon it would be too goddamned much to suppose they be waving a white flag of truce?"

"They be waving the guns and swords," Hob said. "We ought to wave a few of our own."

Spider sighed. "I just want to go home, goddamn it." Then he spat. "Well, then. We have a fight on our hands, and not a lot of weapons. Odin, Hob, grab anything you can kill with and come with me. Fuck, grab a brand from the fire, too, each of you. Go!"

Odin set the dead Iroquois's pistols on the ground. "Those are primed and ready, for anyone needing one."

Spider turned to the others. "Arm yourselves, sharpen some goddamn branches if you have to. Douse the fire and take cover. Do what you can."

"Just you three going to meet the pirates?" Lazare, the cook, brandished a long knife.

"We have . . . done this sort of thing before," Spider said softly. "Miss Brentwood, wake Mister Wright, gently. . . ."

"He awoke once," she said. "He was disoriented, and I bid him sleep some more."

"Well, wake him again, and explain to him what is happening. He will be groggy. Give him some strong drink. You might need to pour some on his face. But wake him. He is a strong man, and we will need him for this fight."

She nodded. "Take Hadley with you. You are outnumbered, and he is a brave fellow."

Spider looked at Hadley. "You can come with us, too. I'll give you an axe."

"I will stay with Miss Brentwood."

Spider handed him the Iroquois axe. "Very well, then."

Spider turned to follow Hob and Odin, who were already headed to the beach.

"Should you not wait for Nicholas?" Abigail's voice was high and quavering.

"Fuck no," Spider hollered. "No time to spare! Keep him here and let him protect you!"

Spider's legs were not long, but he was fast and agile. He caught up to his friends quickly. They splashed in the creek, Hob and Odin holding their burning sticks high to avoid the water, the rush of air stoking the torches brighter. Spider drew knife and pistol. They ran as fast as they could, without a thought of sneaking, for everything depended upon them reaching the beach before the pirates came too far inland.

The bright sky opened up before them as they neared the edge of the shady woods, and they slowed their frantic pace. A few steps farther and they dove for cover behind trees and boulders, Odin and Hob veering to the left and right. Spider, breathing heavily, uttered a silent thanks. They had made it, and his companions were now crawling toward the spots from which they would spring the trap Spider had devised.

The pirates, six of them, reached the sand. Two of them leapt ashore, crouching with guns ready, eyes peering into the woods. The rest hauled the boat ashore quickly, then turned it broadside and upside down. Then all six men took cover behind the boat.

They had done it quickly and efficiently. *Fuck*, Spider thought, *this might not be so easy.*

Everyone waited, and Spider's heart drummed like a beat to quarters. He wondered if the pirates would notice the thin curling smoke rising from the brands Hob and Odin held in their hiding places. He glanced about and decided they could not have noticed the thin trails of powder leading across the beach; those were concealed nicely behind the mounds of sand that covered the two buried powder kegs. *If only the bastards would come nearer before the goddamned brands go dead. . . .*

Gulls circled, their cries ripping the air. Out in the cove, a bell rang on one of the ships. Spider clenched his teeth and hoped at least one of these men coming to kill him had tobacco or a flask. He craved both and knew he'd desire them more after the fight, if he still lived.

A swarthy fellow with a red scarf tied about his head leapt over the boat and started coming forward. He crouched low, a pistol in each hand and a goddamned battle-axe strapped across his back. Slowly, he crept.

The man with the axe did not get shot, so the other five went over or around the boat and started forward. Confident now, they broke into a slow trot, weapons ready and murder in their eyes.

Spider nodded at Hob, then Odin. Both grinned in reply. They knew what to do next and, unlike Spider, looked forward to the action to come.

Odin and Hob lit the powder trails leading from their hiding places to the hidden bombs. It was a race now. Would the pirates notice the burning powder in time to duck low and avoid the worst of the carnage? Spider, willing himself to remain planted in his hiding place, shook his head. Probably not. And the only real cover was the boat they'd left behind.

Fire and sparks raced toward the buried kegs. The pirates came onward. Small twisting pillars of smoke rose, darkening as they danced toward the buried kegs, and the swarthy bastard with the battle-axe pointed with a gun and cried an alarm.

"Trap!"

Hell, yes, it's a trap. Spider inhaled sharply. *It's a nasty goddamned pirate-killing trap.*

The pirates dove toward the hot sand but not soon enough. The kegs, one to either side of the approaching marauders, exploded in lightning flashes of bright orange and yellow, bellowing thunder. Spider ducked behind his tree, for he knew the nails would fly far.

Once they'd covered the kegs with sand, in spots close to the trees so the spy on the hill could not see what they were up to, Spider had grabbed a couple of sacks of nails from his tool kit and given them to Hob and Odin. They'd packed the sharp bits of metal into the sand covering the kegs, the nails ready to fly with musket ball speed once the ignition came. Those nails, along with splinters from the demolished kegs, chewed up the rushing pirates like grapeshot ripping sails. Flying metal streaked through the air, shedding blood that resembled the tails of tiny comets. A flying spike gashed the trunk of the very tree Spider crouched behind, then whistled into the underbrush behind him.

"*Redemption!*" Hob rushed forth, gun and sword in hand, even before the smoke cleared. Spider and Odin leapt forth from their hiding places and joined him, ducking low to see beneath the black-and-white smoke roiling across the sand. Odin's feather-adorned hat, taken from the Iroquois they'd killed, fluttered to the ground.

Spider took in the carnage, men streaked with blood and faces ripped, before plunging his knife into the neck of a poor bastard who tried to rise. Knowing that fellow would die any second, Spider shot another wailing pirate whose arm lifted a pistol aimed at Odin. The man's back erupted in red, and the banshee howl died with him.

"Ha!" Odin charged toward the swarthy man with the battle-axe who rose, staggering, with two red-dripping nails protruding from his shoulder. The man lifted his axe, and Odin fired both of his guns.

The man fell and twitched in the hot sand as Odin pounced on the axe. "Ha!" The crazy one-eyed bastard then rushed toward a lanky fellow trying to get up. A quick sweep of the axe and that man was nearly decapitated.

Spider, choking on smoke, spun like a dervish. "Hob!"

Spider need not have worried. Hob was neatly slitting one man's throat while another lay quite obviously dead nearby. That poor soul had taken the brunt of one explosion, and his face, full of nails, looked like a red pincushion.

Hob looked up, saw Spider, and grinned. "Look, Spider John! That fucker's arm blew ten feet away!"

"Aye," Spider said. "Aye." He dropped to the sand, breathing hard, and clutched at Em's pendant. *Jesus*, he thought. *Let these be the last men I kill.*

With no one left to fight, Hob and Odin joined Spider on the sand. "I am keeping this axe," Odin said. "Goddamn, I love this!"

"Can I have your cutlass then? We showed them, didn't we?" Hob did not notice his right bicep was bleeding.

"Did they get you, boy?" Spider rose to examine the wound.

"Splinter or nail from our trap. Those ugly shit-eaters did not touch me!" Hob nodded as Odin gave him the sword.

"I'll be wanting that back, Hob."

"Aye, thank you!"

Spider glanced toward the schooner. "There's more ugly shit-eaters over there," he said. "And there is no way they didn't note what happened here."

"Those kegs were fucking loud! Ha!" Odin rose and danced, sweeping his new axe through the air.

"Brilliant idea you had, Spider John." Hob nodded. "Bloody brilliant."

Spider looked at the dead men lying around him. "I wonder how many of these gents wished they could leave piracy behind before they came to such a bloody end. I do not feel brilliant, Hob. I am weary of this."

"We live, and they don't." Hob saluted Spider. "That is all I fucking need to know. Sir."

"Let's get under cover. Yon schooner might hurl cannon balls at us any moment." Spider peered across the sea, expecting to see guns being run out. Instead, he saw another boat plying the waters—and it was flying a white flag.

"What?" Hob exclaimed. "They give up?"

"They fear my axe! Ha!"

"That fellow standing in the rear," Spider mused, pointing, "has long red hair."

"Hell, that's not a fellow," Hob said.

"No," Spider replied. "It's Anne Bonny."

28

"Run, Hob, and warn the others. I am all out of tricks." Spider tried to slow his rapid breath. The scent of burnt powder lingered, and a stream of smoke now and then stung his eyes.

"I count six, aside from her, Spider." Hob held a steady hand against his forehead to shield it from the sun. "They are waving a white flag, but even if it is a lie, I still think we can take them."

"Well, you are bloody wrong," Spider growled. "We are out of powder and already tired from fighting. I am tired, anyway. And I do not trust that woman there; I surely don't."

Hob started to speak but kept quiet for a moment. "Aye, Spider," he answered reluctantly. "What message for the other castaways?" He tucked Odin's sword into his belt.

"Tell them what happened here and what's coming. Tell them to crouch and hide, ready to ambush. And tell them Odin and me aren't likely to stop these bastards if they are intent on killing. The best we might be able to do is slow them down, delay them. Make sure Miss Brentwood hears that. We can't stop them. Go now."

"Aye," Hob said. "But I am coming back."

"Come back quiet," Spider ordered. "And with a primed pistol or two. Maybe we'll need a surprise on our side."

"Aye." Hob ran off.

"So, what do you think we ought to do, Spider John? I am out of guns, but I can swing this goddamned thing." Odin's new axe cut the air between them, and he buried the blade in the hot sand. "Line the bastards up for me; I'll lop off three heads in a single stroke!"

He pulled the axe head from the sand and kissed it tenderly.

"I deem you a friend, Odin," Spider said, "but you scare me near to pissing my britches."

"Ha!"

Spider eyed the approaching boat and reached toward the belt of the nearest dead man. He found a flask and a pouch of leaf. "Well, then."

Spider took a deep swig, delighted to discover the flask contained good Porto. He sighed with satisfaction and tossed the pewter flask to Odin. Then he pulled his pipe free, stuffed it with the dead man's tobacco, and looked about for a burning keg shard to light it. In a moment he had it going, and two deep draws later he almost felt as if he could relax. "I aim to ask that lady some questions, and I will talk and talk and talk to give our friends in the woods as much time to arrange a defense as possible."

He palmed the hilt of his throwing knife, tucking the sharp blade up along his forearm and concealing the hilt behind his hand. "And I aim to sell my life dear if they decide to fight. They might be of a mind to avenge these bastards."

Odin nodded. "They will find us tough to kill, goddamn it. You are a damned good man, Spider John. Fine as any." Odin turned his eye toward the oncoming boat. "Don't know why they would avenge these useless louts, though. Ain't worth it."

"We shall see what we see. Be ready for anything."

The boat approached the sand, and Anne Bonny leapt out with a splash. She strode through the water, smiling widely, and waved at Spider as the men accompanying her pulled the boat up next to the one already on the beach. One of those men planted the white flag's pole into the sand with a heavy thunk.

Truce flag or no, Spider remained alert.

Anne Bonny had a sword and guns in her belt, but her hands were stretched out as though she was preparing to hug someone.

Spider's grip on the knife tightened.

"Well, John, you looked better to me before you drenched yourself in other men's blood—but that has a certain appeal, too, I dare say." She winked. "How came you to be such a mess? From what I saw, yon dead fellows here nary put up a fight."

She waved her hands over the scattered dead, as though she were asking a theatrical troupe to take a bow. Then she leaned forward, scooped a wickedly bent nail from the sand, and grinned. "Lovely little trap you set up."

She tossed the nail behind her.

"We were outnumbered, so we tilted the scales a bit."

"Indeed. I saw the bombs go off. Nicely done." Meanwhile, her men looked as though they wanted a little violence.

Spider bowed. "We always aim to give a good account of ourselves."

Anne Bonny looked at him as though she expected more.

"Are we going to have a dispute, Anne, over the bloodshed here? Over Sam Smoke?"

"You need not worry, John." Anne glanced around at the carnage. "These poor souls were sent to their fate by Pete Reese, not by me. I'd have had the good sense and forethought to have warned them about potential traps, were they my men. But they knew there might be opposition, and they knew every day on the pirate account might be their last. May God bless them, or damn them, as he pleases. Or the devil take them, for that matter. It is not my concern."

Anne laughed, and Odin roared along with her.

"They had a spy on the hill, an Iroquois, I think. And what of Sam Smoke? I know you did not care for him, but your lads here—Pete's men, I presume, don't recognize them from *Redemption*—might be in a vengeful mood." Spider measured the distance he'd have to throw his knife to take down the nearest fellow with ready guns while Odin sidestepped to the left, knuckles whitening as he gripped the haft of his axe.

Anne shrugged. "The lookout is unknown to me, and these men are no longer Wicked Pete's. They are mine." She turned to the men who had accompanied her. "Do any of you wish to avenge the lookout?"

Indifference was the only answer.

"There you have it," she said. "As for Sam Smoke, no one on the high seas had any love for that vicious cock save for Wicked Pete Reese, and he is in no position to avenge anyone. Ever."

Spider nodded, glad to feel his muscles loosen and his breath come easier. "You seem to be in far better standing than I would have expected, Anne." He sucked from the pipe and blew a great cloud out of the side of his mouth. "How do you come to be still alive?"

Her men formed up in a crescent behind her, and Anne grinned. "Wicked Pete Reese welcomed me with a smile. He was still smiling at the very end. I killed Pete without so much as a hello. Cutlass, right straight up through his crotch."

Her eyes danced when Spider winced.

"Then once across his throat for good measure. I think it best to be thorough." She winked.

Spider cleared his throat. "And Ned Low?"

"Ned Low, alas, was not with them," she answered. "Ned is still out there somewhere, roaming the sea. He gave Pete command of these ships. I have no business with Ned and hope to avoid him. Anyway, once I had given Reese exactly what he fucking deserved—I had intended to keep his head as a souvenir, but you may have seen one of my overeager gents toss it overboard . . . no?—well, my business with Pete concluded. I planned to implore these good fellows to take me in as one of their crew, but it turned out that this gent"—she pointed behind her toward a scarecrow of a man, naked to the waist and grinning like a clown—"knew me of old. Didn't you, Sundog?"

"Yes, yes, Cap'n." The man stared at her like a puppy. For a moment Spider thought the man might lick her hand.

"And Koro here remembered me fondly, too, did you not, dear?"

A hard-eyed fellow, with four pistols in a bandolier and earrings that appeared to be made of human finger bones and gold, nodded.

"So, then, Sundog and Koro, knowing my abilities and prowess, put it forth to the crew that perhaps I should be their new captain. And so now yon schooner, *Madeleine Robin*, is mine to command."

The pipe fell from Spider's jaw, and he caught it in his free hand. The other hand still hid the knife, and he half expected to need it. "If you have no ill will toward us, will you take us off the island? Provide passage?" A vision of Em, smiling brightly as he splashed ashore from a boat at Nantucket, filled Spider's mind.

"No."

Spider blinked. "But . . ."

"I said no. I have another man to kill in Nassau, and so my business is there."

"You might take *Robin* to Nassau and let *Redemption* or one of the other ships go north," Spider said. "There is much good hunting north." He bowed slightly, in what he thought might be the proper gesture of a courtier to a queen.

"You daft lobcock!" Anne laughed. "I worked and killed for this, and I damn well will enjoy the fruits of my labor. I wish to keep yon *Redemption* for my own. She is a fine, fine ship. I'll not send her to Boston. I will sail her to Nassau and perhaps swing my prey from her yardarm. And the lads aboard yon *Thorn* and *Dark Treasurer* have plans for raiding already, and they are good plans; I approve heartily. My new crews and I shall profit greatly. And I must keep in mind Ned Low, of course. Should our paths cross, he might take the unreasonable position that all these ships are his, not mine. I will need my ships, should that occur. I shall need manpower, too, I dare say."

Spider nodded and sighed. "Aye."

"You have shown yourself to be a man, John." Her gaze traveled up and down his lean body. "Resourceful. I adore that trick with the powder kegs. Capital thinking, that. And you don't frighten easily. I watched your face when Sam Smoke had a gun to your head. You were steady, calm. And you got your knife into his neck damned quick. I could use you, and your friends, too. I have a burgeoning new fleet, and I believe in strength in numbers."

Spider said nothing, but his mind raced. The last few years he'd spent on the pirate account flooded his thoughts. All the bloodshed. All the fear of being caught, of being hung. He could not return to that. He could not.

"I mean to say you are welcome in my crew, John. You might find it to your liking." She reached for her right breast, cupped it a moment, then brushed back a cascade of red hair.

No, he thought. *Not a bloody chance.*

Spider blinked. "I, uh . . . I have a wife and a boy."

Anne winked. "So?"

Spider scratched his head. *Is she trying to keep me off-kilter? Is she about to shoot me? Or stab me?*

Nervous, he stuttered onward. "I just want to see them. Her. Her and the boy. Little Johnny. Seven or eight, he must be. I ain't seen him or her since he was a baby."

"Seven or eight?" She licked her lips. "You must have been quite young when you fathered him."

"Aye. Aye." *Quite young, indeed,* he thought. Em had been his first, and she'd needed to show him what to do, even. Em was the only one who had mattered.

Anne Bonny stepped closer, nearly touching him, and stared into his eyes. Spider wanted to stop talking, but he couldn't. "We married, me and her. Em. Emma. She and me. Quiet, but we married. Her father is a preacher."

"Let me guess." Anne tickled Spider's crotch. "You got her with child, first, and then married her. Aye? Her father encouraged you to go to sea, to support your little family."

"Aye." Spider stepped backward, but Anne just stepped forward.

"And you are convinced she has spent all this time, all these years, pacing a widow's walk, watching the horizon for your triumphant return? How precious, that!"

"I do not believe . . ."

"And you've been chaste all this time?"

Spider felt himself growing hard. "No. I mean, well, no. There have been times . . ."

"There can be more times," she whispered. "Join my crew."

Spider backed away. "I have reasons to be elsewhere in the world, Cap'n. Sorry."

"Very well," she said, mocking him with a frown. "John is a saint. So then, how many in your company?"

"I think, um, I mean, I believe, about twenty. Not quite two dozen, surely." Spider glared at Odin, who kept looking back and forth between Spider and Anne and grinning like a madman.

"Very well." She tilted her head in thought. "You have your boat, and I shall leave you one of mine, for I like you, John, even if you won't join my crew. I will take on any who will come, provided they know they must fight if called upon, and any of your lot that won't throw in with me may take those boats and go where they please. Nassau or the Turks, or Jamaica. Anywhere you please. And I shall wish them well. And you."

Spider nodded.

"You may not even need to reach a port," Anne continued. "I imagine that handsome fellow Price might yet be out there looking for *Redemption*. Or, more likely, for pretty young Abigail."

"Could be the navy is looking for us," Spider said.

"You should join me, John. I may just become the scourge of the high seas."

Spider sighed. "No, Cap'n. I lived the pirate life a few years. I am done with it. I will not speak for all our company, but I will not go with you, even if I must remain here alone."

"Well then, bathe, John. I may yet have you work off the cost of the boat." She winked again. Odin laughed and punched Spider on the arm.

Hob rushed out of the island shade. He had a gun, but it was tucked into his belt. "So it all seems well, then?" His glance went back and forth between Anne Bonny and Spider, and he seemed quite concerned.

"I doubt we deserve such luck, but aye," Spider said. "It all seems well."

Hob bowed to Anne. "Congratulations on your captaincy, miss. I overheard. I was waiting in secret, lest we needed a surprise attack!"

"How courteous, and that was an excellent strategy, sir," she said quietly. "You are well formed." She stepped toward Hob and grasped his bicep. "Strapping, aren't you?"

"Aye, and not half as blood-smeared and sweat-soaked as Spider John."

"Spider John?" Anne rubbed her chin. "I heard that name in Port Royal. You killed a naval officer, I believe."

"So they say," Spider answered, glaring at Hob.

"Well, then," Odin said. "If no one here is going to kill anyone, or screw anyone, can you finally tell us all who killed the goddamned cap'n, Spider John? You had it narrowed down, as I recall."

"Do you still think I killed him?" Anne asked.

"I cannot help but notice you arrived exactly where you wished to be, where you could kill Wicked Pete." Spider's fingers prepared for a knife throw. "Not certain that would have happened without the cap'n's death, and I hate coincidences."

"Koro, Spider John has a knife hidden in his hand. Kill him if that hand moves."

Koro drew two pistols. "Aye, Cap'n."

"I think you should drop the knife, John." She cooed the words, as though she were asking him to buy her a pretty hat.

Spider dropped the knife into the hot sand.

"Spider John, know this. I followed Sam Smoke, because I knew that he eventually would lead me to Wicked Pete. I did not kill Captain Brentwood. If I had, I would have done so openly, and I would have dared you or anyone else to do anything about it. I do not pounce like an eel hiding in a reef. I approach openly, blade and gun in hand. When I kill a man, I want the whole bloody world to know it."

"You did not kill the cap'n, then convince poor Nicholas Wright to come this way?" Spider could easily imagine how she might have won the young man over.

"No, Spider, I surely did not. Wright is a finely built man, and I enjoyed turning his head, but if anyone led him to these waters it was Sam Smoke, not me."

"Hmm." Spider drew hard on the pipe. "I thought it possible you killed him to arrange all this, yes, but now . . . I am thinking it would not be your way of doing things. I do not believe you killed the cap'n."

Spider grabbed the flask of Porto from Odin. He took a deep swig and dropped the empty vessel on the beach. "Very well. Hmm."

He popped the pipe back in his mouth.

"You seem confused?" Anne's brows arched above fine eyes.

"Aye," Spider said, bending to pick up his knife, slowly, while Anne told her men the danger had passed. He tucked the knife into his belt. "I am wondering why you came ashore, if not to avenge these dead men. You could have sailed away and left us to rot. Your coming ashore seems, I think, unnecessary."

Anne smiled. "I came ashore because I figured it out, Spider. I know who killed the captain! And I like the girl enough to want to tell her." She batted her eyes. "Perhaps she will reward me."

"That is all, nothing more?"

"You are a suspicious bastard, Spider John."

"Aye. Let us rendezvous with the others, then. Hob, you go ahead and tell them it is safe, so they do not fucking shoot us. And we'll all gather and find out who killed the good cap'n."

29

"Good, everyone. All is good. The danger, I believe, is past."
Spider urged them out of hiding. Thomas the cat was first,
rushing to Odin and rubbing against the man's wet, bloody britches.

Anne Bonny and company, at Spider's suggestion, stood with out-
stretched arms, and Koro waved the white truce flag. Still wary, the castaways from *Redemption* kept weapons to hand, and all gazes remained
fixed on Anne's dangerous-looking fellows.

Spider took a position in the center of their makeshift camp on the
stream's southern bank. The campfire was still going, despite Spider's
earlier order to extinguish it, so he refilled his pipe and lit it.

Abigail, slowly shaking her head, broke the uneasy silence. "Anne,
these men with you . . . what is happening here? Tell me, please, as my
declared friend."

"These men answer to me, and you need not worry, Abigail." Anne
turned slowly, drawing a pistol from her belt. "I like you, dear girl, and
no one who answers to me shall hurt you. This, I swear. Indeed, there is
but one person here who needs to fear me, and that is the person who
killed your father."

Spider heard a few gasps.

Anne strode toward Abigail, halted abruptly, and whispered, "I
know the man who did it, girl!"

Abigail shook. "Who?"

"That bastard right there!"

Anne Bonny lifted her pistol and took aim at Rufus Fox.

Bloody hell, Spider thought.

Spider's shoulder collided with Anne's belly just as she fired, and the errant ball ripped leaves from trees. Spider and Anne rolled on the ground, and once he'd untangled himself from her he looked up into the barrels of six guns, all wielded by Anne's men.

"Hold your fire, gents," Anne ordered, though she glared at Spider.

Odin, on the perimeter, held a gun in each hand and swept both weapons back and forth, making sure each of Anne's men felt like a potential target. Hob drew a pistol, too.

Thomas scurried into the brush.

"Yes, wait!" Spider held his open hands up and rose slowly. "Let us hear the case! If your cap'n proves his guilt, you can all shoot Fox! But let us hear the case!"

Once he determined no one was going to shoot him this instant, he picked up the pipe and stuck it in his mouth.

"I will prove it," Anne said, rising. Her men lowered their guns. She looked at Spider and winked. "You may be as quick a man as I have ever seen. If I do not end up killing you over this, you still might be of use on my crew."

Spider nodded. "Just tell us why you think Rufus Fox killed Cap'n Brentwood."

"He could not have," Abigail whispered as her gaze shifted across the ground. "It is not true."

"I have killed no one!" Fox threw his hat in anger. "This charge is preposterous!"

"Present your case, Cap'n." Spider kept his gaze on Fox, and his fingers near the throwing knife.

"When Abigail persisted in her belief that her father had not taken his own life," Anne told them, "I began to believe it, too. She knew him best of anyone in the world, and the man she spoke of, I believe, would not have killed himself."

"He most certainly would not have done so," Abigail said.

"I could not figure why anyone would kill the man, though," Anne continued. "He seemed a decent sort. Then I thought maybe that bastard Sam Smoke did it. That useless son of a whore would kill anyone and would need no reason at all. He liked watching men die.

But it could not have been Sam, could it? Sam does not have the cleverness to kill a man in a locked room and make it look like a suicide. He simply doesn't. And once I came to that conclusion, I thought of other objections. I supposed Sam Smoke would be unable to have committed the crime without torturing the captain. He'd never have been able to resist cutting him, making him beg. This killing was done with one quick, clean shot to the head. That is not the way Sam Smoke ever killed anyone."

Anne smiled, pleased to have everyone's attention. Spider noted Hob, gazing stupefied.

Anne continued. "If Smoke was not the killer, then, who might have done it? I could see no reason in it. But then I noted how much attention Fox had lavished on Abigail. How he always seemed to be looking at her. How maybe the captain was an obstacle in his suit for the girl's hand, and how he might feel she had nowhere else to turn if that obstacle was removed."

"Of all the monstrous . . ." Fox looked as though he wanted to scream, but his words caught in his throat.

"And you are a clever man, too, are you not?" Anne slowly drew another pistol. "You are good with tools. If anyone could make a contraption to shoot the captain in his own cabin, I figure, it had to be you." She aimed at Fox's chest. "Shall I kill him, Abigail? Or would you prefer to pull the trigger yourself?"

Spider gulped and stepped between the gun-wielding woman and the nervous Quaker. "Is that all of your evidence?"

Anne laughed. "What more is needed?"

"Well, let me tell you some things I noticed," Spider said as calmly as he could. "Then we can decide whether to shoot this man, or shoot someone else."

"You think I am wrong, Spider John?"

"Perhaps, Cap'n. Hear me out." He turned toward Abigail. "I told you I would try to sort this all out. I believe I have. Will you hear me out?"

She nodded.

Spider looked at Anne. "One big objection to your idea is that the cap'n had a gun in his hand and a note on his desk. Do you think Fox arranged all that through the grating?"

She blinked. "Well . . ." She lowered her pistol. "Very well. Speak, John."

Spider cleared his throat. "Miss Brentwood. You said you did not believe your father had killed himself, and I believe you."

Abigail looked confused. "Yes. I am sure he would not have taken his own life."

Wright groaned with pain. Abigail returned to sit by him and wiped his damp forehead. Wright, plopped up on a blanket, took her hand. Abigail shook her head. "Father would not do that. He thought suicide to be a mortal sin, a coward's way out, and about the worst thing one could do with God's gift. But we know he did not kill himself. Do we not? It was that horrible Little Bob. John reckoned it all out. Bob hated my father. He killed him, I am certain of it. It was just like you described earlier, John. Bob hid in the clock and killed my father."

"Little Bob did not kill him," Spider said. "Bob's a hateful, spiteful wretch, but he isn't clever enough to have murdered your father. He's dull as a turtle, can barely remember how to shit."

"It required no special cleverness, I should think," Fox said tersely. "Bob hid in the cabin. Perhaps in the clock, or in an empty trunk. He was a small man, could hide almost anywhere. He fired the fatal shot; then he hid and snuck out later."

"That's a clever thought," Spider said, looking Fox in the eyes. "And I considered it, too. Eyed the cabin myself, looked at the clock. I opened it up, too, fully expecting to find Little Bob Higgins hiding inside. He wasn't."

Fox objected. "Perhaps you looked too late."

"Perhaps," Spider said. "But I do not think so. It is not easy sneaking about on the deck of a ship, men everywhere, and Little Bob could not blend into a crowd. He was a very small fellow, and we all knew him. He'd stand out, wouldn't he? It'd be like a tuna in a pile of squid."

"Stilts," Fox said.

Spider laughed, despite the tension. "Stilts?"

"Indeed," Fox said, his brow creasing and his head weaving about as he thought. "I have seen them at circuses; they make a man double or triple in height, perhaps more. Bob might have used such to blend in. A long coat, I dare say, and he could appear to be a man of a normal stature."

The Reverend Down stood next to Fox, looking dubious. "I believe that wretch Higgins killed the captain, Mister Fox, but this . . . this theory of yours, it sounds as preposterous as your views on the epistles. Stilts? I do not believe it would work. A long coat, for instance, in this climate? I think that should have drawn attention. And stilts on a rolling deck, I think, would be very difficult, even for a veteran sailor." The preacher smirked, appearing to enjoy having the upper hand against Fox in a debate on any topic.

"Nor do I think stilts were involved," said Spider.

"Little Bob could not walk from the mainmast to the forecastle without starting a fight with someone," Hob declared.

"That's gospel, Hob." Spider drew hard on the pipe, then blew out a long stream of smoke. "No, sorry, Mister Fox. I worked with Little Bob long enough to know he isn't so smart, nor so agile, as all that. You will not convince me he managed it, not if you swear on a Bible."

Fox grinned nervously and spread his hands. "Well . . ."

"You are a clever man, sir, and you can't help but try to figure out how things work and how to solve problems." Spider took a couple of steps toward Fox. "Tell me this. The cap'n was killed in his locked cabin. We all heard a shot, rushed in, and found him dead. We even found a wee bit of a note he'd written, an apology. But I am dead certain he did not kill himself. He had been sad, yes, but he was showing interest in things. Sailing again. The ship. His daughter's future. That clock. Even that damned poor mouser of a cat, Thomas. Cap'n Brentwood was not a man about to shoot himself in the head, no matter how he missed his wife. And I know by other signs, too, more certain ones, that he was killed. Tell me now, Mister Fox, how would you go about it? How would you kill a man in a locked cabin?"

Fox was flustered. "Do you think, John, that I would . . . ?"

Spider continued. "Think on it, Mister Fox. Suppose you want to kill a man. You want everyone to believe he killed himself. How would you go about it?"

"I would not contemplate such!" Fox's face was bright crimson now, like a good tomato. "He was my friend! And it is not man's place to take a life! That sad task belongs to God!"

"You have said we are here to do God's work," the Reverend Down said softly. "Your friend was suffering, despondent. You even mentioned, in private moments, that Captain Brentwood had considered taking his own life not so long ago. Did you act as God's agent, Mister Fox? Did you help the captain do what he lacked the courage to do himself?" The pastor's expression left no doubt whatsoever that he dearly hoped Rufus Fox was a murderer.

Abigail gasped. "That is not possible."

"I apologize, Miss Brentwood," the reverend said. "These things, perhaps, are not for you to hear."

"I will know the truth," she said quietly, her gaze locked on Fox.

"Then know that I helped your father by reminding him how much he had to live for," Fox said through tightly clenched teeth. "Our time is measured to us, and I would not dare presume to overrule the Maker on such a thing."

Spider turned quickly to Abigail. "You are a lovely girl," he declared. "Suitors aplenty, I reckon?"

She stammered, gawked, and scrunched up her brow in confusion. "What's this? I have had suitors. I do not understand why you ask."

Fox huffed loudly. "You press too far, John."

Spider shrugged. "I pry with purpose." Indeed, he planned to fire questions now in rapid succession, a full broadside. *Keep them off balance, leave them no time to think, see who rattles and breaks.* "Did you and your father discuss a suit from Mister Fox?"

"What? No!" She clearly considered the idea preposterous. Wright's expression said he, too, thought it a ludicrous notion.

"John!" Fox spat the word. "How dare you? No such thing was discussed!"

"I believe you," Spider answered. "I believe him," he added, this time directly to Abigail. "Your father discussed suitors with you, I reckon?"

"Yes, but never a suit from Mister Fox." She looked at the man, not unkindly, but he did not notice. Fox stared at the ground, his face a sunset red.

"Hadley! He loves the girl!" That came from Lazare, the cook. "And the captain, he would never condone such a union, with a black man!"

Hadley took two long strides toward the cook, knife raised. Hob jumped into his path, pointing a gun, and growling low. "And you had a key to the cabin, you bastard."

Hadley froze.

Spider looked the young man in the eye. "Hadley."

The man gulped and stared at Hob's gun. "Yes, John?"

"I never once thought you killed him. Not for a second."

Hadley lifted his gaze from Hob's gun. "I didn't."

"I know."

Hadley nodded at Hob, then stepped back.

"He had the key in his chest, Spider John." Hob shot a glance at Spider, then returned his attention to Hadley. "Do not forget that!"

"I do not forget, Hob. Do not shoot Hadley just yet, though."

Hob lowered his gun reluctantly.

"I did think, like Anne did, that Mister Fox killed him, though," Spider said. "It was a clever murder, and I thought Mister Fox might be the only person aboard smart enough to plot it, and I thought maybe he had desires your father had thwarted, Miss Brentwood."

Spider turned his attention back to Fox. "I am sorry, sir. You are a good man, but a clever one, and I did suspect you. But I was wrong."

Fox sucked in a huge amount of air and glared at Spider. "Yes. Yes, sir. You were very wrong."

"Aye," Spider said. "But think on it. How would you have committed this murder? It was a damned clever thing."

Fox shook his head and spread his arms wide. "I do not know; we all heard the shot. . . ."

"We all heard a shot," Spider John said. "But it was not the fatal shot."

Fox stared at Spider blankly.

"What we heard was not the shot that killed Cap'n Brentwood," Spider said again. "He was already dead by then."

Fox's face lit up. "Already dead . . ."

"Aye, shot earlier," Spider said. "Remember Thomas? Where was that blasted cat when we heard the shot?"

Abigail spoke up. "Sitting by my father's cabin door."

"Aye, Miss Brentwood. And where was that damned cat every other morning?"

She scrunched her face up in thought, then nodded slowly. "In the cabin, with my father. Father would not sleep without Thomas!"

"Aye," Spider answered. "I should have seen that right off, but it was a rough morning." He decided not to mention how much rum he'd had the night before. "Any other morning, that cat is in there with the cap'n until the cap'n comes out himself. Not that morning. That morning, Thomas was out and about, because your father had not let him in the night before. He could not let the cat in. Because he was already dead."

Mutters and whispers whizzed back and forth, and people looked about them, wondering who the killer might be.

"We all heard a shot," Spider continued, "and we all were supposed to hear a shot, by God, but it was not the shot that killed him. Cap'n Brentwood was already dead."

"How the blazes . . . ?" Hob scratched his head.

"The blood on the cabin walls," Spider said. "It was already thick, already run its course to the deck by the time we got in there. Not flowing like a goddamned river the way Sam Smoke's blood did when Odin shot his fucking head off."

"Aye," Odin said. "Ha!"

Spider went on. "The blood, already sticky on the bulkheads. It should have been flowing, trickling down. But it wasn't, was it? It was thickened already, sticky, not oozing. It had already been there a while."

Heads around him nodded.

"And there were other clues, too. Where was the gunpowder cloud? If the cap'n had just shot himself, as we all were supposed to believe, the cabin should have been heavy with it. We all should have choked on it and coughed on it in that tiny space. But it wasn't there. I smelled blood, but not gunpowder."

He could see the dawn breaking in many faces around him. Spider wiped sweat from his brow and continued. He plucked the pipe from his mouth and pointed it at the Reverend Down. "The cap'n was killed the previous evening."

"You accuse me?" The dour man gawked, and Spider grinned inwardly.

"I have not accused anyone, Reverend Down. Not yet, anyway."

"Enough!" Abigail covered her face with her shaking hands. "John, or Spider John, or whoever the hell you are, you act as though you know. Who killed my father? And why?" She wiped away a steady stream of tears, but her blue eyes burned with cold fire.

Spider softened his voice. "Miss Brentwood, how did you know about your father's love of this island?"

"Nicholas told me of it."

"Nicholas? Not your father?"

"No. It was not something he ever mentioned to me. Perhaps to Mother, but . . ."

"I remember Cap'n Wright mentioning an island to you, a place your father told him of, before we sailed," Spider said. "I overheard that. You did not seem to know of the island. Odd, is it not, that your father would mention an island to Wright but never to you? Did anyone else aboard speak of this island? Did anyone else talk to you about it?"

She frowned.

Spider pressed. "Anyone else aboard *Redemption* ever mention it?"

"Why, no."

"Wait," said Lazare, the cook. "If the captain was killed the evening before, we would have heard the shot."

Spider turned toward the man, ready to hurl a curse, but he was interrupted.

"We heard a lot of shots!" Fox clapped his hands together. "A great deal of shooting, in fact!" Enlightenment dawned on him, and the man's natural curiosity overwhelmed his earlier embarrassment and anger.

Spider nodded. "Aye, sir. Sam Smoke was up on the poop, blasting away at a sorry piece of wood afloat behind us, and a lot of other fellows were shooting at it, too. That is when the murder happened. Plenty of noise to cover the shot that actually killed the cap'n."

"Then Sam Smoke killed my father?" Abigail ran a hand through what used to be long, beautiful hair. "How could he . . . ?"

"He couldn't," Spider said. "He was above, the whole time, when the murder happened. But he was providing cover for the person who shot your father. A great deal of shooting and blasting and gun smoke to conceal the bloody deed. Sam Smoke was up there raising an unholy ruckus of gunfire so a coconspirator could kill Cap'n Brentwood. No one would notice one lone shot in the cabin amid all the other shooting. It was like hiding a goddamned herring in a whole school of herrings."

"But what was it we heard the next morning, if it was not the shot that killed the captain?" Lazare's eyebrows danced, and his gaze darted about. "We all heard it."

"Aye, and we were supposed to hear it." Spider was waving an index finger now. "I suspect what we heard was a bag of powder, set off with a slow fuse, from the stern gallery. And it was set off when we were all gathered for the Sunday service and the cap'n was locked in his cabin, so we would all assume he had shot himself."

"Some sort of timer, a clockwork?" Fox rubbed his chin.

"Simpler than that, I reckon," Spider said. "Although, I must admit, I thought of that, and that made me suspect you. No. I reckon it was lit on the poop deck, with a fuse, then dropped to the stern gallery, where it exploded. Right behind the cap'n's cabin. To us on the deck, it sounded like it came from within, and when we found the cap'n, we thought he'd committed suicide. But he hadn't killed himself. Once I figured out the timing, I went out to the stern gallery. I found black smudges on the deck, where the powder bag exploded."

"Brilliant," Anne Bonny said.

Odin uncrossed his arms and held his guns level. Eyes in the crowd shifted. Abigail looked at Fox, at the Reverend Down, at Odin, at Spider. "This is . . . this is what must have happened!"

"Aye," said Spider. "Tell us the truth of it, Cap'n Wright."

Abigail gasped, rose, took three steps, glared at Spider, then glared at Wright. "Nicholas?"

Wright stared at him blankly. "This is all ridiculous," he said. He started to rise but sat back down when Odin aimed two pistols at him.

"You were up on the poop when the shot we all heard went off. You had a pipe going, too." Spider narrowed his eyes. "Easy enough to light a slow fuse with a good pipe going. I reckon you had a bag of powder and a fuse under your shirt and lit your little bomb with the pipe. You stood behind the helmsman, lit your fuse, dropped your bomb onto the stern gallery, and waited for the blast."

"You do me wrong, carpenter," Wright snarled.

"No. It was you."

"You lie," Wright said. "And your lad there, he said Hadley had a key! Aye? Why should Hadley have a key? He stole my key, so he could kill the captain!"

"No," Spider said. "You tossed your key into Hadley's chest. Miss Brentwood started talking about how her father couldn't have been suicide, aye? And there was that handsome lieutenant, Price, being all gallant. Suppose he started taking Miss Brentwood's idea of a murder seriously? Started poking about more. He might have figured out it wasn't all as simple as it seemed. So you needed another plan and put a key in Hadley's trunk. Planned to make him your scapegoat, no doubt. He was a potential rival for the girl's attentions, aye? But Hadley had no reason to kill the cap'n. Hadley would not ever do a thing that would hurt Miss Brentwood. Not ever."

Spider sighed. "No, you killed him, Wright. I did not want to believe it, because I actually thought you a good man. But I was wrong, more than once. I thought you acted foolishly in coming here to this island, doing a goddamned reckless thing out of love for Miss Brentwood. Then for a while I thought maybe Miss Bonny here had used her charm on you, convinced you to steer here, so she could take care of her own business, set *Redemption* on course for her vengeance. But I have talked to the woman with weapons in hands, looked her in the eye, and . . . no. She might have rounded up some men; hell, Hob would have followed her lead in a heartbeat, and I don't think it would take her long to win some fellows over. She could have taken over the ship and headed here. It would have been easier and a more sure plan than this sneaky murder and convincing you to deceive Miss Brentwood just to get us here. So why didn't she do that? Because she didn't know Ned and Wicked Pete would be here. She was just following Sam Smoke, thinking he'd lead her to her prey."

Anne took a theatrical bow.

"But if Anne did not know of the island rendezvous, and if the only one who knew about this island was you, Wright, then . . . it had to be you that killed him. Once the cap'n was killed, you could steer the ship anywhere you wanted. The cap'n never loved this island, did he? Maybe never even saw it. That's why his daughter never heard tell of it before you mentioned it to her. It was a lie so you could send this ship westward toward Ned Low."

"Listen, John, everyone, this is madness." Wright started to rise, saw Odin leering behind a pair of guns, and sat again.

"It was you who ordered me to make that stupid target for Sam Smoke, a key part of your plot, to provide cover for the killing," Spider said. "And I don't recall you being around for the shooting contest up on the poop, although it's the kind of thing you normally would wager on. You weren't on the weather deck or forecastle at the time either, near as I can recall."

"I was there," Fox said. "I shot with Sam, and you did not rule me out as the killer."

"You left before Sam's ruckus ended." Spider shrugged. "A clever man might have wanted to be seen up on the poop, shooting, so he could persuade people later he could not have been in the cabin shooting the cap'n. Sorry, Mister Fox, but you are a clever man, and I had to think of such notions. Hell, you even had a goddamned blanket about you, and I thought maybe you left the poop, snuck in and killed the cap'n, and let that blanket catch all the blood spraying, and then you chucked it overboard. That was the very thing that first got my eye on you, sir, the blanket. I really thought you had worked it all out. In an odd way, it's a sign of respect. I really figured you smart enough to have planned this all out."

"The blanket? It is still in my bunk." Fox scratched his chin. "But would not Nicholas have been covered in blood, if he killed the captain?"

"Anyone would have." Spider nodded. "I don't see how the killer could have escaped that. But shortly after the murder Hob went chasing after Miss Bonny while she was talking to Mister Wright. Not far from the cap'n's quarters, by the way, and not long after the murder had to have happened, if I am right. And Mister Wright swung a duffel or sack at Hob. Remember that, Hob?"

"Jesus," Hob said. "Yes!"

"I'll bet that was full of bloody clothing," Spider said. "Wright probably took clean stuff from the cap'n's things, after getting drenched with blood. . . . Sorry, Miss Brentwood."

Fox turned his gaze on Wright. "But you . . . you profess to love her."

"I ordered the target made, yes," Wright said, smiling, his teeth bright in a face quickly flushing crimson. He spoke softly, the way he did with the crew when things were going well. "Sam wanted it, and I obliged. He was a paying passenger. Someone else must have done the deed in the captain's cabin, though! Not I!" He turned his face toward Abigail. "Not I, Abby. You must believe me."

"Don't believe him," Spider said. "I thought you were trying to honor her father, Wright, when you slipped off from the convoy in the night. I thought you were trying to please Miss Brentwood, win her favor. But your every decision since the cap'n's death was aimed at putting this ship into Ned Low's hands. Wasn't it?"

Wright's eyebrows arched. "No. No. Sam Smoke must have had an ally aboard, someone who plotted with him. I would not . . ."

"The bloody pirates knew we were coming," Spider said. "And they knew we would not put up a fight. Sam Smoke was aboard to make sure you did not back out of your goddamned bargain. I have seen pirate attacks. They come at you growling, howling like a mad mob, anything to put fear into you. Anything to make you piss your britches and decide not to fight, because they would rather just take your goods and be on their way as fast as may be. And they come at you in numbers to overwhelm resistance from the start. These lads did none of that. They took their time setting up their blockade, fired some shots—salutes, I reckon, or signals to their spy on the hill, or their agent on *Redemption*, by thunder! That was Smoke's job, right? Make sure you did not stray from your course? But they did not fire anything, did not do any menacing, anything that would cause fear. They sent just a handful of men over to our ship. That is not the pirate way. It sure as bloody goddamned hell ain't Ned Low's way. Overwhelming force is what pirates rely upon. Why send only a few men? Because they knew there would be no fight. They knew it. We did not stray into a trap. We were making a goddamned rendezvous."

Wright, red-faced now, bellowed, "Because they knew Sam Smoke was aboard! They knew he would secure the ship for them! It was him! It had to have been him!"

"No," Spider said. "Sam never left the poop deck when the killing must have happened. And Sam Smoke did not order us away from our escort in the night, did he? Sam Smoke did not hold a gun to our heads and command us to sail to this island, did he? And Sam Smoke did not make a move to secure *Redemption* for Ned Low, not until he thought you might lose your nerve and make a run for it."

"Nicholas?" It was a whisper, a pleading, and Abigail's eyes welled with tears.

"How could you have endangered her so?" Spider asked. "You had to know what would happen to her in the clutches of those men."

"I would have protected you!" Wright's hands covered his eyes. "God, God, God!"

"How much money did you owe Ned Low? Lose a few bets, did

you?" Spider brandished his knife. "This ship was intended to pay off a debt. You couldn't resist a wager. We all joked about it, but our games were for low stakes. But they play for higher stakes in Port Royal, don't they? I am thinking you got into a game with Ned Low, or Wicked Pete, or someone else of their crew. You lost a lot. You made a deal to turn over *Redemption*. Smoke was aboard to make sure you turned over the vessel, is that right?"

"It was supposed to be my command," Wright said, his hands still hiding his face. "The captain and Abby, neither of them was supposed to be aboard. Neither of them was going to make this trip! The plan was laid long before the captain decided to make the journey, before he decided to bring Abby along, and I was just going to slip away from the convoy and meet Ned Low here. Abby was not supposed to be here! The captain was not supposed to be here!" He spoke through giant sobs. "I was supposed to command, hand over the ship, pay off Ned. And when that changed, when your father decided to command and . . . oh, God . . . to bring you, Abby, I . . ."

"You killed him during the shooting contest," Spider said. "When you went up to the poop the next morning, the day of the Bible reading, you had a bag of powder and a fuse tucked away."

Wright, unnerved now, nodded furiously.

"Lit it with your pipe."

More nodding.

"Dropped it to the stern gallery."

Wright uncovered his face. "Yes! I admit it."

"Cowardly bastard," Spider said.

Wright ignored him and turned pleading eyes toward Abigail. "I told Smoke we needed to change the plan. Find another way. He told me he would kill you, Abby, if I went back on my word."

"Your word . . ." Abigail's eyes blazed.

"I would have protected you, Abby. No one was going to hurt you so long as I had blood in my body!"

"They'd have shot you dead without hesitation, Wright." Spider shook his head. "Ned Low does not make deals he intends to honor."

Abigail spoke through clenched jaws, barely audible. "My father hired you, taught you . . ."

"Your father denied me your hand!" Wright clenched his teeth tightly, too, as if he were baring fangs. "Your father took this command from me! He thought me inferior . . ."

"He saw potential in you." She reached behind her back, freed the gun Spider had given her, and aimed it at Wright's forehead.

Wright held his breath.

Abigail's arm tensed.

Wright made no move to stop her, or to escape.

Everyone else stood frozen, not breathing.

"I love you, Abby."

Abigail shivered. The gun in her hand shook, and Spider began to fear she would pull the trigger by accident, and the ball might pierce anyone at random. He stepped forward to take the gun, but Anne Bonny got there first.

The redhead grasped the gun gently. "Abby, dear. Give it to me. Give it to me."

Abigail relinquished the weapon. Wright sighed.

"I showed you how to use this," Anne said. "This is how."

She shot Wright between the eyes.

Spider and Odin looked at each other. Everyone else did the same. No one said a word for a long, long time as Abigail stood over the dead body of Nicholas Wright. Her gaze remained locked on him.

Anne draped an arm around Abigail. "You had every right to kill the bastard. I am happy to have done it for you."

Fox looked as though the world had vanished beneath his feet. The Reverend Down stared wide-eyed, prayed quietly, and shook. The rest of the gathered men nodded.

"No one will say a word," Lazare said.

"I didn't see anything happen," Odin growled. "Nor did anyone else. And I will kill any man who says otherwise."

Abigail stared at Wright. Wright stared up and through the canopy of trees and into the Caribbean sun—but did not see it.

Spider found a hogshead and sat. He brushed sweat and grass from his face. The mystery of the captain's death, which had nagged him like a gnat swirling about his head, was resolved, and the cowardly murder was avenged. He sucked on the pipe and wished to God he had whiskey. He glanced toward a hogshead of rum, but Fox was sitting on it.

Spider closed his eyes. He had been on edge for days, and here, for now, there was no immediate mystery, no present enemy to fight.

For now, Spider could sleep. He drifted off, and soon Emma's smile and crinkled nose greeted him on a Nantucket pier. She was teasing him because he wanted to show Johnny and Hob how to drill a proper hole, and the boys wanted to rush off on a lobster boat.

30

Spider stood on the beach, watching Anne Bonny's fleet disperse. Her boat had been used by Hob and others to take her back to her flagship, and now they were rowing it back toward shore. In the morning, Spider would see that the two boats in their possession were seaworthy, and they would discuss who among them might be able to navigate. A couple of fellows among those who had not joined Anne's crew had been naval midshipmen once upon a time and figured they could reach Nassau, or the Turks, easily enough.

From there, Spider would find another ship and sail to Em's arms. He stared to the north, and the pendant's reassuring weight against his chest calmed him.

He took a fat swig of rum, tossed aside the empty flask, and resumed smoking his pipe. "Good to not be sailing on the devil's wind, don't you think, Odin?"

The one-eyed gentleman merely grunted and stretched out on the sand, being nearly drunk enough to piss himself. Spider was surprised Odin had not joined Anne's crew. "I'll stay with you, Spider," the old man had said by way of explanation while he was still a little sober. "Otherwise, you are fucked. Ha!"

Spider was not at all surprised to hear Little Bob and his friends had decided to go pirating with Anne. It was the only choice for them, really, for no one remaining on the island would have them around. Anne had taken them on with some reluctance, but pirates nearly always could use more hands.

To the west, *Madeleine Robin*'s silhouette pierced the setting sun. She would carry Anne to Nassau and to her next victim. The remainder of the lady's small fleet veered toward the Bahamas to seek prey and plunder. No part of Spider longed to be with them. He had seen all the bloodshed he ever wanted to see.

Behind him, men sang and drank around a huge bonfire. Abigail walked farther up the beach, Rufus Fox by her side.

Odin sat up. "Drink alla rum?"

"Yes, Odin, I drank all the rum."

"Thought you tryin' a quit."

"That was yesterday." Spider blew a long stream of smoke into the wind. "This is now. Here comes the boat."

The rowers jumped out in the shallows and brought the craft up on the beach. Spider jogged toward it and called out. "Well then, Hob, does she ride nice and steady? We'll give her a look in the morning."

He got no answer.

"Hob?"

Spider ran. "Hob?"

Once he got close enough to make out faces, Spider's jaws clenched and the pipe stem snapped in his mouth. "Where the bloody hell is Hob?"

"He stayed with the red-haired woman," one of the boat crewmen said.

Spider stared into the sun's burnt orange disk. *Madeleine Robin*, now a mere smudge, crossed it.

"Goddamned fool, I was," Spider said. "Goddamned fool. I should have seen it. I should have put the stupid fucker in chains."

He was still staring west long after *Madeleine Robin* vanished from sight.

Author's Note

*A*ll of the characters who figure in this story are fictional, save two.

Anne Bonny, indeed, raised bloody hell in Caribbean waters with Calico Jack Rackham and was reputed to have fought as well as any man. She was captured along with Jack's crew and sentenced to death, but pregnancy delayed her execution. She was the daughter of an Irish attorney who owned property in the Carolinas, and his connections may have helped her, too. There is no record of her execution.

I have no real reason to believe that Anne Bonny returned to the Caribbean and hunted down men who wronged her, and she may well have settled down somewhere in the colonies or the Bahamas with a new name and identity, but her whereabouts during the period of my story were vague enough to give me some leeway. I could not quite resist the opportunity to include her in this novel. If scholars one day prove she was somewhere else at this time, please remember I am a storyteller, not a historian.

Edward "Ned" Low, sometimes spelled Lowe or Loe, also was real, and by all accounts he was as sadistic and horrible as he is portrayed in my story. His bloody deeds were compared to those of the Spanish Inquisition. The unfortunate fate of Ed Pigeon described in my novel is entirely fictional, but Ned Low was, indeed, reputed to be a sick and violent man. It is said that on occasion he cut off men's lips, boiled them, and forced the poor souls to eat them. His whereabouts at the time of this story are unknown, but his reputation was such that anyone sailing these waters in 1723 certainly would have feared running into him. If later research places him elsewhere during this period, well, please forgive me.

Acknowledgments

There are so many people to thank: Everyone at Seventh Street Books, my agent Evan Marshall, my friends and inspirations Tom Williams and Tyrone Johnston, and, of course, my wife and child, Gere and Rowan. Mom and Dad, too, bless them. Subtract any one of them from the equation and this book would never have come to be.

The other authors at Seventh Street Books have been very welcoming. Our publisher offers a wide array of crime fiction, from funny to gruesome to thought-provoking. I am proud to have conned my way into such a fine crowd of writers.

I also want to thank Robert Louis Stevenson, whose *Treasure Island* will forever stand as the yardstick by which all other pirate novels are measured. I read that book again every few years, and it never disappoints.

Other writers whose works fueled my desire to write, in no particular order, are Arthur Conan Doyle, John D. MacDonald, Mark Twain, Ellery Queen, Rex Stout, Patrick O'Brian, C. S. Forester, Fritz Leiber, Ursula K. Le Guin, Alexandre Dumas, Rafael Sabatini, J. R. R. Tolkien, Robert E. Howard, and Daphne du Maurier. I do not write like any of them, nor am I able to do so, but all of them shaped me.

I also want to mention Phoenix Brewing Company in Mansfield, Ohio, where portions of the first two Spider John novels were written. Mighty fine brews can be found there.

Lastly, I want to thank you. Not enough people read these days. I am exceedingly happy that you do.

About the Author

Steve Goble is the author of *The Bloody Black Flag*, the first Spider John mystery novel. A former journalist, Goble now works in communications for a cybersecurity firm. Previously, he wrote a weekly craft-beer column called Brewologist, which appeared on USA Today Network–Ohio websites.

Author photo by Jason J. Molyet